CW01669496

Foı

This work is a work of fiction. The names, characters and incidents portrayed in it are works of the author's imagination. Any resemblance to actual persons, living or dead or localities is entirely coincidental.

RAF Harrowbeer opened in 1941 and was a Fighter Station for the remainder of WWII. Hawks Tor was operational as a Chain Home Low Radar Station between 1940 and 1942. In this novel the dates have been changed to suit the narrative.

ISBN: 978-1-7385793-0-3

The game of consequences

The game of consequences originated in 19th-century Britain and emerged as a favoured parlor game among the literary and elite circles. The random nature of the emerging narrative invariably led to amusing outcomes. Whilst the connections we make in real life may appear less random, the choices we make can still lead to unexpected consequences.

Consequences

Margaret and Ken 1940 – 1955

Margaret
And Ken
Met at the village hall
She ordered a cream tea
He made a promise
She said "No regrets"
He said "I can't forget you"
And the consequence was

Jim and Christine 1965 – 1998

Jim
Met Christine at the library
He drove her home
She made a decision
He said "I love her"
She said "You did me a favour"
And the consequence was

David and Erin 2004 – 2023

David
And Erin
Met online
She found a letter
He told his mum
She said "I'm sorry"
He said "And now we're here"
And the consequence was

Erin 2004, Vancouver Island

The car behind her decided now was the right time to overtake, even though a car was driving straight at them. As a cyclist, Erin assumed that all drivers were arseholes, so she had already started to apply her brakes just before it swerved back in front of her, narrowly avoiding a collision.

"You jerk!" Erin shouted loudly at the driver, but he'd already put his foot down, a clear indication that he knew he was in the wrong. Another day she would have noted his registration number and reported him, but, as usual, she was running late. Instead, she took a deep breath, checked her tyres were still in one piece, and pushed off again.

She was on the way over to her grampa's old home, a bungalow in Oak Bay, on the outskirts of Victoria. Last week she helped him move into a retirement village, and last night she received a phone call from the new owners telling her that they had found a few items that had been left during the move. Erin had the summer to herself after finishing university in May. She had opted to do her degree in Oregon, but she was happy to be back in Vancouver and was looking forward to a couple of months of doing nothing before she started her first job in September. The fact that her interregnum coincided with her grampa's move was a happy coincidence. He had always been such a supporter of hers, and she was glad she could repay some of his generosity. Her grandparents had moved into a bungalow when the family farm was sold. They hoped it would see them to the end, but after her grandma died, her gramps decided he didn't want to live with the memories. The flat at the retirement village was a fresh start for his twilight years.

The move last week had gone well. Her dad hired a van, and together they made several trips back and forth, bringing across everything they could manage. Her grampa had taken downsizing to heart and done a great job clearing out things there would be no room for. Even so, there was a lot to move, and his new flat still had boxes piled high in one corner of the lounge. She wasn't surprised they had forgotten things, and she was happy to go and collect them. The new owners said it was mainly paperwork.

She jumped off her bike, took her helmet off and rang the bell. It was strange not to see Grampa's head in the window or his broad smile when he realised it was her. The new owners were a couple in their 70s. The wife answered the door and looked confused for a moment.

"Hello, I'm Erin. You rang to say some paperwork needed to be collected."

"Yes, my dear," the woman said, slowly recognising the stranger at her door, "Do come in. I'll ask Bill to find it for you."

Erin walked into the once-familiar hallway. It still looked like her grampa's place, but the unfamiliar new residents made it feel different. A cat rubbed against her leg as if to say, 'This is my home now.' She waited awkwardly for a few minutes before the aforementioned Bill appeared, clutching a package to his chest.

"Hello, dear," he greeted her.

"Hello. I've come to pick up some of my grampa's things," Erin explained.

"Yes, yes. It's only this," he said, handing over a buff-coloured parcel.

"Did Gramps leave this here?" Erin asked, taking it from him.

"No, I don't think so. It just got delivered the other day." He turned the parcel over and pointed out the return address. "It looks like it's come from England. It's quite heavy. It must have cost a lot to post," he offered.

Erin took the parcel from him and examined it. The return address was to a woman in Windsor. She wondered who her grampa knew in the UK. She hadn't ever heard him mention anyone. She was tempted to look inside but instead popped it in her backpack.

"Thank you for letting me know," she said to the gentleman. "Do ring if you find anything else we've forgotten."

She jumped back on her bike and started off towards her grampa's new flat. She would take this to him and have a cup of coffee. Hopefully, he would have cleared a few more boxes. She would pop the package into his desk until he had.

Part One: 1940 - 1955

Margaret
And Ken
Met at the village hall
She ordered a cream tea
He made a promise
She said “No regrets”
He said “I can’t forget you”
And the consequence was ...

Margaret

Walking through London on a beautiful late spring day, it was hard to believe there was a war on. Yesterday, the king had asked Winston Churchill to become prime minister and, had she been paying more attention, Margaret would have noticed the blackboard at the news stand on the corner of Shelton Street announcing 'Chamberlain Resigns, Read All About It'. Instead, for the last ten minutes, she'd been trying to avoid walking on the lines between the paving stones.

She wasn't sure what had started her off. An old poem had popped into her head just as she'd got off the train at Tottenham Court Road, something about bears gobbling you up, and it suddenly became incredibly important not to tempt fate. The mere thought of lunch at Lyons Corner House with her mother had her avoiding every line between Soho Square and Shaftesbury Avenue. At one point, she had made such a dramatic change of direction that a man walking towards her ended up performing an impromptu Paso Doble with her. Now, on top of everything, her shoes were starting to hurt. She cursed herself for wearing the new pair of Oxfords, but she'd wanted to impress her mother with how well she was doing, so she'd purchased a new cardigan and shoes and applied a splash of lipstick before leaving her flat this morning.

Her flatmate Cynthia had laughed at her. 'You're only having lunch with your mother; anyone would think you were on a date!'

Margaret knew it was ridiculous, but there was something about her mother that made her feel like a naughty child.

She didn't understand why her relationship with her mother was like this. She and her sister had enjoyed a lovely childhood, relishing the long country walks with their father. Released from the straitjacket of parlours and drawing rooms where one had to be 'seen and not heard', Margaret had flourished. She had learned the names of the birds and the trees by heart, using her binoculars and a little moleskin book to record her sightings. Sometimes she would accompany her father on his fishing trips. She delighted at the coloured lures glistening in the sunshine, pretending to be jewelled dragonflies and fooling the fish into biting. Her father would stride into the river in his waders, determined to catch them a trout for tea, and she would sit quietly on the riverbank, awake to any sounds from the surrounding trees that might alert the fish. Her father was a patient teacher. He knew everything and relished the opportunity to pass his knowledge on to his youngest daughter. And, in return, she adored him.

Mother had been a different kettle of fish. Her preference was for an indoor life surrounded by polite society. She had her social circle of acquaintances, changing into her afternoon dress to receive guests after lunch and asking their 'daily', Vera, to serve tea in the drawing room. Her mother always seemed exasperated by Margaret's physicality and enthusiasm for life. She made excuses for her in front of the guests, and Margaret wondered if she would have been happier without any children.

There were occasions when Margaret thought she loved Vera more than her mother. When she returned home from adventures with her father, there would always be a pot of tea and buttered crumpets waiting by the fireplace. Vera would sit patiently and listen to Margaret as she went through her moleskin, showing her the names and descriptions of all the birds they had seen and then creating a story or poem based on them. Daddy once said their mother needed 'a lady that does' because she was a 'lady that doesn't'. Margaret intuitively understood that this was not to be repeated.

On occasions, their mother would ask her two daughters to entertain her friends. Margaret always seemed to disappoint with her laboured playing of *Greensleeves* or an overly enthusiastic rendition of a poem she had learned specially for the occasion, whereas her sister would earn the rapturous applause of the audience as her voice soared to the highest notes in *O for the Wings of a Dove*. Perhaps, thought Margaret, it wasn't a case of her mother being happier without children, more that she would be happier without her.

Margaret passed The Globe on Shaftesbury Avenue where last week she and Cynthia had watched *Cousin Muriel* with the wonderful Peggy Ashcroft. Afterwards, they had sat in the pub and Cynthia had announced that she would 'henceforth call her Peggy' in honour of the actress. Margaret rather liked it, but she knew what her mother would say. Perhaps she would save that particular bombshell for another day. She arrived at the corner of Coventry Street just after 1 pm as many of the clientele were spilling out and hurrying back to their jobs. Margaret could see her mother through the leaded windows, already seated on the far side. She reached for her powder compact, checked her face, re-applied her lipstick and stepped inside.

"Hello, Mummy."

Margaret had been shown to the table by a 'nippy' with a very modern bob that Margaret rather coveted. Her mother, who as usual had secured a window table, glanced at her watch as Margaret arrived.

"Hello, darling. I thought we said 12.30. Is that a new cardigan?"

Her mother was a stickler for both punctuality and smartness. She was always early for any appointment and dressed for the occasion. Today, she wore a light brown tweed suit with a hat and gloves. Margaret instantly felt underdressed.

"It is, Mummy. I got it only yesterday at Derry and Toms. Do you like it?" Margaret asked.

"Well, I'm not sure the colour is the most flattering. It makes you look a little pasty."

"Cynthia said it looked very nice, but perhaps it's a little modern for your tastes."

Margaret rarely stood up to her mother, but even this jibe seemed not to permeate her mother's notoriously thick skin.

"I'm not sure you should take the opinions of your flatmate over your mother, Margaret. And Cynthia doesn't mix in the same circles as we do, now does she?"

"Honestly, Mother, these opinions about people and the circles they mix in aren't relevant anymore. You do know there's a war on, don't you? Adolf doesn't care which school you went to or how good your elocution is. We're all in it together now."

"Well, I don't know about that, but it does matter to me, and I really wouldn't want you to take fashion advice from a shop girl whose parents hail from the East End."

Margaret realised there was little point in continuing the conversation in this direction. Her mother always thought herself better than other people. Since Margaret had been very young, she had dictated with whom her daughter could and couldn't be friends, based entirely on what their parents did. But today Margaret was on a mission and needed her mother on her side, so she decided to change the conversation to avoid getting into another row.

It had been Cynthia who had first planted the idea in her head. They shared lodgings, two bedrooms, and a bathroom in a house in South Kensington. The owner lived downstairs with her two children. Her husband had recently signed up and was now 'somewhere in France'. The children, who were evacuated to friends of the family, had recently returned when the expected bombing of London had failed to materialise. The whole setup was perfect for Margaret. It meant that she could finally leave the constraints of living with her mother and start to have a social life. After a day in an office, the hubbub of family life made her feel at home, and even with all the uncertainty caused by the war, having the children around helped everything feel more normal. And Cynthia was a breath of fresh air.

Cynthia was already back from her job behind the glove counter at Derry and Toms and she leapt on Margaret almost before she had got through the door. She was clutching a copy of The Daily Telegraph and pointing to an advertisement with such animation that Margaret worried it would fly out of her hands.

"We should do this, Margie, we really should." Cynthia was more excited than Margaret had ever seen her.

"What are you talking about, Cyn? I can't see what it says while you're bouncing around like that."

Cynthia caught her breath, grabbed Margaret's hand and pulled her up the stairs and into the bedroom. She spread the paper out on the bed.

"This is what I'm talking about." Cynthia pointed at an advert. Margaret quickly skimmed the text:

Help the Royal Air Force... We are looking for young women of good education for Special Duties in the Women's Auxiliary Air Force... Go to the R.A.F section of your nearest Recruiting Centre.

"Well, I don't know about me," Cynthia announced, "you wouldn't exactly call my education good, but this could be perfect for you... and Special Duties... how exciting... imagine the adventure."

Margaret was only half listening to her friend now. Her brain was racing, and she had a feeling in the pit of her stomach that this was the day when her life was about to start.

Cynthia was right about Margaret's education. Her father had first raised the idea of boarding school with her during one of their long walks. The previous summer, on their annual holiday in Whitley Bay, they had stayed in the same guest house as two sisters who ran a boarding school in Eastbourne. They had seen Margaret playing on the beach, and her mother had taken the opportunity to share her concerns about Margaret with them.

"She has far too much energy," Margaret had heard her say to the elder sister. "She's always been like that since she was a toddler. It's put such a strain on me. On the whole family, really. She's like a wild thing, always running around the house and constantly asking questions. It's not good for my nerves."

Margaret knew she shouldn't listen to other people's conversations, but it was about her, and her mother wasn't exactly whispering. It was almost as if she had wanted her to overhear. She had gone to the sea for a swim and hadn't heard the rest. On her return, her mother was still in conversation with them, and at tea that afternoon she had seen the younger sister hand her mother a booklet about Fairfield Lodge Boarding School for Young Ladies. At nine years old, Margaret didn't feel like a young lady, so she wasn't particularly worried. She should have been.

The following April, as she walked across Houndkirk Moor with her father, he had broken it to her that, come September, she would be heading to a boarding school in Eastbourne, which was 250 miles away from her home, her beloved sister, and her weekend walks with her father. It took her a while to understand what he was saying. Father had tried to make it all sound wonderful: the seaside, lots of girls to play with. Time would fly by, he promised, and she'd have the holidays to look forward to.

Looking back, she imagined that her father had tried everything he could to get Mother to change her mind. She knew he loved to have her around and would miss her terribly, but she also knew that what Mother wanted, Mother usually got. Perhaps her mother thought it would be the making of her, but the truth was, Margaret had been unhappy at Fairfield Lodge. Rather than sparking the curiosity and natural intelligence of their wards, the spinsters who ran the school focused instead on preparing the young ladies to be good wives and mothers in the future. All that had done was make Margaret more determined to rebel, which meant she was constantly getting herself in trouble for the smallest of misdemeanours.

Fortunately for Margaret, fate had intervened three years later, when her father had secured a more prestigious position and moved to London. Her family bought a house near Windsor, and Margaret, who had made no secret of how unhappy she was in Eastbourne, had finally moved back home. The school had seemed relieved that she was leaving Fairfield Lodge, and despite some veiled comments in her report about being high-spirited and strong-willed, they didn't stand in her way when she left mid-term. From then on, she thrived academically, first at Windsor Grammar and then at Notting Hill Collegiate, where she passed her School Certificate with distinction.

Margaret hugged Cynthia and re-read the advert.

"Yes, Cynthia, this is perfect," she gushed. "Let's get down to the Recruiting Centre immediately."

"Only one problem with that," Cynthia replied, "they're not open until tomorrow!"

At lunchtime the following day, the friends met at the Recruiting Centre. They only had an hour for lunch and were shocked to see the queues forming outside. Margaret worried she would have to head back to the office when they finally made it inside. A middle-aged woman dressed in uniform gave them forms to fill in and asked them for their educational records. Soon after, Margaret was called into a small office with 'RAF' written neatly on the blackboard outside.

The sergeant looked up from his papers and asked Margaret why she wanted to join up. Thrusting the advert towards him and talking at pace, she explained the qualities she believed would make her an excellent candidate for special duties. She knew she was rambling, but ever since Cynthia had shown her the advert, she'd had butterflies. She had barely been able to sleep last night, her thoughts running away with her, and her stomach churning with a mix of apprehension and nervous excitement. Aware that she hadn't drawn breath since she entered the office, she paused. The sergeant, finally given space to speak, smiled in her direction.

"Well, I can see that you are very enthusiastic about the opportunity," he said, not unkindly.

The next few moments passed in silence as he looked through her paperwork and asked a few ancillary questions. Finally, he looked at Margaret, smiled, and told her to expect a letter in the next week. The whole interview had taken just ten minutes. Cynthia was already waiting outside.

"How did you get on? Will they have you for the Special Duties?"

"Yes, I think they will." Margaret replied. "They've told me to expect a letter within a week!"

Cynthia had been right about her lack of education, but she was excited enough, as they had asked her to join the army as a driver.

"Imagine, Margie – I'm going to learn to drive and map read and everything!" she enthused.

As they had waited for the bus to take them back to work, they talked of the adventures ahead of them. They knew they would be posted to different parts of the country, but with the optimism of youth, they promised they would be friends for the rest of their lives. Margaret jumped off the bus and waved goodbye to Cynthia as she carried on her journey to High Street Kensington. Taking a deep breath, Margaret had paused for just a moment before skipping up the steps of her office, bursting through the front door, and promptly telling her colleagues the news.

"And how is Father's work?" Margaret enquired, changing the subject to get onto safer ground.

"You know, darling, it's all a bit tricky now with all the younger men signing up. He's going to be so overworked, and I worry that he won't be able to help me at home anymore."

Since the move to Windsor, her mother had relied on Margaret's sister to help with the chores. Now, with both sisters in London, looking after the house fell solely to her mother, and she was ill-prepared for the task. Margaret worried about her father as he loved his food and would miss the Lancashire Hot Pot and Game Pie that Vera had been so adept at making in Sheffield.

"We're all going to have to do our part, Mummy," Margaret rallied, trying to sound sympathetic. "Compared to all those brave young men, managing the laundry alone isn't such a hardship."

"Of course, I know that," her mother countered. "I've been talking to my cousin about joining the Women's Voluntary Services myself. They are doing wonderful work, and the Harris Tweed uniform is very fetching."

Margaret smiled to herself. Who else would see fashion as a motivation for joining the war effort?

"Well, that's very public-spirited of you, Mummy," she said with as little irony as she could muster. "I've been thinking about joining up myself."

"To the WVS, darling? That would be wonderful. Perhaps you could move back home and be around more to help. You know how much Daddy misses you."

Margaret couldn't help but bristle at this. After all, Daddy's feelings hadn't mattered much to her mother when it came to sending her away to boarding school!

"No. Actually I was thinking of the WAAF," she countered.

"Oh, don't be silly, darling. Why on earth would you want to do something like that? Do you even know if they'd have a girl like you?"

"Yes. As it happens, I do," Margaret smiled triumphantly, pulling the letter out of her pocket and handing it to her mother.

Her mother replaced her teacup on its saucer and skimmed the words on the page before refolding the letter and putting it back in the envelope. She had never before seen her mother lost for words. The moment stretched between them like a river awaiting a bridge. In the silence, Margaret could hear her heart pounding and feel her hands grow damp. It surprised and annoyed her that her body was giving away just how much she wanted her mother's approval.

Her mother beckoned the 'nippy' over and asked for a top-up of the tea.

"Well, I suppose we'll have to manage without you," she acknowledged. "At least one of my children knows where her priorities lie."

But even this slight couldn't dampen Margaret's enthusiasm. She was finally going to be able to break free from her mother and her constant disapproval, and the rest of her life was about to begin.

And Ken

"Pass the sprouts."

A girl of about eight or nine in a green paper hat was swinging her legs and kicking Ken's leg excitedly.

"And the gravy." A younger boy sitting to his left was now doing the same.

"Pass the sprouts, *please,*" said the mother, smiling apologetically at Ken.

"I'm sorry about their manners," she continued. "It's always like this at Christmas, but we don't usually have guests to think about!"

Ken and his friend had received the invitation to Christmas lunch a couple of weeks ago. They'd been in a pub on their first weekend of leave and had started playing dominos with the locals. The conversation focused on the terrible bombing raid that had happened the previous year. Many Canadian and American airmen had been killed, with the Germans targeting the hotels where they were staying. Ken had heard stories of the raids during his training. They tended to emphasise the positive stories, including the miraculous escape of one airman who, having been blown out of a window at the Metropole Hotel, survived by having his fall cushioned by the hot air generated by the blast. The reports were that he landed on the pavement, dusted himself off, and then ran back into the building to help rescue his comrades.

Ken imagined the residents of Bournemouth might not be best pleased with the Canadians, Americans, and Australians who were making their town such a target. The reverse was true. Come the end of the evening, one of the men they had been playing dominos with invited them to Christmas lunch, saying it was the very least he could do. True to his word, a week later, they received the invitation, sent via the Reception Centre to the hotel where they were staying.

It felt like everyone in Bournemouth had opened their doors to the overseas serviceman, many of whom, like Ken, were celebrating their first Christmas away from home. His friend claimed it was because they brought a whole box of goodies not on the ration list of English families. Ken doubted that the fruit juice, evaporated milk, bacon, sugar, coffee, and lard they gave the family, made up for the inconvenience of hosting two young men for the day.

The English family was not that different from the one he had left back in Vancouver. And while he was grateful to be enjoying turkey with all the trimmings with an English family, it made him realise just how much he was missing everyone at home. He'd arrived in Liverpool on a packed troop ship from Halifax, Nova Scotia, just two months ago. The crossing had been rough, and Ken had been pleased he'd listened to the advice from his brother and opted for a top bunk to avoid being vomited on from above. Once they'd landed, they'd had a couple of days in Liverpool before being moved down to the Bournemouth

Reception Centre to await an onward posting. The two months had passed slowly for Ken, a strange limbo period for young men eager to get their wartime experience properly underway. Most of the men who signed up in 1943 had either been too young to volunteer at the start of the war, or, like Ken, too important for their families to let go.

Ken was the second child, nestled between an older brother and a younger sister. As three children separated by only five years, they had always been close, developing sibling rivalries based on their position in the pecking order. Everything was turned upside down when, out of the blue, and ten years after his sister had been born, their parents had sat them down and told them they were expecting another baby. They had all reacted differently. It had worried his brother the least. At fifteen, he considered himself an adult and couldn't see how another baby in the family would change anything for him. He did admit to feeling sick at the idea that their parents were still able to have babies at their advanced age, a thought that had completely bypassed Ken. When another girl was born in 1935, his sister's nose had been well and truly put out of joint by the realisation that she was now neither the only girl nor the youngest child. This situation was only rectified when, as a teenager, she started to see the advantages of her parents still being preoccupied with a younger child.

Ken was entranced with the idea of a baby from the start. He'd always been close to his mother, happily helping her collect the eggs every morning and going to the market with her to sell the jars of jam she'd been making all week. As her tummy swelled, he was fascinated to feel the kicks and see the shape of a foot, or an elbow emerge unbidden. And when his baby sister was born, Ken was the first of her siblings to hold her.

"You always were a big softie," his mother had said, ruffling his sandy hair. Secretly, she had been pleased that her youngest son was still the sweet boy he'd always been, despite growing almost four inches in the last year and developing wispy hairs on his chin.

"Anyone for Christmas pudding?"

The shout roused Ken from his reminiscences. They'd sat down in the living room after the turkey dinner and were now listening to the king's speech on the radio.

'Your thoughts will be in distant places, and your hearts with those you love,' the king said.

There was something very moving about the idea that, around the Commonwealth, people would be tuning in and hearing the very same words. He imagined his sisters sitting in the parlour with his parents, and his brother, stationed in Yorkshire, listening with the rest of his squadron.

"I'd love some pudding, ma'am," Ken replied as the children came running down from their bedrooms clutching their new toys.

"Can we have the threepenny bit if you find it?" the little girl demanded, keen not to miss out on the fun of finding buried treasure, whilst being too full to eat another mouthful.

“You certainly can, little lady,” Ken replied. although in the end, his friend emerged victorious, only just avoiding swallowing it whole.

It was strange to think that had his father not decided to move to Canada as a young man, Ken might have been living in a house just like this. Life on the farm had not been easy for his parents. His father had moved to Canada from Scotland in 1911. Attracted by the opportunities promised by ‘the most fertile country in the world’, he had purchased the 16-acre farm with an inheritance left by a childless great-uncle. Like many others, he’d returned home to fight in the First World War, and then, scarred by the memories and determined to put it behind him, he’d married his childhood sweetheart, and they had sailed to Canada to start their new life together on Vancouver Island.

When Ken had been born in 1923, there had been no indication of the impending depression. His parents had expanded and diversified the farm. Buoyed by high yields and good summers, they had borrowed to buy a combine harvester, one of the first on Vancouver Island to do so. Ken remembered an idyllic childhood – playing amongst the haystacks, fishing for newts and tadpoles with his net, and enjoying picnics packed with the best of the land: sweet corn dripping with butter, bread piled high with jam and plums so sweet you had to eat them in the river, washing your fingers and mouth thoroughly before the wasps came for you.

By the time his baby sister had arrived, those days were long gone, together with the combine harvester, which they were lucky to sell to a neighbouring farm at a loss.

Hard work and sheer bloody-mindedness had helped them keep their heads above water during the great depression, paying off their debt and eating up the savings that his parents had managed to bring with them from Scotland. They had been lucky to survive. Many other farms hadn't, and it had made his parents increasingly cautious. Where other farmers started to take on help, they continued to manage without, meaning that Ken and his brother took on more and more of the jobs. When war broke out in Europe, both brothers had wanted to sign up. After long years of relentless hard work, a heady mix of patriotism for their parents' country of birth and the promise of travel and adventure proved hard to resist. Ken would never forget the day they had walked into their parents' parlour with all the family present and announced their intentions.

His baby sister had burst into tears. His other sister, usually so calm in a crisis, had stamped her feet, shouted that it was 'so unfair', and stormed out of the house. Their father, keen to avoid the inevitable confrontation, ran after her, and their mother sat silently, her needlework abandoned on her lap, with tears welling up in her eyes.

Within a minute, all the excitement and purpose that the brothers felt was punctured, and they stood there deflated, unwilling to take back the words that had ripped like a tornado through their future plans, but uncertain what to do next. For the next few hours, nobody spoke about their announcement. Ken even wondered if it had all been a dream and that they had thought the words and not said them out loud. Eventually, after his sisters had gone to bed, their mother and father sat them down at the kitchen table and talked.

"Your father and I have been fearing this day for months," their mother had begun. "And the last thing we want to do is stand in your way."

"We're proud of you, of course we are," their father had added, "but we just don't know how we'll cope on the farm without you."

They'd talked for most of the evening and finally agreed that his brother, as the eldest, would go. Ken would stay at home to help manage the farm. It hadn't been the outcome that Ken had hoped for, but he'd never been able to hurt his mother, and he could tell that both her sons going off to fight would have broken her heart. Over the next eighteen months, Ken had thrown all his energy into managing the farm. All Canadian farmers were expected to 'Grow for Britain', so he and his father had made changes, growing more crops and selling their cows to other farms so they could concentrate on the food that would most help the war effort.

Ken knew what they were doing was important, but with every friend that volunteered and every letter home from his brother, he became more frustrated with his lot. In the end, it was a chance encounter and a bit of luck that had sealed his fate. He had been at the next-door farm one day, tinkering with the tractor, when his neighbour had mentioned that the university in Vancouver was looking for people to undertake a sixteen-week electronics course.

"You're pretty handy with that sort of thing," his neighbour had continued. "Why don't you think about applying?"

Those who did well were selected for further training and then shipped to England to undertake vital work there.

Ken was flattered that his neighbour thought him good enough, but worried about getting his hopes up.

"I don't know though, sir," Ken had replied. "It sounds great, but my parents wouldn't be able to cope without me."

At that moment, two girls walked past. One of them turned and smiled at him, her dark hair and green eyes lighting up as she caught his stare.

"Who are they?" he asked, aware of his neck growing hot under his collar.

"That'll be our new farm cadets. They're here for the summer, maybe longer, to help out around the farm."

Ken had heard about schemes to get girls and young women to help on the farms whilst the men went to war, but he suddenly saw a way through. If he could find some cadets to help his parents, then maybe he could sign up for the electronics course and finally get to follow his brother to England.

Over the next few weeks, he had worked hard to get his parents on board with his idea. Surprisingly, his sister had become an ally, and with the arrival of the farm cadets on the next-door farm, Mary was keen to show that anything the boys could do, she could do just as well. It only took a few weeks for his parents to agree to the idea, and by then the three girls had become firm friends. Most evenings, Ken would hang around with his sister and the girls. From the start, it was clear that one of the girls was interested in Ken. Laurie had rosy cheeks and a gentle manner, and her face lit up whenever Ken was around.

"You know she's sweet on you?" his sister would say when they sat together on the verandah at night. She was only pointing out what everyone else could see. And whilst Ken definitely felt something back, he also knew that this was his chance for adventure, and however much he cared for her, nothing and no one was going to stop him from joining up. While he was at the University in Vancouver, he would come home to see Laurie and his family most weekends, but once he moved to Clinton for radar training, they'd kept in touch with letters. After his training finished, he had returned home for a few days' leave before departing for England. It was a strange few days, with Ken excited to be leaving, and his family and Laurie finding it hard to imagine life without him around. On his last evening, he and Laurie had sat on the haystacks, holding hands and looking at the stars.

"It's the same stars in England, you know," she'd said, "So you can look up, and I'll look up, and it will be just like we're sitting next to each other."

He'd kissed her then, but even though they were both caught up in the moment, he'd been careful not to take advantage of her obvious adoration. Who knew what would happen in the future? The last thing he wanted to do was break her heart, but it was surprisingly comforting to know there was someone at home waiting for him if he ever made it back.

They finally left the Christmas celebrations at 6 o'clock, full of good food and cheer. They had just enough time to get back to the hotel and change into their uniforms before an evening cocktail party at one of the larger hotels on the front. It was a cold, clear night, and Ken and his friend chatted amiably as they made their way along the front.

"What do you think about the posting, Ken?"

They had heard two days ago they were being posted to Devon. They were very different characters, but they'd grown close over the past couple of months, and Ken was pleased to have someone to navigate all these new experiences with.

"I'm looking forward to it. It feels like a long time in the making."

"I know. I thought the war might be over before we saw any action."

The posting was to RAF Harrowbeer, a base full of American and Canadian Airmen. They would be working between the airbase and RAF Hawkstor, a Chain Home radar station just a few miles away. As soon as they had got their postings, the hunt was on to find out what the living quarters were like and what opportunities there were to socialise with the opposite sex. The word from others was that it was all a bit basic, but there was a high WAAF contingent at Hawks Tor.

"Did you leave anyone special at home?" Ken asked. They had swapped family details but not mentioned any sweethearts they'd left behind.

"Nobody special. You never know what's facing us over here."

"Or who'll we'll meet." laughed Ken.

By now, he'd expected to be missing Laurie more than he was. It made him feel guilty.

"Come on, slowcoach, race you back to the hotel," his friend shouted ahead of him.

"Give me a minute. I need to tie my shoelaces."

It was a very dark, clear night. Ken looked up at the sky and located the three stars of Orion's belt.

"Happy Christmas, Laurie," he whispered before sprinting after his friend.

Met at the village hall

"Are you wearing your blackouts tonight, Peggy"

"Not if I can help it," Margaret replied, stubbing out the end of her cigarette and jumping to her feet. The two friends sat outside enjoying their cigarette rations, watching the March sun slowly disappear across the moor. They were supposed to wear regulation uniforms at all times, including the dreaded underwear, but a recent assignation with an American airman had secured her friend some silk from a German parachute. Margaret had not pressed too hard for details of what was expected in return, delighted instead that a) she was her closest friend and b) her friend's sister-in-law was such a skilled seamstress that she had been able to fashion two pairs of exceptionally fine cami knickers from the material.

Margaret had arrived at RAF Hawks Tor via Gloucester, Yatesbury, and the Isle of Wight. Basic training in Gloucester had passed in a whirlwind of uniform fittings, dental inspections, square-bashing, and aircraft identification. In Yatesbury, she signed the Official Secrets Act and was initiated into the secrets of radar. Understanding just how important her job would be almost made up for the sleepless nights that followed hour after hour of focused concentration. Finally, in Ventnor, her wartime experience began in earnest. Following the intensity of the training, life on an RAF station was a breath of fresh air. She found it easy to make friends; a shared dormitory and long night duty shifts created a strong bond with the other girls, while regular trips to the pub and local dances gave Margaret her first experience of the opposite sex. It was in Ventnor that she met Jim.

Jim came from the East End of London and had joined the RAF from technical college, although he claimed to be the least technical person there was. Without the war, their paths would never have crossed, yet they had clicked straight away, meeting behind the scenes at a pantomime he had written – a modern version of Cinderella, full of in-jokes and witty songs. He had played Buttons to rapturous applause, and Margaret had found him charming. Her parents wouldn't approve of their friendship, but that hadn't stopped them from spending time together. Long walks on the coast and visits to the cinema led to kisses, but never anything more.

When she was posted to Hawks Tor, they promised to keep in touch, and she received a long letter every week full of funny poems and limericks that made her laugh out loud. Two months ago, he had written about an overseas posting. She had written back with all her news, but Margaret wondered if her fondness for him was more sisterly than anything romantic. The war had heightened her senses, but life on the base was always busy, and sometimes Margaret went many days without ever thinking about him.

Since Christmas, the Germans had embarked on a renewed bombing campaign, which the papers called the Baby Blitz. The raid last week on Bristol had been a spectacular disaster, with many of the bombs ditched harmlessly into the sea around Poole and Bournemouth. With very few losses on the Allied side, the mood in the station was upbeat, the chatter in the dorm all about the dance at Horrabridge. The friends walked back into the dormitory. The few lucky enough to be off duty tonight were trying and failing to keep their excitement to themselves. One was holding up a small mirror and applying the Victory Red lipstick her mother had sent her last week.

"I can't wait for tonight!" she intoned dramatically, lying back on her bed and clutching her knees to her chest. It seems months ago that we let our hair down and put on our dancing shoes."

"It was only two weeks ago, and unless you want to be put on report, we'll have to wear our clodhoppers as usual," replied another.

"It's just so unfair," the first girl continued. "How can we compete with the village girls in their pretty dresses? We look so dowdy by comparison."

"They say that some men prefer a girl in uniform. It adds a touch of mystery."

"I don't know about that. I've heard that the Americans call blackouts 'Passion Killers', or 'Harvest Festivals' because everything is safely gathered in!"

The room dissolved into hoots of laughter, and two of the younger girls stood on their beds and started a lighthearted pillow fight.

At this, her friend nudged Margaret conspiratorially and pointed at the brown paper package on her bed.

"No blackouts for us tonight, Peggy," she whispered.

Margaret was slightly in two minds about the dance tonight. On the one hand, she loved to dance. Since the Americans had arrived, she and her friends spent hours practising the jitterbug on their time off, each taking their turn at leading. They had built up quite a repertoire of steps. On the other hand, she was worried about going out and enjoying herself with Jim so far away. She had never made him any promises, but as she looked forward to the dance tonight, she felt guilty that her thoughts were not with him, but on the Canadians she might dance with later.

"Shove up! I don't think I'll survive another bump."

Margaret and her friends had managed to bag a lift to the dance in a truck and were sitting haphazardly in the back, being thrown about by every lump or bump in the road. The driver had had other deliveries to make before getting them to the village hall at Horrabridge, so it was nearly 9 pm when they arrived, and the dance was in full swing. The friends made straight for the cloakroom, where they combed their hair and reapplied their lipstick.

"Do you think the Canadians will be here tonight?" Margaret ventured. "I've heard so much about them."

"I do hope so, Peggy. The GIs are nice, but they can be a little full-on. The Canadians are more like our boys..."

The reference to 'our boys' brought Jim to mind. Margaret wondered, not for the first time, whether Jim had seen their relationship in a different light.

"... except with more money and a lovely accent! I'm a sucker for the accent, I must say."

Margaret put any further thoughts of Jim to the back of her mind.

"Let's go and get a drink and see if we can spot any that we want to dance with," she countered.

"Righty-ho! But don't go and leave me on my own, unless I make it clear that things are going OK!"

"Of course. I wouldn't do that to you, and we'll leave together come what may," Margaret promised.

Ken was in two minds about going to the dance tonight. He'd only recently arrived at Harrowbeer, and most nights it was as much as he could do to write his diary before he was out like a light.

"You can't let me go on my own." After a week of night shifts, his pal was keen to see what the local area had to offer. "And just imagine all the beautiful women you could be missing out on."

Nestled on the edge of Dartmoor, the airbase was well equipped for socialising. Every month there would be a dance in the mess and the onsite cinema provided a welcome distraction from the daily stress of sorties and strikes. Tonight's dance was off base at the village hall at Horrabridge, and many had decided to attend, buoyed by rumours that the local land girls would be there in force.

"I love a girl in dungarees," Ken's pal said mischievously, "although they have a very strict 'no male visitors after lights out' rule at the local WLA hostel."

"You love a challenge," Ken laughed, although he doubted his friend would have the guts to try anything. He was much too respectable for that. Few of his friends had much experience of the female sex unless they happened to have sisters – in which case, they knew just how fierce they could be.

All this talk of land girls brought Laurie to mind. The latest letter from his mother had reassured him they were all doing well. Despite the rationing, they were eating better than they had in years. His mother had been busy home-canning the plums and pears from their orchard as part of the Jam for Britain campaign. Yesterday, a parcel had arrived for him that was jumped on by his fellow Canadians. Although he was missing home, Ken hadn't found that absence made the heart grow fonder when it came to Laurie. He enjoyed reading the letters she sent, but he couldn't summon up the feelings he had felt when sitting beside her at the farm. It was good, in a way. At least he didn't feel homesick.

Ken felt guilty about how little he thought about his girl back home. The other day, he had been to Hawks Tor to help out. The winter cold and flu season had hit them hard, and they were desperate for trained operators. He had finished his six-hour shift and was getting ready for the ride back when he made eye contact with one of the WAAFs. She was tall and slender, and her brunette hair had a natural wave. As he'd walked out of the Operations Room, he'd held the door open for her, and as she smiled and thanked him, their eyes had met for the merest of moments.

"A penny for them, Ken?"

"Sorry, I'm not sure I'd be the best company tonight. I wonder if I've caught the 'flu they all had at Hawks Tor."

“That’s a shame,” his friend replied mischievously, “only I've heard there’s a big contingent of WAAFs coming to the dance tonight.”

“Is that true, or are you just hoping to talk me around?” Ken asked. He had briefly mentioned the green-eyed girl he’d seen last week, and he wouldn’t put it past his pal to make things up to persuade him to come tonight.

“God’s honest truth,” Bill replied, drawing a cross over his heart, “and I might not be able to stop dancing with them myself!"

“OK, you’ve got me good and proper. Give me ten minutes to get ready, and I’ll see you on the truck,” Ken replied. However tired he felt, if she was going to be there, he couldn’t risk missing seeing her again.

Her friend went to buy them a Gin and It while Margaret surveyed the packed dance floor. The recent Baby Blitz meant there were a great many airmen in tonight. She recognised a few of them from other dances and knew which ones to decline politely, either because of their two left feet or their propensity for becoming overly amorous. In one corner of the hall, she noticed the distinctive uniforms of the Canadian airmen. Perhaps it was the lack of familiarity, but she found them particularly attractive. Her friend returned with their drinks as the band struck up a foxtrot. The local girls in their civvies started dancing arm in arm with each other, hoping to gain the attention of the GIs, who tended to stay by the bar drinking and smoking until the band played the Lindy Hop or the jitterbug. It was hard to compete with all that colour,

Margaret thought, although her illicit silk underwear did make up for things a little!

She saw one of the officers from the local base walking towards them and was relieved when he asked another girl if she would like to dance. He was pleasant in a dull sort of way and would have been deemed a suitable catch by her mother, but after Jim, Margaret found herself put off by the stiffness and old-fashioned manners of these well-educated boarding school boys. Not so her friends, who made no secret of their desire to 'bag an officer' who could keep them in a style to which they would love to become accustomed. Margaret finished her drink and was thinking of getting another when the band started to play *The Blackout Stroll*, and one of the girls she had shared a truck with grabbed her arm. "Come on, Margie, we can't stand around drinking all night. We need to find ourselves some handsome partners," she implored. "Let's start together, and then make our way over to the Canadians. When the lights go out, we'll make sure we get the best-looking ones," she continued, delighted with her plan.

Margaret glanced casually towards the section of the room where most of the Canadian airmen were assembled, hoping she wasn't being too obvious. The girls picked up the tune and, taking care not to stand on each other's feet, manoeuvred around the room. It was hard to judge when the lights might be extinguished, so as soon as they were in position, they turned circles on the spot.

"We can't stay here all night," Margaret whispered, "People will guess what we're up to."

"Don't worry, I bought the band leader a drink," her friend laughed, and suddenly the room was plunged into darkness. "Operation Canada Duck successfully completed," she whispered back as she dropped Margaret's hands.

Taking a deep breath, Margaret walked in a straight line and, almost immediately, her hands were taken in a firm, confident grip. Something was thrilling about starting to dance with someone you couldn't see, as if fate had intervened. She could tell that he was tall, certainly taller than she was, and he led with confidence. Within a few seconds, the lights went up, and she blinked as her eyes slowly became accustomed to the light.

"Wow," he mouthed. Then, recovering his manners, "I'm so pleased to be acquainted with you."

Margaret's heart was beating ten to the dozen. She tried to take in his features while continuing the dance. He was tall, over six foot, and had one of those friendly faces that kept breaking out into a smile. He had twinkling green eyes and dark sandy hair, which he wore with a side parting. She realised he was waiting for her to say something, but her mouth had gone dry, and she was finding it hard to form any words.

"I saw you as soon as you came into the hall," he said flatteringly. "I couldn't take my eyes off you."

"I'm sure you say that to all the girls," she stumbled, blushing slightly.

"I did. I was waiting for the opportunity to come and introduce myself."

The music stopped.

"Shall we get a drink?" he asked.

Margaret suddenly felt in urgent need of another drink. She couldn't make head or tales of her reaction to this man. He was just another airman, like all the others she worked alongside. Before the war, Margaret never had much contact with men, just expecting them to be like her father. Since joining up she regarded them mostly as colleagues to share a joke with, or as companions on visits to the pub. None of these men had made her stomach turn somersaults or her neck turn pink the way it was doing now!

"Do you want a cigarette?" she asked, hastily pulling a packet of Players from her jacket.

"Don't mind if I do," he responded, guiding her to the bar. "What are you having?"

"I'll have a beer, please."

As he got the drinks, Margaret composed herself. Gradually she became aware of what was going on around her. She could see one of her friends standing with a Canadian, and yet another dancing with the officer from earlier. The cigarette was calming her nerves, and she was starting to feel more like herself. The next minute the band struck up a jitterbug and all the Americans swarmed onto the dance floor, grabbing the local girls out of the arms of their current partners. Not that they looked like they minded too much. At one dance on the Isle of Wight, there had been a scuffle between the British boys and the GIs, but in general, most Brits knew they were beaten when it came to any form of jive. They just weren't built for it in the same way.

Margaret glanced at her handsome Canadian.

"Shall we?" he enquired, glancing towards the dance floor.

"I'd love to," Margaret replied, stubbing out her cigarette and putting her glass on the table.

Immediately, they were caught up in a flurry of activity as couples competed to show off their best moves. Initially, Margaret felt shy about letting go with an unfamiliar partner, but before long the practice with her girlfriends paid dividends, and she got into her stride, buoyed by the confidence of her Canadian. It was one of the things she loved most about dancing. It was so physical, you just lost yourself to the music and let your body take over. And this partner was good, twisting and turning, jumping and jiving with the best of the Americans.

Compared with the local girls, Margaret and her WAAF friends were inhibited by their uniforms, but looking around the dance floor, all Margaret could see was a whirligig of unashamed happiness. Earlier in the war, some had criticised the decision to allow dancing at a time of national emergency, but no one now would deny the brave young pilots the opportunity to let their hair down when no one knew what their future might hold. Many nights Margaret would lie awake, listening for the sound of the planes taking off and then returning hours later, counting them out and counting them all back home safely.

As the band stopped playing and people left the dance floor, Margaret assessed her partner. Even dishevelled by the dance and with sweat gathering on his upper lip, she wasn't disappointed. In fact, she wondered what it would be like to kiss those lips and allow herself to be enveloped by those broad, masculine arms. He smiled quizzically, as if he had somehow guessed what was going through her mind. She grinned back.

"That was quite something," she acknowledged, finding her beer and taking a sip to give her time to steady herself. "Wherever did you learn to dance like that?"

"I could ask you the same thing, ma'am," he teased.

"I've been practising with my girlfriends for just such an occasion," she offered in a conspiratorial tone. "We didn't want to be outshone by the local girls."

"There was never any chance of that," he countered. "I can't imagine there would be many that would outshine you, in any way at all."

His eyes twinkled as he spoke, and Margaret realised she'd never really been courted before. Her dates with Jim had come off the back of going out as a group of friends, and whilst they had cuddled and kissed at the cinema, she'd never really seen him as anything more than a friend. What she saw in her Canadian's eyes was something quite different. It was the look Humphrey Bogart gave Ingrid Bergman in *Casablanca,* as if she were the most beautiful and desirable woman in the entire world. Margaret broke his gaze, embarrassed and confused by the emotions he was stirring within her. At that moment, her friend arrived.

"Hello there," she giggled, "Aren't you going to introduce me to this handsome fella?"

"Of course, silly me," stumbled Margaret, "This is Mary, the friend I just mentioned, and this is..." Margaret realised that she didn't know his name.

"This is Ken," he replied.

She ordered a cream tea

Give me your hand, and I'll help you to the top," Ken offered, reaching down towards her.

"I've managed this far. I'm sure I can make it on my own," Margaret replied, breathing hard as she made the final effort and emerged triumphantly at the very top of Smiths Cliff.

They had set out early this morning, grabbing a lift with air crew that were being transferred to Davidstow, and then catching the bus to Boscastle before walking along the coast to Tintagel. Since meeting at the dance in March, Margaret and Ken had spent most of their free time together, but this weekend was the first time they had managed to coordinate their weekend leave.

In the intervening months, they had learned more than many couples learn about each other in a lifetime. Ken was a natural storyteller, entertaining her with tales of his family in Vancouver – his brother, who was soft on a girl that he had met at a school dance, his older sister, who loved to knit and had made Ken a wardrobe of socks before he left for England, and his baby sister Beth, who was just eight when he left for the war, a miracle sibling born to his parents in their mid-40s. Each character was described so vividly that Margaret felt as if she had already met them.

As they spent long days walking across the moors, Margaret shared her own stories. She told him about the day her father had come home soaked to the skin after he had been pulled into the river by an enormous trout he had tried to land. She opened up to him about the strained relationship with her mother, and how abandoned she had felt when she was sent to boarding school. As the memories threatened to overwhelm her, Ken held her tight and told her that he would never send her away from him.

Their lives had been different, but despite growing up nearly 5,000 miles apart, they had much in common. They loved the great outdoors and often tried to outdo each other with their knowledge of trees, flowers and birds. They had developed a point system for each discovery. On the walk today, Margaret spotted a Felwort, a rare plant she'd seen in a book her father had given her for Christmas. Margaret claimed five points for rarity to put her into the lead, while Ken argued that her local knowledge gave her an unfair advantage, and it should be downgraded to three. As they got their breath and looked out to sea, Ken put his arms around her and rested his chin on her head. They stood quietly for a while, taking in the freshness of the sea breeze and watching the gulls as they hovered and glided above the waves, looking for lunch.

"I think that's a Herring Gull." Ken pointed to the distance.

"It's a shame we haven't got radar to identify it properly," Margaret laughed.

One of the pleasures of spending time together was they could talk about their work.

"Are you feeling homesick?" Margaret asked.

"A little, I suppose. I miss Mom's home cooking, but this almost makes up for it." He squeezed Margaret a little tighter.

"Almost?" Margaret turned to face him. "Perhaps this will help."

She kissed him lightly and then pressed more firmly until his lips parted. Ken moaned and kissed her back.

"OK, not just almost; entirely, completely. You have no idea what you are doing to me."

"I rather think I do," laughed Margaret as they set off again along the coastal path towards Tintagel.

By three o'clock, they had reached the castle, and before visiting the ruins, they stopped for a cream tea at the local tea rooms.

"You know there's etiquette involved with a British cream tea?"

Margaret had already ordered scones with clotted cream and a pot of tea for two.

"I wouldn't want to be taken for an uncouth foreigner, so do fill me in immediately," laughed Ken.

"In Devon, you put the cream on first and then the jam, whereas in Cornwall, they would shoot you if you did that," Margaret explained.

"I don't see any pistols under their aprons," Ken replied.

"It's simply not worth taking the chance," Margaret laughed, adding the cream on top of the thick layer of strawberry jam.

Sitting enjoying a cream tea on a warm May afternoon, it felt like the war was a million miles away. The news recently had been more positive, with the failed bombing of Bristol giving everyone hope that, finally, the Germans were on the back foot. After four long and difficult years, Margaret allowed herself to think about life after it was all finished. Funny though it sounded, the war had suited her. She was no longer the same person who had sat nervously with Mummy at Lyons Corner House, desperate for her approval. In the WAAF, she had relished finding something she was good at and enjoyed the respect that came with it. And she had made friends for life with others who were as quick-witted and competent as she was. The icing on the cake, she'd found her Ken, or fate had intervened and they had found each other.

"A penny for your thoughts?" said Ken.

Margaret smiled back. She had been teaching Ken English idioms, and she loved that he was now using them with her.

"I was just thinking how much I'm enjoying the war," Margaret started. "Well, not enjoying, that would be an awful thing to say. I just mean that you make me very happy," she stumbled.

"You make me very happy too."

Ken held her hands in his and kissed them lightly, hesitating as if there was more to say.

"What is it?" Margaret prompted. She saw the merest hint of something in Ken's face that she couldn't place. Fear perhaps, or regret.

"It's nothing. I can't believe that less than a year ago, I hadn't met you, and now I can't imagine life without you." Ken's words were laced with emotion.

They paid the bill, thanked the waitress, and set off to explore the ruins of Tintagel.

Like many Canadians, Ken was fascinated by English history. Margaret bought a guidebook from the small hut at the entrance and read passages as they strolled between the walls, catching glimpses of the Cornish sea below.

"In the 12th century, the cleric Geoffrey of Monmouth wrote the History of the Kings of Britain," Margaret began.

"I love your accent, Peggy," Ken grinned.

He had started calling her Peggy the first time they met at the village dance. To most of her friends, she was Margaret or occasionally Margie, but Ken had adopted Peggy as his pet name for her, and she rather liked it.

"Stop interrupting, or I'll have to throw you over the parapet," she said bossily.

"In it, he tells the tale of Uther Pendragon, King of Britain, who was driven mad with his lust for Ygerna, the wife of Gorlois of Cornwall. Aware of his rival's desires, Gorlois imprisons Ygerna in an impregnable stronghold on the coast – the castle of Tintagel."

"It doesn't look terribly impregnable to me," interrupted Ken.

"Shh, I'm reading."

"But then, rather stupidly, he goes to live in a fortress nearby. When Uther sees the castle, he realises that no ordinary attack can succeed. There is only one way in, and the guards could easily hold out against a small army," Margaret continued, ignoring the interruptions.

"Exciting!" exclaimed Ken.

"Idiot!" laughed Margaret.

"Seeing Uther's despair, Merlin the prophet uses a magic potion to transform Uther into the exact likeness of

Ygerna's absent husband. The guards fall for it, and so does Ygerna, who takes him to her bed. That night, she conceives Arthur, later to become King Arthur."

"Who would have thought history could be so thrilling?" said Ken.

"More legend than history, but yes, it is amazing the lengths some men will go to get a woman into bed," concluded Margaret. They continued the tour hand in hand, Margaret reading excerpts from the guidebook and Ken interrupting.

They were surprised when the man from the kiosk came to tell them that he was about to shut the gates. It had been a beautiful day, and neither wanted it to end. On the bus back to Boscastle, they sat in companionable silence, Ken reading the rest of the guidebook while Margaret let herself imagine what life might be like after the war was finished. Everyone knew it was foolish to make plans during wartime because you never knew what was around the corner. But with her head resting on his shoulder, she daydreamed about setting up home with Ken. She didn't know what that life would be like, or even which country it would be in. If push came to shove, she wondered whether she could leave her family and friends behind and move to Canada, or convince Ken to stay in England? Would she persuade her mother that this charming Canadian would be a good catch for her least favourite daughter?

Before she knew it, the bus was stopping, and they were back in Boscastle.

"Come on, Peggy, you were miles away!" said Ken, grabbing her hand as they jumped off the bus. Tired but happy, they walked back up the hill to The Wellington Hotel.

The hotel stay had been her idea, a way for them to have some proper time together rather than the evenings at the pub or local dances that had inevitably been shared with friends. As she dressed for dinner in her single room, she wondered whether that had been her only motivation for suggesting the holiday. Like most girls of her background, she had been warned about being alone with men who 'were only interested in one thing'. Conversations with friends in the WAAF suggested that women often enjoyed this one thing just as much as men and that wartime provided the perfect excuse to find out. As their kisses had become ever more passionate, Margaret felt herself yearning for something more. A few months ago, she'd had a letter from Cynthia, who had told her about a friend who had decided to 'go all the way' with a soldier on home leave. When the friend heard that he had been killed in action, she had been pleased that they had been intimate and comforted by the precious memory. Margaret briefly wondered whether this had happened to a 'friend' or whether Cynthia was trying to tell her about her own experience and had worried that Margaret would be shocked by the admission.

She certainly wasn't shocked, although a few years ago she might have been. Her mother would have dismissed it as something that 'girls like Cynthia' do, but that well-brought-up young ladies would never consider until their wedding night. As if being born in the East End bred into girls a willful disregard for the natural order of things and left them bereft of morality. Had her mother expected these lessons in morality to be instilled into her daughter by two spinsters at Fairfield Lodge, she would have been sorely disappointed. All that experience had given her was a certainty that she was not cut out to be a good and dutiful wife in the image of her mother. The war had come at just the right time for Margaret; without it, she would have been reduced, for a reduction it would have been, to marrying some nice but dull man who met her mother's unwritten standards of class and social standing.

What the war had done spectacularly well was rip apart all the previous social norms. By putting young people, men and women, rich and poor, educated and uneducated in a melting pot, adding a uniform, and stirring in a heady cocktail of national pride and excitement, the war had created a generation unprepared to accept the previous rules. Perhaps that was what her mother had seen in her all those years ago, the potential for disobedience, for holding her own opinions and making up her own mind. Disobedient, she might be, but she wasn't unkind. For the last few months, she had worried that Jim felt more for her than she did for him. He had been away for nearly two years, and while neither had promised to be faithful to the other when they parted, she wondered if he had misinterpreted the signs. His letters to her were full of humour and warmth and he talked endlessly about rekindling things on his return, and how much he missed her. She always signed her letters, *Yours Ever, Margaret*, but she meant nothing more than they would be friends forever.

It wasn't friendship she felt when Ken kissed her, but the rush of something she had no words for in parts of her body that felt awake for the first time. She had to find out if she could trust these feelings and whether what she felt for Ken was more than mere desire.

That night, Margaret got dressed more carefully than usual, and by the time she had slipped on her silk underwear and dabbed a little Chanel behind her ears, her heart was beating faster than she could ever remember it beating before. The perfume had been a 21st birthday present from her sister. She couldn't think about her family now, or she might lose all courage at the last minute. She checked her hair for the last time in the mirror, slipped on her shoes and went downstairs to meet Ken for dinner.

Ken was already seated in the dining room, looking out of the window towards the sea. Margaret took a few moments to renew her resolve, before walking to the table. It amused her to think that Ken had no idea of her plans. She assumed that he was more experienced than she was, but perhaps when the time came, he would be too much of a gentleman. She had no idea what she would do then. Until that moment, her idea had felt thrilling, but now in the cold light of day, she started to feel a little sick.

When Ken turned round, everything was alright again. He was just her Ken, and she was herself, not some scarlet woman about to seduce him. It was all going to be fine.

The next morning, Margaret woke feeling completely happy. Next to her, in the tiny single bed lay her big Canadian bear. She lightly tousled his sandy hair and wondered what she had done to be so lucky. She had surprised him last night; being the gentleman he was, he had not considered the possibility that they would sleep together. Happily not such a gentleman that he had refused. They hadn't been able to resist each other. And despite her inexperience, Margaret found she gave him pleasure without any embarrassment. For her part, the wave of desire she felt when he kissed her had travelled to every part of her body, making her toes curl and her fingers tingle. A surge of pleasure that she was unable to contain had finally exploded in her brain like fireworks on New Year’s Eve.

“Wake up Ken,” Margaret whispered as she nuzzled his neck. It was nearly 8.45 am, and breakfast was finishing soon. Ken stretched out luxuriantly, almost forcing her off the single bed but grabbing her just in time.

“I think this is the happiest I’ve ever been, and the best I’ve ever slept,” Ken yawned.

“Probably because you took up most of the bed,” Margaret laughed. “Anyway, I am famished and breakfast finishes in half an hour, so I think we'll have to find a way for you to go back to your room without anyone seeing you, and then we can meet at breakfast like perfectly respectable folk.”

“We are perfectly respectable,” countered Ken. “It’s just that we can’t keep our hands off each other.”

Margaret pulled him to her and kissed him deeply. Ken groaned as the effect she had on him made departure from the room impossible.

“Perhaps we can miss breakfast just this once,” said Margaret, as she pulled him close to her.

He made a promise

"Is everything OK, Ken? You've hardly touched your pint?" With all the noise, no one noticed how quiet Ken was. Peggy was deep in conversation with her friends. She saw Ken out of the corner of her eye and mouthed, "Are you OK?"

Ken nodded and pretended to be interested in the latest gossip. He usually loved evenings like this, where the drinks and laughter flowed. His heart wasn't in it tonight. On Monday, his commanding officer called him into the office to tell him he was being posted as part of a top-secret mission. Since D-Day there had been rumours of a second invasion in Southern France that would trap the German war machine between Normandy and Marseille. Those rumours were now becoming reality and Ken would be part of a mobile radar unit designed to provide the Allies with as much warning as possible during the invasion. He would be leaving from Plymouth next week.

Ken should have felt honoured, but from the minute he left the office, he felt sick at the prospect of leaving Peggy. He couldn't explain how he felt about her. Nothing he had experienced so far had prepared him for these feelings. After their weekend in Tintagel, he'd hardly slept for days. He had expected his feelings to settle with time, but even now, every time he thought of her, his heart would beat so fast that he had to breathe deeply and slowly to bring his pulse down. He supposed he must be in love with her, but nothing had prepared him for this. Sometimes, when he and Margaret were together, he felt as if a fever had taken over his entire body – he was intoxicated by her.

As the week progressed, he became increasingly anxious about telling Margaret. He convinced himself that once they parted they would never be reunited and he was sure that he would never get over it, never get over her. Where before, he would have engineered reasons to bump into her between shifts, he now found ways to avoid her. He knew that as soon as she looked into his eyes, she would know something was wrong, and he couldn't bear it. In his misery, he contemplated disappearing without telling her, but he wasn't a coward. Instead, he spent the time rehearsing what he was going to say, going over and over the words in his head, desperate to find a way to reassure her about how much he loved her, without letting his fears surface. He had his speech planned, but when they got to the pub, surrounded by friends, he would have done anything to put it off. As those around him drank their beers and gossiped, all he could hear was the clock on the wall counting down relentlessly to the moment he had been dreading all week.

"Right. Who wants a lift back to base?"

A voice from across the table broke into Ken's consciousness. The night was ending, and people were picking up their things and getting ready to leave.

"Yes, please. Bagsy the front seat!" Margaret answered for both of them.

"Would you mind if we walked?" Ken asked quietly.

"Really? It's two miles at least. Wouldn't you rather cadge a lift with the others?" Margaret turned to look at him.

"I need to talk to you about something, and I need some air," Ken answered.

"You're scaring me," Margaret replied, the warm glow of the pub and the effect of the brandy and ginger ale quickly fading as she registered the tone of his voice. Ken made their excuses to the others. There was the usual laughter and innuendo from the other men about why they might want to be alone together. Margaret tried hard to act normally. She waved to her friends, but her smile was fixed, and she could feel the anxiety rising like acid in her stomach. She had a sixth sense for bad news. She vividly remembered the morning her mother told her about boarding school, her tone all soft and lilting. Margaret hadn't been fooled. Had her mother really believed that adopting a fake voice would somehow lull her into joyfully accepting the horrible news? Ken didn't play these games with her, he seemed to pick up on her feelings and anticipated her thoughts. It was one of the things she loved about him.

"I'm afraid I have some bad news, Peggy."

Ken's use of his private name for her brought a lump to her throat.

"I thought that might be the case," Margaret choked. Different scenarios were running through her head. None of them were good. "Go on then. I can take it," she managed, sounding more courageous than she felt.

"I've been posted," Ken continued, keen to get the bad news out of the way so he could take Margaret in his arms and comfort her. "It's top secret, but they urgently need more mobile radar units. They've asked for a Canadian unit, and I fit the bill."

"I suppose it's an honour for them to ask you?" Margaret managed, trying to hide her disappointment.

"Yes, they saw it that way. Although I wouldn't say they asked, exactly. I'm ready to do my duty, I just wish…" Ken's words trailed off into the night air.

"No point wishing. If wishes were horses, then beggars would ride," Margaret said softly.

"Is that another of your quaint English sayings?"

"It's Scottish, I think. My father used to say it to me when we were out walking."

"What does it mean?"

"I think it means that if wishing could make things happen, then even the poorest of people would have everything they wanted."

Margaret suddenly felt unbearably sad. All her hopes for the future. She and Ken getting married, sharing adventures, maybe starting a family, and growing old together. It all seemed ridiculous now, just silly dreams brought crashing down to earth by reality. Not for the first time, Margaret reflected on how strange the war had made everything. Without it, where would she be now? At home, probably, still being treated like a child. No doubt she'd be doing some dull shorthand typing job and being introduced to the 'suitable' sons of Mummy's friends at weekends. The war had given her so much more. The chance to do important work, to meet people that would never have been in her social circle, to drink, dance and smoke if she wanted to. To fall in love. With a Canadian, no less!

The fact that a single woman would go away for a weekend unchaperoned, would have been unthinkable before the war. She smiled, imagining Mummy walking in on her and Ken in bed together. Unthinkable. They walked in silence, not knowing what to say. The night was still, and the earthy smell of heather was hanging low on the developing mist. It was Ken who broke the silence. He stopped, pulled Margaret towards him, and encircled her in his big, comforting arms.

"I promise you that this will not be the end of us," Ken started in a low whisper. "The war is ending, everyone can feel it, and when it does, we will find a way to be together. I can come and live here, or you can come and join me in Vancouver. My parents will love you as much as I do. We can do some travelling. I can show you Canada, or you can show me Europe. It will be the two of us again, with our whole future to write."

Margaret buried her head deep in his shoulder, taking in his scent and feeling the weight of comfort in his hug. While he held her, she let herself believe it. She knew he had meant every word. But believing it didn't make it true. There were so many ways this could end, and Ken's way was just one of the possibilities. For the moment, his way was enough, and Margaret clung onto him as if, by doing so, she could make his promise come true.

Margaret couldn't believe how packed the train had become. When she boarded at Plymouth, she found an almost empty compartment well located between the buffet car and the toilets. But now she was at Taunton, every seat was taken, and she was pleased to have a window seat. Looking out as the fields sped by, Margaret could hardly believe how much had changed for her over the last two months. The trip back to London had been a last-minute decision, and she was lucky that Mary had agreed to swap her weekend pass. Margaret had told her enough to persuade her of the importance of the trip without burdening her with all the details. She didn't feel ready to do that yet. She wasn't sure she ever would be.

She was pleased that Jim had driven her to the station. He'd arrived back in England just a week after Ken had left. It was like one of those theatrical farces her mother was so fond of, with a man leaving by one door and another arriving by the other. It had been a joy to see Jim again, and he'd done much to lift her spirits. He had such energy and kept them all entertained at the pub with impressions of people he had come across on his posting to Italy. She had forgotten how charming he was, and despite missing Ken terribly, she could feel herself being drawn back into the comfortable friendship they had shared before. He was easy to talk to and without revealing too much about Ken, a good solid shoulder to cry on. With her own heart in quite a fragile state, she was embarrassed to say that she found his attention flattering. At the back of her mind, Margaret worried that this was because he felt more for her than she felt for him.

She hoped she wouldn't break his heart. They had got to Plymouth with only a few minutes to spare, and Margaret had quickly jumped out of the truck.

"Do think about what I said," Jim had said earnestly, handing her the suitcase. "I meant every word."

"I know you did Jim, and I promise I will think it through carefully. I just need some time to weigh everything up in my mind. I'll be back on Sunday night, and we can talk properly then," Margaret replied, kissing him on the cheek.

"Try not to miss me too much," said Jim, blowing her a kiss as he jumped back in the truck and drove away.

Without any warning, the train lurched forward and came to a sudden stop. A kit bag belonging to one of the soldiers fell out of the luggage rack, just missing a little girl seated opposite. Margaret rose to make sure that her luggage was secure.

"I hope we're not stopped here too long," the girl's mother exclaimed. "A couple of months ago we ended up almost sleeping on the train we were here so long."

"I think, ma'am, that was when they were moving all the troops ready for D-Day," a GI, sitting in the corner, responded.

"You're probably right, but it was no fun at all, was it, Nancy?" the mother grumbled. The child snuggled closer to her mother and buried her head into her shoulder, uncomfortable at the prospect of speaking in front of adults.

D-Day had felt momentous for the country. Eisenhower's plan and the ingenious deceptions that were put in place had finally put the Allies on the front foot. It had been followed in August by Operation Dragoon and now the news was much more positive. People dared to hope that this might be the beginning of the end. It seemed peculiarly cruel to Margaret that an event that had been the fulcrum for so much hope for the country had also been the focus of her own distress. The train starting up again jolted Margaret from her thoughts.

"Thank goodness for that. At least we'll be home for tea now, Nancy," the mother said.

"Can I have a sandwich to keep me going?" Nancy asked, and her mother took a fish paste sandwich from her bag.

"Sorry about the smell, but it's better than Nancy moaning for the next half an hour," the mother said laughingly to the rest of the carriage. Margaret smiled and took the opportunity to go to the toilet as she was bursting. The trip to London was long on the best of days, and this was not one of those. As she opened the compartment door on her return, she was struck by the strong smell of fish and had to work to counter an overwhelming sense of nausea. She breathed deeply and returned to her seat. Margaret had been feeling sick on and off for the past few weeks. It seemed that any strong smell set her off. The nausea had started soon after she missed her period and further confirmed what she already knew.

So far, she had managed to keep her pregnancy secret from her friends on base. It was not an easy thing to do when they were billeted together. She hated lying, so instead, she pretended that her period had come as usual, even complaining of tummy cramps to buy herself some time. She had no idea what she was going to do. She hardly knew how she felt. It was all so complicated and tied up with her feelings for Ken. She did feel shame. Getting pregnant was, without a doubt, the most shameful thing a girl could do. But alongside the shame was a feeling of outrage. She hadn't got herself pregnant, quite the opposite. And how could something that happened naturally between two people who were in love be shameful? It made no sense to her.

Her immediate problem was time was running out. After Ken had told her about his posting they had managed to secure extraordinary weekend leave. With little time to plan, they visited Plymouth, forged a make shift wedding ring from some copper wire, and spent two days holed up in a small hotel on the front. She was fortunate her pregnancy wasn't showing yet. But that wouldn't last forever. There was no room to hide in a WAAF uniform. Some days she would be so absorbed in her work that she could almost push the pregnancy to the back of her mind, but then a wave of nausea would hit her, and with it, the realisation that this was a problem that wasn't going away. The trip to London provided valuable thinking time. For a few hours, she didn't have to pretend that everything was fine, but she was so exhausted that all she wanted to do was sleep. Burning a hole in her pocket was the latest letter from Ken. It had arrived this morning, and she had skimmed it whilst waiting for Jim to pick her up. The train journey gave her time to read it properly and write a reply. Trembling, she took the letter from her bag and started to read.

My darling Peggy,

I can't believe that it's been a month since we kissed goodbye. I can honestly say that absence does make the heart grow fonder. Except I couldn't love you any more than I did on that day we parted.

It's so wonderful to receive your letters. When I read them, I can hear your voice speaking the words to me, as if you are right here beside me. Did I tell you how much I love your voice? How much I love all of you?

Margaret smiled to herself. How strange his accent had sounded when they first met. It was part of the magic. He sounded like a film star.

I'm sure you must be getting the news at home. I can't say much, but now we are making more progress, the mood is much more positive amongst the men. My one consolation for being away from you is that what we are doing seems to be making a difference. Hopefully, that means we can be together again very soon.

Being away from you has stirred up so many emotions, and seeing so much horror has made me hungry for your sweetness. I've had many letters from home which have left me homesick for the quiet and solitude of our little farm. I lie awake at night and imagine us on that farm together, you collecting the eggs in the morning and then us sharing a full English breakfast, like the one we missed that morning in Boscastle. Perhaps in a few years, we will buy a place of our own, and start a family.

Margaret instinctively touched her stomach. He had no idea, of course, why would he? She was sure he would do the right thing and marry her, as soon as he returned from France, but reading his vision for their life together, she felt a wave of anxiety. Did she want to be a farmer's wife, and would she want to live on the other side of the world, away from her family and friends? More pressingly, it seemed unlikely that Ken would get back before the baby was born. Her head in a whirl, she returned to the letter.

My darling, I know I am springing so much on you at once but thinking about our future is the only thing that keeps me sane. I love you so very much, and I would marry you in a heartbeat if only you'd have me. Please write back soon and tell me your answer.

Whatever the future holds, I will have no regrets because I have loved the best girl ever.

Your very own,

Ken

Margaret placed the letter on her lap and wiped her eyes with her handkerchief. The letter cemented the decision she had been wrestling with. She knew what she had to do. It would be the hardest thing she'd ever done, and it would cost her everything, but perhaps that was the price she had to pay for the months of happiness she shared with Ken. Only time would tell.

She said “No regrets”

“Come on Stan, help me tie this bunting up at the windows,” Queenie shouted up the stairs. Margaret was emerging from another uncomfortable night in a small single bed, but she couldn’t help but smile at the enthusiasm emanating from her mother-in-law.

“Margie, do you want a cup of tea? Shall I bring one up to you?” Queenie asked. “Today’s not a day for lingering in bed, even in your condition,” she laughed.

“A cup of tea would be lovely. Give me 5 minutes and I’ll be down to help,” Margaret answered, looking around for her dressing gown and manoeuvring herself into a more comfortable position.

Margaret stroked her bump affectionately, “Come on, little one. This is a day we will never forget.”

As she sat up and put her feet into her slippers, she glanced at the wedding photograph in proud position on the chest of drawers. She and Jim were smiling happily in the middle, Queenie and Stan were on either side of them with Cynthia, and Jim’s best friend, completing the wedding party. It had been a small gathering, organised so quickly that, thankfully, her own family had been unable to attend. Margaret was already three months pregnant, but Cynthia’s skills with the sewing machine meant that no one but Cynthia and Jim would ever know. Margaret was fortunate that her bump was small, and even though she was due any day her new parents-in-law believed this was a honeymoon baby.

When Margaret had confided in Jim about her condition, it was to show how impossible his proposal was. She has wanted to be honest about her feelings towards him. She saw him as a friend and nothing more. She glanced down at the wedding band. Her fingers had swollen during the pregnancy, and the ring was now impossible to remove. It was as if her body was confirming what she already knew. The decision she had taken was irreversible.

When she had told Jim about her pregnancy, what had she expected? Outrage? Hurt? Embarrassment? She hadn't wanted to break his heart, but she couldn't let him continue to think that their relationship had a future. But she had underestimated Jim, or at least she had underestimated how much he felt for her. Of course, he was shocked by the revelation, but if he was hurt by her betrayal or shocked at her indiscretion, he didn't show it. And then, 24 hours later, he was waiting for her at the end of her shift.

"I've been thinking," he began, "that if you'd have me, I'd be honoured to be your husband and to look after the little one as if they were my own…"

Hearing Jim, usually so funny and irreverent, sounding so serious and grown up, brought tears to Margaret's eyes.

"… and I know you don't love me yet, but we get on, don't we? Maybe that will be enough, or maybe, in time, you will learn to love me back." His voice crackled with emotion.

Margaret had been speechless, and then she had started to cry properly with big, splashy tears pouring down her face. For the life of her, she couldn't decide if they were tears of joy or sadness. Later, as she was sitting on the train to London, the situation became even more surreal. For there in black and white was her second proposal in less than 48 hours, although this time it was from the love of her life and the father of her unborn baby. And it wasn't exactly a proposal, more a confirmation of their love for each other: 'I would marry you in a heartbeat.'

Seeing her parents and her sister that weekend had helped Margaret make her decision, and when Jim met her at Plymouth on Monday evening, she wrapped her arms around him and told him that she would happily accept his proposal. Two weeks later, with help from a weekend pass, they were married at a church near Jim's parents in Leyton. When Margaret's friends asked about Ken, she had spoken sadly of a letter she'd received where he'd mentioned a childhood sweetheart and a desire to get back to Canada as soon as the war was over. At least that part was true. If anyone was surprised at how quickly she'd transferred her affections to Jim, they were too polite to say. A new posting for Jim helped explain away the rush for a wedding, and when six weeks later Margaret announced her pregnancy, no one suspected a thing.

The hardest part of all had been writing back to Ken. She had thrown away so many drafts before she found the right words. She had known that it would destroy him. It made her heart ache.

My darling Ken

It was wonderful to receive your letter. I could hear you speaking the words to me as if we were in the same room, not hundreds of miles apart.

My life has been reduced since you left for France. Every day is busy, but without you to share it, my life is empty. I long to touch your face and kiss your lips. My memories of our time together are my constant companion. I miss you with all my heart.

I scour the papers every day for news. We have been sheltered from the worst atrocities of the war in England, and even the bombs falling during the Blitz can't compare with the horrors we are hearing about on Omaha Beach. I pray that you are safe.

During our time apart, I have been thinking about our future. You write that you are missing your family and the quiet solitude of the farm, and it makes me think how much I would miss my own family if I were to come with you to Vancouver. You know how much Mummy infuriates me, but I would find it hard to leave them all behind. Does that sound selfish? This time apart has shown me how hard it is to be away from those you love.

I will always love you Ken, and some part of you will always be with me, but I know in my heart that I can't come with you, and I love you too much to ask you to stay with me. We should have, as you say, no regrets for I have loved the nicest guy ever.

Your very own

Peggy x

She blotted the ink and folded the paper quickly, worrying that, at any moment, she might change her mind. For the week after she had posted it, she had disturbed nights and vivid dreams. In the small hours of the morning, she couldn't stop herself from imagining Ken's excitement as he first recognised her handwriting, and then his despair as he read her words. But even with these reservations, she knew that she had followed the only course of action open to her and that Ken would ultimately be happier. Within a year, he would probably have forgotten all about her and found someone else to love. She hoped so. And because he would never know about the baby, he could never have any regrets, only happy memories of their time together.

Now, as she sat in Jim's childhood bedroom listening to the sounds of the East End waking up to a momentous day, she'd almost convinced herself that the baby was Jim's and that she wasn't due for a few more months yet. Jim's parents had been so good to her, taking her into their home and treating her like the daughter they never had. Of course, she could have gone home, but Mummy was so busy with her WVS activities that Margaret would probably get in the way. And to be honest, Mummy wasn't terribly keen on Jim and certainly gave the impression that Margaret could have done so much better for herself. Little did she know.

Margaret regretted leaving the WAAF, but once her pregnancy was obvious, there had been no question of her remaining. It had been kind of Queenie and Stan to take her in. At least she'd been able to contribute some extra orange juice and milk from her pregnancy rations, although no one seemed keen to share the cod liver oil. Margaret finished getting dressed and tied her hair up in a red, white, and blue scarf. Today promised to be quite a day, with a street party planned and talk of going to Buckingham Palace later to see the king and queen, and maybe even Mr. Churchill on the balcony.

She was keeping her fingers crossed that Jim would be able to join them. They had spoken on the phone last night, and she knew he was doing all he could to make it back today. Margaret joined Queenie in the kitchen.

"Hello, love. How are you feeling this morning? Did you sleep any better?" Queenie asked.

"I slept like a baby," Margaret replied, although the combination of the baby kicking and her father-in-law's snoring vibrating through the paper-thin walls meant that she'd hardly slept at all.

"I don't know why they say you sleep like a baby unless they mean being woken up every few hours for a feed or a cuddle!" Queenie laughed. "I don't think I got a full night's sleep until Jim was at school."

Margaret couldn't quite believe that all of this was nearly upon her. She had no experience with babies, and the mere thought of bathing and feeding them brought her out in a cold sweat.

"Is there anything I can do to help?" Margaret asked, keen to distract herself.

"Could you start peeling the parsnips and turnips for the Woolton pie?" Queenie asked. "It's Jim's favourite, so I hope he makes it home in time for the street party."

Queenie disappeared into the kitchen to make the pastry, and as Margaret reached for the knife, a sharp tightening in her stomach caught her by surprise. It only lasted a few moments, but it was enough to take her breath away. She briefly held onto the back of the chair, closed her eyes and counted slowly to ten. By the time she got to seven, the pain had faded. She took a deep breath, sat down and continued to peel the rest of the vegetables.

By her reckoning, she was already two weeks late. It shouldn't have surprised her that the baby would make its presence felt today. Who wouldn't want to join the party? The news of Victory in Europe had filtered through yesterday, and many had celebrated all night. Margaret wondered whether Jim had been one of them, and if he was in a fit state to travel. She hoped so. If the baby came today, she would need him by her side. Finishing the vegetables, she took off her pinny and told Queenie she was going to hang out more bunting. There was no need to worry her yet. Instead, she walked to the corner of the street and waited in line outside the phone box.

As far as the eye could see, multi-coloured bunting was hanging from street lights, and Union Jacks were billowing from upstairs windows. A group of revellers, many in uniform, ran arm in arm, stopping occasionally to link arms with strangers and twirl them around. She wrapped her coat protectively around her bump as one party approached. As they drew alongside, Margaret spotted the distinctive blue of the Canadian Royal Air Force. Without warning the wearer broke ranks and threw his arms around her, planting a kiss on her cheek. As he ran off to join his friends, Margaret felt another strong tightening across her tummy and breathed deeply to try to stem the pain. It had been at least half an hour since the last one, so she knew the baby wasn't coming immediately, but she was sure that today was the day.

The man coming out of the phone box kissed Margaret's hand as he exited. He was about to swirl her around when he caught sight of her bump.

"You should call her Britannia," he hiccupped, clearly a little the worse for wear.

Margaret popped her pennies in and quickly dialled the number the doctor had given her for the district midwife.

"Hello," she began, "I realise it's rather inconvenient, being a national holiday and everything, but I rather think my baby might be coming."

Jim had received the telegram from his mother this afternoon: **BABY COMING EARLY STOP GET BACK SOON STOP**

Despite his best efforts, there was no way he would get back to London before tomorrow. VE Day celebrations were well underway at the base, and even if he'd been able to find any transport, it was doubtful that anyone was sober enough to drive him to the station. He knew Margaret would manage without him, but he felt awful that he wasn't there to play the dutiful father in waiting. He should be pacing up and down outside the ward, cigar in hand, waiting to wet the head of his firstborn. Instead, he was nursing a hangover at an RAF base in Suffolk.

Jim was determined to be a proper father to Bump, the nickname he and Margaret had used for the baby throughout her pregnancy. When he first suggested marriage, he had just returned to England after more than two years away. During his time in Italy, he had witnessed terrible atrocities and seen close friends wounded and worse. It had made him homesick for family, and he promised himself if he made it out in one piece, he would do better. He would be better.

When Margaret had told him about Ken and the pregnancy, he was still riding a wave of euphoria. He was home, and he was alive. After a week with his parents, he had taken the train to Devon, hoping to surprise her. It was he who was surprised. They walked for miles whilst he told her about his time in Italy and the terrible atrocities he had witnessed, the friends he had lost. She held his hand tenderly and embraced him when it got too much. When he tried to kiss her, she turned her face away. He cupped her chin in his hands and asked her what was wrong. That simple action unlocked a flood of emotion. The story poured from her, how she and Ken had met, their first time together, the shock of his leaving. When she told him about the pregnancy, the tears flooded down her face. Jim might have felt hurt, rejected even, but instead, he felt a strange urge to protect her, and with very little thought, he'd asked her to marry him, as if it were the most obvious thing in the world.

The doubts started to set in as he'd waved Margaret off on the train to London. Would he be able to love another man's child? Did he love Margaret? But it was all too late. He should have thought before he spoke. It had seemed like the right thing to do. A grand gesture.

Ever since he'd been a young boy, Jim had wanted people to like him, so he told people what they wanted to hear. During the war, this had served him well. He'd charmed his superiors, made his colleagues laugh, and was always popular with the ladies. In Italy, several local girls had fallen for him. Taken in by his good looks and words of love, they traded their affections for his promise to return to find them after the war.

“How on earth do you get away with it?” his friends demanded.

“I just tell them what they want to hear,” Jim replied.

The proposal to Margaret had been at a different level and not one he could get out of as easily. Whilst Margaret was in London, he had held onto the hope that, with time to reflect, she might turn him down. But that hadn’t happened. He had made his bed, and they would both have to lie in it. Now, six months on from their wedding, Jim was determined to make the best of it. His parents had accepted her immediately and were thrilled that they were to be grandparents. He and Margaret had continued to grow close. He loved her; he just wasn’t sure he was in love with her. For now, they had a secret to keep and a child to raise. Anything else was for the future. He sent a telegram by return: **HOLD ON STOP ON MY WAY STOP SHALL WE CALL HIM WINSTON STOP**

In the end, baby Gwen wasn’t born at home on VE Day but two days later in hospital. The lack of midwives and concern that she was going into early labour meant that Margaret was told to go straight home, pack a bag and make her way to the local maternity hospital. Sitting up in bed, surrounded by other new mothers, Margaret was rather pleased with how everything had turned out. The extra day had given Jim time to get home, and she hadn't completely ruined everybody's celebrations.

The birth had been excruciatingly painful, but in the hospital, she had been able to have gas and air, which had taken the edge off the contractions. When Gwen was finally born and weighed in at 8lb 3oz, everyone seemed delighted that she was such a healthy weight. If any of the doctors were suspicious of her dates, nobody said anything, and when Jim came to sit with her later and gently kissed Gwen's downy skin, she knew that she had done the right thing.

With visiting hours over and all the babies in the nursery for the night, Margaret finally had time to gather her thoughts. She had felt sure the baby would be a girl from the first time she felt her move and had already decided on the name Gwen Alice. Gwen, after the wife of Merlin to remind her of her magical weekend in Cornwall, and Alice because that was Ken's mother's name. Not that Jim knew any of this. She was just pleased that he liked the names and didn't ask any more questions. The one request Jim made was that she didn't speak of Ken again and that no one, apart from Cynthia, would know that Jim wasn't the baby's father.

For all the love that he had shown her, it was a small price to pay, and a secret she was happy to take with her to her grave.

He said "I can't forget you"

"Do you have time for a cup of tea?" her friend asked. "Since the girls started at school, I don't seem to see anything of you."

"Go on then," laughed Margaret. "I think the housework can wait for one morning."

Since moving into Holyrood Avenue, Margaret had developed a good circle of friends, many of whom were either pregnant or planning to have babies soon. After the war, it seemed as if everyone was having babies, and as a mother, Margaret was in high demand for advice from these nervous new mums. She didn't see herself as an expert, but she remembered how much Queenie had helped her in the early days and how clueless she had felt.

Her mother had proved worse than useless at any practical help. But then, her generation had always had nannies or lady nurses on hand to look after the baby. At least the wealthier ones had. The only advice that her mother had given her was to prioritise Jim over the baby, get her figure back as soon as possible, and give up breastfeeding at the earliest opportunity. Jim's mother Queenie, on the other hand, spent hours with Margaret, offering countless cups of tea whilst she sat feeding. And she had shared all sorts of tips, such as the best way to stop

Gwen wriggling like an eel when bathing her, and a very clever way to fold and secure nappies with only one hand.

Tips like these had positioned Margaret as some sort of baby guru with the new mums of South Harrow. Although she felt a bit of a fraud, she was happy to help as she remembered only too well how overwhelming it could all feel. When she and Jim had finally been able to afford their own home, Margaret was devastated that she would no longer have Queenie on hand to offer advice, although she knew in her heart of hearts that Jim's parents had done more than enough for them already, and that Jim's single room probably wasn't the best start for them as a married couple.

It had been her father who had set the wheels in motion for the move. He had spoken to a friend of a friend who ran a small advertising agency in London and asked if there might be something suitable for Jim. Since leaving the RAF, Jim hadn't known what peace-time work would suit him, and his early attempts at DIY made it clear he wasn't cut out for a trade. What he did have was a talent for writing. During the war, he'd kept everyone entertained with the funny sketches he'd written, and this way with words proved the ideal background for a junior copywriter role. With the end of rationing and the invention of new products, this was an exciting time to be working in advertising, and it seemed that Jim had a flair for coming up with headlines for the latest soap powder or hair cream.

Although Margaret was pleased he was happy and doing so well, she couldn't help feeling sorry for herself. It seemed that now the war was over, people just expected women to return to the home and forget that they were more than capable of doing important paid work. Whilst Gwen was a baby, the novelty of it all had helped to distract her, but now that Gwen was at school, she was bored of the monotony of shopping and housework. She'd recently applied for a part-time job to give herself something more to think about than what to cook for Jim's evening meal.

"How is Gwen settling in at school?" her friend asked as she popped the kettle on.

"She's loving it, although she is tired at the end of the day. All that playing with the other children. They spend their first few years with their mothers and then boom, there's a whole new world of playmates out there."

"I know. I think it's particularly true for the first child. For years they have had you all to themselves, and then suddenly they've got to fit in with all the others. Sally's always had her sister around, so she knows she doesn't get my undivided attention!"

"I can't believe any mother can give a child their undivided attention. The other day, I walked out of Woolworths thinking I had forgotten something, only to realise I had left Gwen inside!"

Her friend howled with laughter at this. When Margaret had first met her at the doctor's surgery, they had hit it off immediately. They lived at different ends of the same road, and with daughters the same age they quickly became firm friends. She was older than Margaret, and as she already had another daughter, she was happy to take Margaret under her wing and introduce her to her other friends in the area.

“I was wondering if I could ask you a favour. Would you be able to have Gwen for lunch on Thursday? I'm going into London, and I won’t be home early enough to pick her up.”

Margaret hated to lie. It made her palms sweat. She wiped them surreptitiously on the chair. She waited a few seconds before sipping her tea.

“Yes, of course I can," her friend replied. "Are you doing something nice?”

“Not particularly, just meeting my mother and sister for lunch.”

“That sounds nice to me. Especially if they pay!”

“I know. It's just that since I married Jim, I think they see me as a bit of a disappointment. They don't think Jim's good enough for me, and my sister has just got engaged to an officer, so I doubt I’ll hear the end of it."

Once she had told the first lie, Margaret found the rest came naturally. Not that anything she said was untrue. She just wasn’t meeting them for lunch.

The truth was difficult even for Margaret to believe. A month ago, she had received a letter from her old Section Leader at Hawks Tor, who was now happily married to an RAF pilot and still living in Devon. Towards the end of the letter, which was full of information on how many children and dogs she now had, she got to the point.

Imagine my surprise when I was forwarded a letter from one of the Canadians, who was briefly posted to Hawks Tor in 1944. Do you remember them? They certainly livened up the dances, didn’t they? And so much more civilised than those awful GIs! This particular Canadian asked if I was still in touch with any Radar operators and, specifically, if I had any forwarding information for you, Margaret.

It seems he is travelling to England in October to show his wife where he was stationed in the war, and he wants to catch up with some of his 'old pals' whilst he is over. I remember that you stepped out together for a few months, so perhaps that's why he wants to get in touch. Although, it seems a bit odd that he wants to introduce his wife to an ex-girlfriend!

To cut a long story short, I didn't feel as if I should give out your details without your permission, so I wrote back and said that if he sent me the details of where he was staying, I would be sure to send them over to you.

Just today I received a second letter telling me that from the 17th – 20th October he will be staying at the Cumberland Hotel in London, and he would love to hear from you.

So, there you have it. Assuming you want to meet up with him, I'm sure you will find the number in the London phone directory. I'm not sure that I would want to. It all feels such a long time ago now and we've all changed so much since then.

She had finished with the usual pleasantries and told Margaret to pop in to see her if she was ever in Devon. Margaret's head was spinning, and she had hardly taken in anything beyond the news that Ken would be in London very soon. Well, that and the fact that he was married. It was hardly a surprise, but it still hurt to think he was. What had she expected? That he would see out his days as a bachelor, sitting on a tractor and unable to get 'darling Peggy' out of his mind. She had sat on the letter for a week, unsure what to do with this information. She couldn't tell Jim. The one thing she had promised him was not to mention Ken again, so that she was contemplating meeting up with him, felt like a huge betrayal. The only other person she could confide in was Cynthia.

After the war, Cynthia had struggled to settle back into civilian life. Being an army driver had let her travel the world, and she had enjoyed the adventure. Since then, she found it hard to find any job that interested her as much. There seemed to be an unwritten rule that women should return to their 'normal' lives, whatever that meant, or better still, get married and have babies. The only problem was that Cynthia didn't have a maternal bone in her body. When she agreed to be godmother to Gwen, she had promised to always be there for her, as long as she didn't have to babysit or change nappies. Eventually, Cynthia got a job as a clerk for BOAC, working at Heathrow Airport. They spoke regularly on the phone, and Cynthia often popped over to see her and Gwen. Last weekend they had gone for a long walk in the park. The conversation, as usual, started with Cynthia updating her on everything that was happening in her life.

"I'm loving the new job, Margie. I might be starting as a clerk, but eventually, I'm going to be a pilot."

Margaret knew better than to stem her enthusiasm, although she doubted this career path would ever be an option for a woman! But you never knew with Cynthia. Perhaps she'd end up travelling the world as an air hostess, although she couldn't imagine Cynthia dolled up the nines pouring drinks for entitled travellers. Nearly an hour later, after countless attempts to steer the conversation in the right direction, Margaret decided she would just have to jump in and say it.

"I got a letter from Ken the other day," Margaret started.

Cynthia, who was bending down to tie her shoelace, almost took a tumble.

"You did what? Which Ken? Do you mean your Ken? Do you mean ..." she lowered her voice, "... Gwen's Ken?"

"It wasn't directly from Ken," she explained, "It was from my old Section Leader. Ken had managed to track her down and asked her how to get hold of me. Cyn, he's coming to England. Actually, I think he's already here, but next week he's going to be in London."

They walked in silence while Cynthia took everything in.

"I think I'm going to meet him," Margaret began. Cynthia's face said everything. "Don't get cross with me. I know you think it's a bad idea, but we never got to say goodbye, not properly. And he's come all this way..." Margaret's words petered out. Her reasons had seemed so much more convincing when she had practised them in her head. She ploughed on. "I want to see that big, friendly face one last time."

"Are you sure this is such a good idea with the problems you and Jim are having?" Cynthia asked.

"Just because we aren't getting on doesn't mean I'm going to fall into the arms of a married man who is going back to Canada in a few days," countered Margaret. She was feeling uncomfortable and angry at the same time.

“The problems with Jim run slightly deeper than that, don’t they, Margie?” Cynthia continued softly, “You’ve hardly had sex since you got married, and now he’s finding reasons to stay out later and later.”

“I knew I shouldn’t have told you anything.” Margaret could feel the colour rising in her cheeks, “I knew you’d taunt me with it at some point. I thought you were my friend.”

“I am your friend; I’ve always been your friend, and I will always be your friend, but I’m concerned that seeing Ken again might bring back all sorts of emotions and feelings that might not be as locked away as you’d thought. That’s all.”

Sitting on the tube as it trundled into Baker Street, Margaret was a mass of emotions. She had kissed Jim as he left for work and then dropped Gwen at school before walking to the station.

“You look nice, Mummy,” Gwen had said, as Margaret wiped the lipstick mark off her cheek with her handkerchief, “and you smell delicious.” Gwen was always experimenting with new words. Margaret loved the expressions she came up with.

“Thank you, darling." Margaret squeezed her hand, "I’m going to see Granny and Aunty Pamela for lunch, so I thought I should wear perfume. Don’t forget you are going to Sally's for lunch today. I’ll pick you up from school later.”

“I won’t forget. Have a lovely time Mummy and send Granny my love,” Gwen had replied as she skipped into the playground.

How easy she found it to lie to Jim and Gwen. Perhaps that's what happens when your whole relationship is built on a secret. When she'd decided to marry Jim, she was sure it was the right thing to do, but five years on, her high hopes of a successful marriage hadn't materialised. Initially, she blamed the living arrangements at his parent's house. But even after they'd moved, things hadn't been right in that department. Gwen was in the next bedroom, and she had never been a good sleeper, but however hard Margaret tried, Jim never seemed to be able to relax.

They would kiss and cuddle, but nothing more. Jim would make an excuse about being too tired or hearing Gwen moving about next door, and the moment was gone. Margaret had assumed that Jim had lovers before they married, but now she wondered if she had misread his confidence for a different type of maturity. Her experience was limited to the brief romance with Ken. Their lovemaking had been so uncomplicated, and they found it easy to tell each other what they enjoyed. In and out of bed, they had been the perfect fit.

She had tried with Jim but found his rejection hard to take. He seemed to want her, but as soon as the lights went out, he would turn over and go to sleep. On the rare occasion that they had made love, she was so worried she would do something wrong that she couldn't relax and lay there hoping that he would finish. The only person she could talk to was Cynthia. Everyone else believed that Gwen was the proof that there were no problems in the bedroom department.

She tried talking to Jim, but it seemed to make things worse, and recently they just stopped trying. They'd give each other a hug, kiss goodnight, and then turn over to go to sleep. So perhaps Cynthia was right, and maybe seeing Ken today was a mistake. Maybe it would just serve to show her what she had lost.

Ken sat at the desk, picked up the phone, and called the operator. They'd arrived at The Cumberland earlier, having taken the sleeper train from Scotland last night. Laurie was exhausted, so she'd gone for a lie-down. When Ken had looked in on her, he'd found her fast asleep. The whole trip had been a whirlwind, trying to combine visiting some of the places he'd been posted in the war with seeing where his parents had grown up.

They'd sailed into Liverpool, bringing back so many memories for Ken. Then they had gone to the Lake District where his mother was from, before travelling to Scotland to visit a couple of cousins who still lived there. The idea for the honeymoon had been Laurie's. When he'd returned to Vancouver in 1945, Laurie had been waiting to greet him. She'd taken to farm life so well that she'd stayed working at the neighbour's farm after the war and was now almost part of the family.

The farming community on Vancouver Island was a strong one. During the war, they all worked together and helped each other out. So it was natural that Laurie and his older sister had become close friends, hanging around with each other in their time off, often with his baby sister in tow. In his groom's speech, Ken had joked that he never stood a chance. Everyone already loved Laurie and it was natural that he would too. On the surface, Laurie and

Peggy couldn't have been more different – where one was tall, the other was short, and where Peggy was happy to be one of the boys, Laurie was made to be a homemaker. But under the surface, they shared many of the same qualities. He was sure they would get along if they met.

When they'd planned their trip, Laurie had asked if there was anyone he wanted to catch up with from his wartime days. He had mentioned a few names including Peggy's, and Laurie suggested he tried to get together with them while they were in London.

'I can go shopping or visit the museums. The last thing you want is me hanging around whilst you reminisce,' she'd said.

It had taken some detective work to track Peggy down, but eventually, Ken had managed, and tomorrow they were going to meet up. It had been over five years since he had last seen her. They were both married now, but his heart was still pounding at the idea of seeing her again. He lifted the handset and dialled the number.

They had spoken briefly on the phone last night and agreed to meet at Baker Street Station. His wife was doing some last-minute shopping before they headed to Heathrow to get a flight back to Canada. The weather was supposed to be fine, so they agreed that they'd walk through Regents Park and end up at London Zoo.

By the time she reached Baker Street, Margaret was starting to feel sick with anxiety. Would she even recognise him? Would they have anything to talk about? Most importantly, she couldn't give him any reason to suspect that Gwen was his.

She would tell him that she had a daughter. It would be strange not to mention it, but she would say that Gwen was four, not five, and Jim's daughter, not his. Before she knew it, she was in the concourse at Baker Street Station. Marching towards her, arms wide outstretched, was Ken, her Ken, and it was all she could do to stop herself running into his arms.

Over the next two hours, it felt as if they had never been apart. Ken told Margaret about his life since the war. He had returned to the farm as expected and soon realised that his parents needed his help more than ever. Over the next few years, he made good decisions about diversifying the business, and a record fruit crop in 1947 meant that they could enjoy 'the fruits of their success'. He had built a second house on the land by the farm, where he and Laurie lived, and his mother and father had treated themselves to an electric refrigerator. Compared with the rationing that England had endured in the post-war years, it seemed that Canada was the land of opportunity.

Margaret gave him the highlights from her life – marrying Jim, falling pregnant with Gwen soon after, and moving into their own home. She almost tripped up when she mentioned looking for a part-time job but recovered by explaining that it was for next year after Gwen started school. They had arranged to meet Laurie at 2.30 pm at the zoo gates. The closer they got to the time, the more the atmosphere changed. On the one hand, there was a cloak of respectability preventing them from saying the things they wanted to say, and on the other, a fear that they would part without saying them. Finally, when it seemed that neither of them would find a way through, Ken stopped abruptly and reached for her hand.

"Peggy," Ken used her pet name for the first time, "I never understood why we ended things. We were so good together. It broke my heart when I got your letter, and I've tried so hard to forget you, but I just can't. You are always there in the background, reminding me that however good my life is, how much better it could have been with you in it."

Margaret didn't know what to say, so she stood there holding his hands in the middle of the park. She could see so much of him in Gwen's face: the same eyes, the same strong jawline.

At that moment she knew that she would always be luckier than Ken because she would always have a part of him with her. And that every time she hugged or kissed her daughter she would be reminded of their happiness. She reached up and stroked his cheek tenderly.

"I know, Ken, I feel the same, but it was the wrong time for us, and it would never have worked. I'm not cut out to be a farmer's wife, and how would your parents have managed without you? We need to be happy with what we have and remember no tears and no regrets."

Margaret wasn't sure where she'd found the strength, but looking at Ken, she could see that her words had left their mark. Despite everything, all the hurt and the love mixed up together, she had said the right thing.

"We will keep in touch?" Ken choked.

"Of course we will," Margaret lied.

And the consequence was ...

Margaret had never been one to make a scene. Her upbringing meant that however hurt or angry she felt, she always kept it inside. But now, on the bus heading towards Slough, she longed to let all her rage out. How could he treat her that way? How could he take her for a fool time after time? Did he really think she wouldn't notice, or did he simply not care?

"Mummy, you're hurting my hand." A voice beside her brought her back to herself. She glanced down and saw Gwen's hand in hers, the fingers squeezed white where she held them in a vice-like grip. Appalled, she dropped her hand, unbidden tears cascading down her cheek.

"Don't worry, Mummy, it wasn't really hurting." Gwen seemed more upset by her mother's soundless tears than anything. "How long before we get to Aunty Cynthia's? I'm hungry."

"Not long now, darling." Margaret managed. She was desperately trying to control her emotions. Automatically, she reached for her packet of cigarettes, only to remember that she had given up a year ago. Never had she felt more like lighting up.

The bus continued its slow progress, each stop hailed by the ding of the bell as afternoon shoppers mixed with children returning from school, their uniforms and general demeanour separating the Catholic school pupils from the local comprehensive. After the summer holidays, that would be Gwen making her way to and from Pinner County. She and Jim had been so proud when she had passed her 11+. The letter had arrived whilst Gwen was at school, and Jim had picked up fish and chips to celebrate. They'd handed Gwen the letter, and she'd danced around the kitchen before jumping into her dad's arms. Always Jim, never Margaret. She was such a daddy's girl, which made this even more difficult than it already was.

"Is Daddy coming to meet us at Aunty Cynthia's?" Gwen asked.

Margaret didn't know what to say, so she patted Gwen's hand and managed 'maybe'. She had acted on impulse. Grabbed some clothes for them both and just about remembered the toothbrushes. The rest was a blur. She had picked Gwen up from friends at the bottom of the close and walked her straight to the bus stop. Gwen hadn't even had tea, no wonder she was hungry. All Margaret had managed to say was that they were visiting Cynthia for a few days. She'd given her neighbour a key and asked her to pop by and feed the cat, because who knew whether Jim would remember. Or whether he would even be there. She had considered leaving a note, but what would she say? *I hope she's worth it*, or *What is wrong with you?* In the end, she had just left. He would soon realise. It wasn't as if it were the first time.

They were approaching Cynthia's stop, and Margaret reached up and pulled the chord. Within a few moments, the bus lurched to a stop, and they pushed their way off. The rush of fresh air was reviving, and Margaret set off on the familiar route with renewed energy. Ten minutes later, they arrived at the maisonette where Cynthia lived. In her haste to get away, Margaret had forgotten to check if Cynthia would be there, and sure enough, there was no answer when she knocked.

When Cynthia arrived home from work forty-five minutes later, she found her best friend sitting on the ground in floods of tears and her godchild standing next to her, small suitcase in hand, patting her mother's head. She instinctively knew what had happened, and her RAF training kicked in. Within half an hour, she had arranged for Gwen to go and play with her neighbour's daughter, had run Margaret a bath, and located the bottle of brandy that she kept for occasions such as these. By the time Margaret had emerged from the bath she had pulled together a chicken salad, uncovered some tinned peaches and evaporated milk, made up a bed for Gwen in the box room and found enough spare sheets and blankets to create a place for Margaret to sleep on the couch.

"How are you feeling now, Margie? Any better?" Cynthia asked kindly.

"I feel numb. Numb and stupid. How could I fall for the same lies, time after time?"

Margaret's cheeks were burning, a combination of the warm bath and the rage percolating inside her.

"You're not stupid. And you are not the first person to believe someone can change. Don't let his faults and mistakes make you doubt yourself, Margie. You've done nothing wrong."

"Apart from marrying him."

“There is that.” Cynthia put her arms around her best friend and hugged her tightly. She had known Margie for nearly half her life and had never seen her as vulnerable as today.

“I'll tell you what we are going to do. I’m going to fetch Gwen from next door, and then we'll have tea. When Gwen’s in bed, we'll talk more, but for now, sit there and drink your brandy. In my experience, there is very little in life that alcohol can’t solve.”

Margaret wrapped her dressing gown around her and went into the kitchen to set the table. It was strange to think of Cynthia living here all by herself. It was such a different life to Margaret’s. Cynthia had work she enjoyed and her own money to spend. At weekends, she took flying lessons at the Airways Aero club, still determined to be a pilot. It was all so much more thrilling than the daily grind of housework and cooking that Margaret endured. When Gwen first went to school, she had taken a little part-time job, but then Jim got a promotion, and they didn’t need the money anymore. So she’d stopped.

Where in all of this was the Margaret who had been specially selected for radar – who had spent the war years plotting fighters, bombers, and enemy aircraft? Or the girl who had driven motorbikes or trucks across open moorland in the pitch black? Who had knocked back halves of bitter at the pub and danced jitterbugs ‘til her feet ached? Who had taken a Canadian to her bed.

Perhaps everyone felt like this as they got older, but when she looked at how Cynthia’s life had worked out, she couldn’t help feeling that hers had gone horribly wrong somewhere. The door opened and the whirlwind that was her daughter rushed in and threw herself onto the couch.

"You'll never believe it!" Gwen intoned dramatically. Margaret couldn't help but smile at her daughter's theatrics. "Susan has a Princess doll, and her mum gave us chocolate cake and milk."

"I hope you've still got room for tea as Aunty Cynthia has gone to a lot of trouble."

"I'll try," promised Gwen, "and then can we phone Daddy?"

Margaret glanced at Cynthia, who dutifully changed the subject.

"Right, upstairs with you. Wash your hands and change into your nightie. It's straight to bed for you after tea."

"It's not my bedtime yet," Gwen replied, but the yawn told a different story.

After tea, they relented and watched 'Double Your Money' before Cynthia took Gwen to bed and read a chapter of 'The Famous Five'. It was nearly nine before the friends could have a proper conversation.

"Do you want to talk, or would you rather just get an early night?" Cynthia asked kindly.

"I don't know Cyn; I feel a bit deflated now. All that fury from this morning has wiped me out."

"Why don't you tell me what happened? It might help you sleep better."

"It's just so infuriating. He's spoiled everything." She started to cry, blowing her nose and wiping her eyes with her pretty handkerchief. "I mean, it's not the first time – you know that. But every time he promises me that it's over and meant nothing. That I'm the only one he wants. I'm the only one he loves."

"How did you find out this time?"

"One of her stockings bundled up in his shirt when I was doing the washing. He said he'd have to stay late in London last week and I believed him when he said he was staying at his mother's. I'm such a fool."

"Does he know you know?"

"I think he'll realise when he sees the washing on the floor. I dropped it where I was standing. His shirt smelt of her perfume..." Margaret's words turned into ugly hiccups, her tears stinging her cheeks.

Cynthia made tea to give her friend time to regain her composure. When she returned, Margaret looked up and managed an unconvincing smile.

"I'm sorry to burden you with all this, Cyn. I didn't know who to turn to."

"Don't be silly. Who else would you turn to than your oldest friend in the world?"

"Some people might turn to their mother."

"Don't be ridiculous, Margie," Cynthia laughed. "Can you imagine it? 'Darling, you have made your bed, so you will have to lie in it' or 'I knew nothing good would come from marrying beneath you'."

Margaret smiled. "Perhaps she was right about that," she managed quietly.

"Oh, come on, it's nothing to do with class. He just can't resist a pretty face," Cynthia added.

"Maybe, but we come from such different worlds, I'm not sure we have much in common. Apart from Gwen, of course, and that's built on a lie," replied Margaret.

“He’s such a good dad to her. You surely aren't regretting your decision?” asked Cynthia.

“In some ways, it makes it worse. Gwen loves him so much I'm not sure I can leave him. I risk her hating me forever. I ruined his life by saying I’d marry him. He probably regretted it the moment he asked.”

Margaret looked over to Cynthia for some response, but she stayed silent. There wasn’t anything to say. They sat in silence, letting the heaviness of Margaret’s words settle. It was a while before either of them spoke. Finally, Cynthia broke the silence. “Will you leave him this time?”

In South Harrow, Jim sat on the bottom of the stairs, the phone beside him. When he got home an hour ago, the house had been quiet. He walked in, half expecting Gwen to run down the stairs and fling herself at him. He opened the kitchen door to be met by a meow and a thud as the cat jumped off the window sill. She was excited for some company, even if it was from her least favourite family member.

Jim started to get that feeling deep in his stomach. It was always the same. The euphoria of the conquest was replaced by the guilt and shame of the hurt he had caused. The abandoned washing told him all he needed to know. How could he have been so careless? If they hadn’t woken up so late. If he hadn’t rushed to collect his clothes, abandoned on the bedroom floor. There had been other times. Plenty of other times. But he had always been ready with a story, an excuse. Enough to provide reasonable doubt. This time he had slipped up, and it would take more than words to repair this schism.

He poured himself a glass of water. He really wanted whisky. Something to burn away the deceit, to absolve him of responsibility. And the worst thing was there was no one he could turn to. No one would understand or listen. He wondered, fleetingly, whether he should ring the girl. Explain what happened. But she wouldn't care. She'd be out with her friends, not giving him a second thought. It had never been more than a bit of fun for either of them. It didn't feel like fun now.

The cat jumped uncertainly on his lap, missing the usual hum of activity – Gwen doing her homework, and Margaret with the radio on in the kitchen making tea. She tentatively nudged Jim with her nose, and he unconsciously stroked her fur.

"What are we going to do now?" Jim muttered to himself. "How do I make this right?"

Lying in bed in the box room, Gwen tossed and turned. The bed wasn't as comfy as at home, and she was missing her cat snuggling into her feet. Today had been an odd day altogether. She hadn't known they were visiting Aunty Cynthia until Mummy had come running up the path and collected her from her friends. They hadn't even gone home first; she'd just been marched to the bus stop. Gwen had visited a few times, but they had always come in the car, and she couldn't remember staying the night before. And Mummy had been so unlike her usual self. She'd hardly spoken to Gwen on the journey and then burst into tears on the bus.

The phone rang downstairs, but no one answered it. Five minutes later, it rang again. Gwen decided to go to the bathroom. Aunty Cynthia had read her a story but had forgotten to remind her to brush her teeth. She hopped out of the unfamiliar bed and walked across the landing.

"She doesn't want to talk to you, Jim."

Why was Cynthia speaking to her daddy? And why didn't her mummy want to speak to him?

After she brushed her teeth, she heard her mother on the phone. Her voice was quiet, and Gwen was sure she was crying again. Perhaps something had happened to Granny or Grandpa. Her other grandpa had died last year, and Daddy cried for weeks. She sat at the top of the stairs and strained to hear, but it was difficult to piece it all together when you only heard one side of the conversation.

After a few minutes, Aunty Cynthia took the phone.

"Just give her some time, Jim. It's been a shock, and she doesn't know what she wants to do. They are both going to stay here for a bit."

Cynthia was quiet as Gwen's father started saying something more, and then she said a little more gently,

"No, Gwen doesn't know anything. She's fast asleep upstairs. I'll ask her to ring you tomorrow night."

Many times over the rest of her life, Gwen would think back to the oddity of that week and reflect on the overheard one-way conversation. Within a year, she had a baby sister to reassure her that her parents were happy together and not going to 'split up' as some of her friends' parents were starting to do.

By the time she left school and embarked on her nursing career, she understood the true nature of her father's infidelities.

But it wasn't until years later, when her parents were both dead and she was a grandmother herself, that she had reason to reflect on the most puzzling question her mother had asked her father. It had been hard to decipher the whispers, but Gwen was sure she heard her mother say, 'Would you have married me if it weren't for Gwen?'

Part Two: 1965 - 1998

Jim
Met Christine at the library
He drove her home
She made a decision
He said "I love her"
She said "You did me a favour"
And the consequence was …

Jim

Jim was driving down the M1 from Headingley with the window wound down, his right hand loosely on the driving wheel and his elbow catching the last of the afternoon rays. It had taken until the middle of July for the summer to arrive, but now it looked like it was set fair for the next month. The cricket had been good, England had won easily, and the crowds had been out in force. The sunshine and cans of bitter had ensured strong sales of the cricket magazine and other memorabilia that his boot had been filled with on Wednesday night.

When he'd applied for the job, his friends in advertising thought it had been a bit of a sideways move, but Jim had always loved cricket, so a job that combined his writing and marketing skills with long summers touring around the test grounds of England felt like a dream job. The reality was a bit different. Navigating the old boys' network wasn't easy with his working-class background and technical college education, but Jim had come across enough officer types in the RAF and seemed to have the knack of making them laugh. It helped that the magazine that he edited was making them money. Most of the time, he was left to get on with things without too much inspection, including signing off his expenses for weekly stays at a mid-range hotel near the test grounds.

If anyone had bothered to think about it, they might have wondered why he needed to transport the merchandise to the grounds himself, or why, with sales teams at every ground, he needed to be there in person at all. But they didn't ask. And so Jim got well acquainted with the hotels and hostelries around Edgbaston and Headingley, Trent Bridge, and Old Trafford. Margaret hated that he was away so often over the summer, and he did feel a twinge of guilt when he missed birthdays or school sports days, but never quite guilty enough to stop him packing the car up every few weeks and going on his travels.

Jim had many faults, but lack of self-awareness was not one of them. He knew that he was self-centred and attention-seeking, and, most of all, he knew he should never have married Margaret. The proposal had been a mistake almost the moment the words were out of his mouth. He and Margaret had never been more than good friends. They had flirted and kissed during their first posting on the Isle of Wight, but it was fueled by the excitement of being away from home for the first time. A holiday romance played out against the backdrop of bombs, made heady by the possibility of never seeing one another again.

When he'd been posted to Italy, they'd promised to write. He was frightened of what he might face and having a sweetheart at home added to the romance of the situation, her photograph a reminder of all they were fighting for. He kept it in his breast pocket next to the military-issue condoms. It was in Italy that Jim discovered he had three unique talents that would see him through the war and set him up for life beyond.

Firstly, he could make people laugh. He had a way with words and knew how to deliver a punchline. In his spare time, he used his writing skills to compose skits and limericks that would have the rest of his unit howling with laughter. Being funny gave him a social standing amongst his peers that belied the fact that he was a short little cockney with a slight stutter.

His second talent was that he was able to make women fall in love with him. Without film star good looks, he relied almost entirely on charm. He knew very few words of Italian beyond *birra* and *sigaretta*, but he was a fast learner, and with his twinkling eyes and ready smile, he seemed to attract the dark-haired Italian girls like wasps to a liqueur. In the outskirts of Naples, where prostitution was rife, the thought of catching an unpleasant disease was enough to prevent him from doing more than share a glass or two with the ladies that swarmed around him. But as the Allies eventually made headway into the North of Italy, he fell in love in every village they passed through on the way. The farmers' daughters he met quickly fell under his spell, as he called them 'molto bella' and promised to return for them after the war.

And so he'd discovered his most powerful talent – the ability to tell a lie and believe it himself. He had been good at this all his life. As a youngster, he found it easy to polish off a second dinner, having already eaten a bag of chips on the way home. When the recruiting officer at his RAF interview asked for his exam grades, he'd inflated them to match what he thought himself capable of, rather than what he had attained. And when he told the girls he met in Italy that he loved them and would return for them after the war, he was only trying to make them feel better about his departure. A white lie harmed nobody, so he continued to tell people exactly what they wanted to hear.

The strategy had one major flaw. What had worked well in the remote villages of Italy regularly got him into trouble in London, where his girlfriends talked to each other and knew he was married. Yesterday, he ended things with the top magazine sales girl after she'd asked him when he was leaving his wife. Jim could say with some certainty that he was never leaving his wife. After one of his early affairs, Margaret had considered divorcing him. She had gone to stay with her friend Cynthia for a week and taken Gwen with her. It had been the toughest week of Jim's life. He had hated being alone in the quiet house, with only his thoughts for company. By the Wednesday he was begging her to come home. He promised her he would change. He would try harder. There would be no more affairs. He even promised to try for a baby with her. When he made those promises, he meant every word.

He finished it with the girl immediately and barely gave her a second thought. It was never about the women, though. He loved to turn on the charm, to flirt a little and prove that little Jim from Leytonstone could amount to something. He relished the chase, and once they fell for him, he didn't want to disappoint them. When the relationship had run its course, he couldn't bear the tears and repercussions, so he just moved on to the next one, hoping that nobody would get hurt.

Seeing Margaret so upset had destroyed him. He saw himself through her eyes, and he hated what he saw. Their relationship had never been traditional, but he loved her deeply and never felt worthy of her. He still didn't know why he had offered to marry her. Perhaps it was guilt after Italy, because he had survived when so many others had not. During the fiercest fighting in the battle for Monte Cassino, friends had died before his eyes. Young men losing everything, whilst he came through unblemished. Perhaps he felt it was his duty to live a good life with a good woman. Margaret was certainly one of those.

Within weeks of his proposal, they had married, citing a short period of home leave before a new posting as the reason for the spontaneity. When Margaret's pregnancy was revealed, his parents insisted that she move in with them until the baby was born, which made any potential intimacy easy to avoid. Once they had moved into their first home, Margaret tried everything to make the physical side a success, but however much she'd wanted to, Jim just found he couldn't. The girls he'd encountered in Italy weren't anything like the woman who had become his wife. And, however hard he tried, and however much Margaret insisted he was wrong, he couldn't shift the belief that it was Ken she wanted, not him.

Margaret had taken Jim's rejection as her failure, not his, and she looked for ways to remedy it. Without a close network of girlfriends, she turned to advice from the agony aunt pages of the Women's Weekly, but when making his favourite supper or running him a warm bath seemed to make no difference at all, she'd simply stopped trying, kissed him on the cheek, turned over in bed and put her efforts into building a home and raising Gwen instead. Jim's approach was to stay later and later at work and flirt with the girls in the typing pool. Within a year of their marriage, he'd had his first affair.

When Margaret threatened to leave, he'd finally understood how much his actions hurt her. Every night, they spoke on the phone and by the end of the week, Margaret's tears and anger had softened. They had talked like never before, a flood of honesty released by the faceless anonymity of the telephone. He had opened up about his fear that he wasn't good enough for her. She had told him how rejected she felt when he didn't want to make love to her. She had feared he was only with her because of Gwen. Little by little their words began to build bridges and heal the hurt. At the end of the week, she had come home. They had both promised to work harder and to talk more honestly. Margaret got a job. Gwen started at grammar school. They went out more, to the theatre and the cinema. And on a Saturday night, they made love. It lacked the illicit thrill of an affair, but it was comfortable and comforting. The following autumn, Susan was born.

In the months that followed, Jim had tried his hardest to be a good father and husband. Margaret hoped that having their own child would bring them closer and finally put to rest Jim's insecurities. Even Jim had thought that some paternal button might be pressed, and he would metamorphose into a hands-on dad, but he was just as unenthusiastic about the disturbed nights and nappy changes as he had been with Gwen, and at least then he had an excuse. With a new baby on the scene, Jim and Margaret never recaptured the closeness or comfortable intimacy they had carved out for themselves after the 'stocking affair', as Jim referred to it privately.

Before Susan was three, Jim was up to his old tricks again. He wasn't sure whether Margaret knew about any of these affairs. He hoped he was more discreet, and Margaret was so tired with a baby to look after, a teenager to support and a house to run, that perhaps she wasn't on the lookout for signs. Either way, their marriage never again reached a point of no return, and, despite not being a conventional couple, they rubbed along well enough in friendly companionship. Jim knew his limits, and when the girl had asked him last night when he would be leaving his wife, he knew he had reached them.

He took the turning for Ruislip, stopped to fill up with petrol, and picked up a bunch of flowers for Margaret. It had been a successful test match, and with his conscience now clear, he felt a renewed sense of optimism about getting home and seeing his girls. Susan would have loads to tell him. She was doing well at school and had won the poetry prize last term. Gwen was also coming home later in the week. She'd just finished her finals and was about to start on the wards at Hammersmith Hospital. They might even go to the Berni Inn on Saturday to celebrate. He turned towards Pinner and drove past the library where he had signed up for a writing evening class. Ten minutes later, he was home.

Margaret heard the car pull up and sighed. She'd been hoping for some time in the garden before Jim got home. The weather was glorious, and she'd been busy at work all day, with no time for a proper break. The cricket had finished yesterday. Jim had phoned to say he needed to stay one more night to pack up properly. She wasn't stupid. She knew what he was really up to. It was just that she didn't mind anymore.

Many years had elapsed since that day when she had turned up on Cynthia's doorstep, full of hurt and rage. And she'd felt so ashamed. What if people found out? What would they say? The time with Cynthia reminded her that what she had with Jim was all she needed from him. Support. Companionship. Friendship. She'd never loved him, and she hadn't expected love in return. So, as long as he was discreet, she didn't mind that he liked to have his little flings, as she called them.

After the hurt of Jim's betrayals had come the joy of Susan. It had been a miracle, given how few times they had made love. She and Gwen had fallen in love with Susan the moment she was born. Margaret had worried that Gwen would be too old and too busy at school to want a baby sister around, but that couldn't have been further from the truth. Susan had brought the two of them closer together.

They had never again spoken about the impromptu visit to Cynthia's, and for a long while, Margaret fooled herself into believing that Gwen had been left unscarred by the events of that week. It had been several years later during a hormone-filled teenage rant, that it became clear that Gwen had been storing away her feelings for years.

"At least when I get married, I won't let my husband go off and have affairs!" she'd screamed down the stairs at

Margaret, just before slamming her bedroom door shut. Margaret had stood staring after her, barely able to breathe, the shock of the accusations winding her temporarily. When she'd finally recovered her emotions, she'd found Gwen sobbing on her bed, tears mixed with snot as she cried with an intensity that frightened Margaret.

"How did you know?" she'd asked softly.

"A woman phoned the other night when you were out," Gwen started. "She wanted to know where Jim was as he hadn't turned up yet. And I just knew." She sniffled, recovering herself. "It all flooded back to me. That week at Aunty Cynthia's, when I'd sat at the top of the stairs and heard you crying on the phone. I knew Daddy had done something wrong."

Margaret gently stroked her thumb across the palm as she'd done as a baby. "Why did you never say anything before? You know you can tell me anything."

"I didn't want to spoil things. And I didn't want you to go away. I thought after Susan was born, everything would be better. That Daddy would love us all again."

"Oh Gwen, he does love us all." Margaret rushed to reassure her. Susan had come in then, woken by the slamming doors and the shouting.

"Why is Gwen crying, Mummy?" Susan rubbed her upper lip with the pink tickle blanket she slept with every night. Margaret gathered them both to her and breathed in all the fear, upset, love and anxiety. She promised herself that she would never put Susan through the emotional mangle that Gwen had gone through. She would do all she could to keep her safe, and if that meant turning a blind eye to Jim's occasional fling, so be it. She knew in her heart that no one would ever take him from them, and right now, that was all that mattered.

The sound of the car door slamming brought Margaret back to herself. She looked forlornly at the garden. No half an hour sit down for her, then. She walked into the hall and saw Jim's blurred frame through the obscured glass blocks that framed the front door.

"Susan, Daddy's home!" she shouted up the stairs, and immediately her daughter came running down to meet him.

Jim strode through the door, and Susan threw herself at his legs.

"Hello, little one," he cried, catching her in one arm and handing the flowers over her head to Margaret. She smiled and absentmindedly twisted her wedding band on her finger.

"I'll go and get a vase, and you two can catch up while I make tea," she laughed. If this is what it took to keep Susan safe from the realities of life, then her own happiness was a small price to pay.

Met Christine at the library

Christine was sitting in the car in the library car park, trying to pluck up the courage to go in. She'd got this far last week and then seen two women get out of another car together and make their way towards the door. She started the engine and left. At home, she'd been so cross with herself. She was a grown woman for God's sake – how hard could it be to walk in alone to a Writer's Circle at the local library? She'd seen the advert on the noticeboard the previous year and written down all the details in her diary. I'll start in the Spring, she'd promised herself. But April had come and gone, and there was always some reason to miss it. And now it was the second week of the autumn term, and she was still making excuses.

Before she changed her mind again, she got out of the car, locked it, and walked towards the door. She would not let this fear stop her from doing the things she wanted. In other aspects of her life, she was fine. She held down a good job as a part-time art teacher at a local primary school, and none of the children or parents would guess about her crippling social anxiety. But put her in a situation with a group of people she'd never met before, and she froze. Her heart would beat so hard she could hear it in her ears, and her palms would sweat. One of her friends suggested that she see a doctor about it, but that was an even more frightening thought than struggling with the anxiety itself. Anyway, she was pretty sure she knew the root cause.

Christine had never been the most confident of children. All these years later, she still had flashbacks to situations where she had felt scared or uncomfortable around other people. She had been born in Romford in 1930. Her parents had met two years earlier whilst working at the Betterwear Factory and married quickly when they found out there was a baby on the way. They had neither the money nor the inclination to look after a baby, and by the time she was 3 years old, Christine's father had left, never to be seen again. For the next few years, Christine lived with her grandparents, and then, on her seventh birthday, her mum announced that they were moving to Gidea Park to live with her new boyfriend. This meant that Christine had to move school, and that was the first time she remembered having the anxious ball in her stomach. Walking into a class full of strangers in the middle of the term, she'd struggled to make friends and constantly imagined others talking about her behind her back.

'Have you seen her shoes; they've got holes in them.'

'Are her mum and dad even married?'

'Don't go to hers for tea, or they'll feed you lard sandwiches.'

Children could be so cruel. And while the grown-up Christine knew that the people gathered tonight would be welcoming, deep down, as she opened the door, she still felt like a seven-year-old desperate to make friends.

She was the fifth person to arrive. Keen not to make eye contact, she made her way to a seat at the end of the semi-circle, leaving a couple of gaps between her and the next lady. Christine had recently turned thirty-five, and she guessed the four women already seated were older than her. Two of them were chatting quietly to each other, and one was searching in her bag for something. The other smiled at her and mouthed, 'First time?' Christine smiled back and nodded. Within a few minutes, a few more had arrived, including the class leader, a younger woman with wild, red curly hair, only just tamed under a bright pink scarf. Following after them, the only man. Most of the other seats were taken, so he walked single-mindedly to the chair next to Christine and sat down. He turned to her to check that she wasn't keeping it for someone and, when she said she wasn't, he smiled broadly, and the smile lit up his face.

"I'm Jim," he whispered, keen not to interrupt the curly-haired woman who had just started to talk.

"Christine," she said just as quietly.

Christine hadn't really known what to expect from the Writer's Circle. The leaflet she had picked up talked about it being a place for anyone who likes to write. Although joining the school at Gidea Park had been a traumatic experience for Christine, she had soon realised that while she would always struggle to make friends, she loved school. Her two favourite subjects were English and Art, and she would sit for hours in her bedroom reading books or coming up with her own stories and drawing pictures to illustrate them.

One of her earliest creations was an invisible mouse called Hugger. In her stories, she and Hugger got up to all sorts of mischief and went on adventures around the world, whereas the furthest she had ever been was to Canvey Island on a brief holiday with her grandparents. She never shared her stories with her mother, instinctively knowing that she would have no interest in them. Instead, her writing became a private pleasure. Every week, she spent her pocket money on exercise books and pencils rather than the sweets and fizzy drinks her classmates bought. The more stories she wrote, the more she created a world away from the dullness of her day-to-day life. Her mother and her new boyfriend weren't cruel; they just weren't very interested in her. It suited them that she would go to her room and read and write, so they could do what they wanted. On many occasions, when she went downstairs before bedtime, she found nobody at home, only to hear them returning from the pub hours later.

"Ok, let's try a writing exercise to warm us up."

The teacher's voice interrupted Christine's thoughts, and she realised she'd been miles away.

"For the benefit of the two newcomers we have tonight," the teacher continued, gesticulating in the general direction of Christine and Jim, "we usually start with a free writing exercise that we do in pairs. I'll give you a scenario."

She used the slide projector to show a painting. Christine could tell it was by Edward Hopper, but she didn't recognise it.

"This painting is called Hotel Lobby. I want you to each choose one of the figures and write a paragraph that explains how that character is feeling. We'll have 15 minutes, and then we'll listen to some of your attempts."

Jim and Christine were sitting next to each other, so it made sense for them to team up. They made their way to one of the tables.

"I wasn't sure what to expect," Christine said.

"No, I wasn't either," said Jim, "although I hoped I wouldn't be the only man!"

"You should have signed up for Introduction to Car Mechanics if you wanted other men," Christine joked.

"That's really not my thing," Jim admitted. "I don't know my spark plugs from my carburettor."

"Even more reason to attend," Christine laughed.

The whole session flew by. Christine was relieved that she and Jim hadn't been asked to read out their first efforts, even though she was pleased with what she'd written. They did a few more exercises, and then two people were asked to read something they had written in the week. The lady who had welcomed Christine earlier went first. She had written a poem about the death of her father the previous year. It was very moving and made Christine reflect on the lack of any father figure in her life.

She had no memories of her actual father, although she did have a few photos that her mother had kept. And the boyfriend, whom her mother had finally married in 1940, had been killed in France just 6 months later. Christine had been lucky to be evacuated at the start of the war. Her mother had said it was for the best, although Christine suspected she meant that it was the best for her. Waiting in a church hall in rural East Anglia, Christine hadn't felt particularly lucky, but being taken in by 'Aunty' Twiggy and 'Uncle' Jack was the best thing that could have happened to her.

When Kate had finished her poem, the teacher turned to Jim and Christine and asked if they wanted to share something they were working on. Christine was eternally grateful when Jim stepped in and offered to read some of the children's book he was writing. It was called *Little Wrinkle* and told the story of a little girl who always told you what she was thinking by wrinkling her nose. The feedback to Jim's story was positive, and Christine could tell he was pleased.

"Well done. That was so good," Christine whispered when they retook their seats at the end.

"I don't suppose you fancy getting a drink? I need something to stop my hands shaking," Jim replied.

Fifteen minutes later, they were sitting at a table at The Plough. Jim had extended the offer to the others, but they'd made their excuses. Some had children to get home to, or husbands waiting to pick them up.

"I loved your story," Christine started, sipping her half of cider. "I've tried to write children's stories, and it's not as easy as it looks!"

"Thanks. I suppose that's a compliment!" Jim laughed.

"Oh yes, it is. Nowadays, I do more illustration than writing, and when I heard about Little Wrinkle, I could imagine her with hair in bunches and freckles all over her nose. Is she based on a real little girl?"

"Yes, she's based on my daughter Gwen. She's all grown up now, but as a toddler, she used to do that thing with her nose."

Christine felt a slight hint of regret. Clearly, he was married with children. Of course, he would be.

"You must have had her very young," Gwen continued.

"She was born two days after VE Day. If she'd been a boy, we were going to call her Winston."

Christine laughed.

"Would you like another half?"

Whilst Jim was at the bar getting them another drink, Christine studied him. He was good-looking, with his dark hair slicked back with Brylcream and a chiselled face that reminded her of a fox. She wondered how old he was. In his forties, she supposed, if his daughter was grown up.

"Do you have just one daughter?" she asked casually when he returned from the bar.

"No, I have two daughters," Jim replied. "Gwen's training to be a nurse – she's just taken her finals – and her sister Susan is nine. She takes up a lot of my time."

"And does your wife work?"

Jim hesitated and looked down at his pint.

"Actually, my wife died a few years ago."

"Oh my God, that's awful." Christine felt embarrassed for bringing the whole subject up. "How on earth do you cope?"

"My wife's sister comes down to stay through the school holidays, and now that Gwen's left home, one of my wife's friends pops around after school to look after Susan until I get home from work. She suggested I come tonight, to take advantage of her babysitting."

Christine's heart was racing. She felt terrible about his wife, but there was no denying they were getting on well together. He was funny and charming and apparently available.

“So tell me more about you,” Jim prompted. “I can’t believe a beautiful woman like you is still single,” he laughed.

“Well I am.” Christine blushed. She knew he was using every cheesy chat-up line, and she was falling for them all.

The truth was that at thirty-five, Christine had never had a successful relationship. She blamed her mother for that. Her mother was a terrible role model and never offered any helpful advice. When she returned home after the war, she had just turned fifteen, and whilst her body had matured, she was still naïve about many things. Twiggy and Jack had been so kind to her, but they hadn’t felt it was their place to tell her the facts of life.

The first thing her mother had said when she came back was ‘don’t you dare go and get pregnant. A baby will ruin your life, just like you ruined mine.’ So Christine had been careful not to make the same mistakes her mother had. By 1946, and already married twice, her mother was engaged again to a man who sold cars at the local Ford dealership. Most nights they went to the pub or the bingo, and Christine was left to cope alone. One weekend, the salesman came home with her mother and made a pass at Christine whilst her mother had gone out for cigarettes. Christine packed a bag and went to live with her grandparents.

She had left school without any formal qualifications, so she went to work in the factory where her parents had met before the war. In the evenings, she went to art classes. She had lost her virginity to the art teacher, a mild-mannered married man who was totally besotted with her. He had admitted to Christine that he and his wife hardly ever had sex as she refused to use contraceptives but was terrified of falling pregnant. Christine wondered if this were just an excuse on his wife's part. Her own mother had said that the only point of sex was to snare a man and that once you had, you spent most of your days thinking of reasons you couldn't have sex that night. She told Christine that she had once pretended to have a three-week-long period, the sanitary towels in the bin the biggest turn-off ever.

Christine recognised something in her art teacher that made her feel sorry for him, and even though he didn't make her go weak at the knees, they had relatively satisfactory sex every Tuesday after art class for the next six months. It had ended when wracked with guilt, he told her that his wife was pregnant, the withdrawal method never being the most reliable form of contraception. Christine hadn't minded too much. Her art had improved, she'd finally lost her virginity, and she'd realised that what she really missed wasn't the sex or the art teacher but the companionship. Two weeks later, she'd received a letter from him and a cheque containing the money he'd earned from the evening classes. With a baby on the way, he had stopped teaching and wanted her to have a holiday with the money. To help her get over him. It was a nice gesture, but she was already well over him, and instead, she used the money as the first month's rent on a flat before offering to take over teaching his evening class.

There had been a few relationships since then, but somehow she always managed to pick a 'wrong un' as her grandmother would say. Often, they were married men. Not that she knew that at first. She'd fall for their charm, and then a few weeks later, she'd notice the telltale signs of never wanting to stay the night or see her at weekends. Sometimes a friend would take her to one side and give her the heads up that they had seen him in Woolworths with his wife and child in tow. Although she hated the idea that she might inadvertently be causing harm to another family, it wasn't just a moral issue for Christine. She was now of an age when she wanted what they had. She wanted a home, a car, a washing machine. She wanted someone to bring her flowers on a Friday night. She wanted to make plans for the future, and most of all, she wanted a baby of her own.

For the last few years, she had stopped dating random strangers and promised herself that she would focus on finding Mr. Right. She avoided the bars where the married men hung out and briefed her friends only to introduce her to eligible and available bachelors. The strategy had not been particularly successful. It seemed that, in post-war Britain, the good men had all been snapped up, and any still available were only looking for a no-strings-attached relationship. Joining the Writers Circle was part of a plan to give up on searching for the right men and broaden her horizons, so it was ironic that it had given her the best option in years.

Christine didn't go into the details of her dating history with Jim. She decided not to tell him much about herself at all. If she played her cards right, she hoped there would be many other opportunities to fill in the gaps. She was excited about the future for the first time in a long time. Perhaps she had finally found someone who could give her the happy ending she was looking for.

"Same time next week?" Jim asked as they parted in the car park.

"Yes, please. I'd love to learn more about Little Wrinkle," Christine replied.

"And I'd love to learn more about you," Jim responded, touching her arm and brushing her cheek with a kiss.

Driving home, she couldn't believe how close she had come to not going tonight, and yet in the space of a few hours, a whole new life now seemed possible. Like in all the best books, she couldn't wait to see what would happen next.

He drove her home

Jim had arrived early at the library and was searching through the shelves of crime thrillers for one he hadn't yet read. Since they first met at the Writers Circle, he and Christine spent most Saturday mornings at the library, and then go for a coffee whilst Susan was at Saturday morning cinema. The timing worked perfectly. Margaret was grateful for having the morning to herself, and Christine enjoyed being out and about 'like a proper couple'.

Jim had found the early days of their relationship easy to navigate. They progressed from drinks after the evening class to visits to the cinema and the occasional meal out. He was always careful to go to places outside his usual stomping ground to make sure they were never caught out by family friends. After their fourth date, when he had pulled up outside her flat, she had asked him in for coffee. The next time, she invited him to stay the night. Not wanting to miss his opportunity, he rushed out to buy a bottle of Liebfraumilch from the Off License, making sure he phoned Margaret from the phone box on the corner to tell her that he had to work late and would stay in town.

He didn't like to lie to Margaret, but Christine made it worth the momentary guilt. She was unlike any of his other conquests. She was smart and funny. They had deep conversations about politics; she'd sit happily on the couch next to him and watch The Big Match. She even enjoyed the wrestling. They had a lot in common, including their love of Leyton Orient. If he had never met Margaret, Christine would have been the sort of woman he would have married. She was also the sort of woman who would run a mile if she knew Jim was already taken, which was why he had to be careful not to get caught.

"Hello, stranger." A disembodied whisper, followed by a slap on the back, brought Jim back to earth. It was an old teammate from a cricket team he had played for briefly after the war. He instantly did the calculations. Did he know Margaret? Had they met? How quickly could he get rid of him?

"Hello there," he lifted his eyebrows in greeting. "Fancy bumping into you in here."

Jim remembered the man as a fast bowler. They'd mainly played in different teams. He thought he was a bit of a drinker. Tim, perhaps, or Tom?

"How's life treating you?" the man asked, clearly keen to talk.

"Yes, good, good." Jim's eyes flashed around the library, desperately looking to see if Christine had arrived. He couldn't be certain whether this chap would remember Margaret, but he didn't want to risk it.

"I'm really sorry," he said, grabbing the nearest book. "I only popped in to get this." He waved the book in his general direction. "My daughter is in the car, so I'll have to run, but it was nice meeting you. We'll have to catch up properly. Grab a drink sometime."

He rushed out of the library, forgetting to get the book stamped, and fled into the car park, where he walked between the cars until he saw the man leave. Then he walked back in, replaced the book, and, slowing his breathing, went over to the children's section, where he could see Christine sitting on a tiny red stool.

"You look like a pixie," he laughed, holding out his hand to help her up and kissing her on the cheek.

"Where did you get to?" Christine asked, "I've been here for ages."

"Sorry, I got held up at the cinema. Had to wait for Susan's friend to arrive before I could leave." He hated that he found it so easy to lie. "What are you doing in the children's section?" He hastily changed the subject.

"Checking out the competition," Christine answered, holding up some books for him to see.

Since the Writers Circle, they had been collaborating on the *Little Wrinkle* book Jim had read to the group on the first night. Jim's idea was to have one book containing all her adventures, whereas Christine thought a series of shorter books, each covering a year in her life, would be better. They had already scoped out *Little Wrinkle Turns Four* and *Little Wrinkle Turns Five*. Research for every year relied on Christine reading the latest children's books to gauge what children liked to read about and on Jim's memory of Gwen and Susan at each age. It became clear that either Jim had a poor memory, or, as seemed likely to Christine, that he hadn't been around much during his children's early years.

"I'll come into my own when Little Wrinkle turns fourteen. I know all about teenage tantrums," he'd promised.

The partnership was working well. First, they would discuss ideas for each book before Jim went and wrote the stories and Christine created the illustrations. To help her visualise the main character, Christine had asked Jim for a photograph of Gwen as a small child. A few weeks later, he had arrived at her house with one in his wallet. It showed a five-year-old Gwen in a seersucker swimming costume and bows in her hair, eating an ice cream. Kneeling next to her, holding her hand, was a young woman wearing slacks and a cardigan buttoned to the top. The woman's wavy hair was being blown across her face, but her eyes shone with laughter.

"Is this your wife?" Christine asked gently, aware that she may have awoken sad memories for him.

"Yes, Margaret and Gwen, in 1950 I think. We had a few days in Whitley Bay. Her parents moved there after the war."

Jim didn't seem too upset to discuss her, so Christine continued.

"How long was this before she got ill?" she ventured.

Jim looked a little distracted.

"It was quite a few years later," he stuttered, which Christine put down to the emotion. "A few months after Susan was born, she found a lump. Even with all the treatment, she only lived a year."

Christine felt the sadness well up in her throat and dug her fingernails into her hand to suppress her own tears from gathering.

"No wonder you don't remember much about Susan when she was young. You must have been distraught."

“It was difficult in the early days. Work was good for the first few weeks, but after the funeral, I was expected to return to normal. That was when the neighbours rallied round.”

Christine put her arms around his shoulders and kissed the top of his head.

“You know I’d be happy to do more to help with Susan, and I’d love to meet Gwen – to see the grown-up Little Wrinkle.”

The change in Jim’s demeanour was dramatic. He’d stood up and turned his back on her.

“I don’t think that would be appropriate,” he’d snapped.

Christine felt as if she’d crossed some invisible line. They’d been seeing each other for almost a year, so she hadn’t thought it too forward, but her suggestion had triggered some raw emotion in Jim. She managed to stumble an apology, although she didn’t know what she had done wrong. To change the mood, she’d taken herself into the kitchen and started on some sketches of Little Wrinkle, attempting to capture the carefree nature of the child in the picture. After a while, Jim came into the room and apologised for snapping. When she asked if she could keep the photo for reference, Jim had taken her kitchen scissors and cut it in two, tucking the picture of his wife back into his pocket. The whole thing had struck Christine as strange, but grief could be like that, so she had put it to the back of her mind.

“Shall we go and get a cup of tea?” Christine found Jim in the crime aisle.

They checked their books out and wandered to the café across the road, where they sat at their usual table at the back. They read the papers in companionable silence and finished their second cup of tea. By the time they left the café, it had started to rain. They walked to Jim's car, huddling under Christine's small umbrella.

"Hop in, and I'll drop you home," Jim offered.

"If you're sure it won't make you late."

Christine unsuccessfully tried to close her umbrella whilst juggling the library books and stopping her handbag from falling off her shoulder. In the end, everything spilt onto the floor. By the time they had got to Christine's flat, she'd gathered everything together. "Don't forget to book your holiday for our trip to Norwich," she yelled as she slammed the door behind her and ran to her front door. She turned briefly to wave to Jim before she disappeared inside.

Jim had forgotten about the holiday. It wasn't easy to get away during test match season, which was why he'd suggested the start of September. He'd have to think of an excuse for Margaret and make it up to her. Perhaps they could have some time away later in the year.

By the time he got back to the cinema, Susan was a lone figure in the car park. She was sitting on the steps, trying to shelter from the rain under a concrete overhang. Jim reached over and opened the passenger door for her.

"Why are you always the last to come?" Susan asked crossly. Her fringe hung limply under the hood of her waterproof jacket. "I could have gone home with Sandra if you'd said."

"Sorry, love, I met an old friend of your mum's at the library and offered them a lift home. Call me a Good Samaritan."

Susan slammed the door, pouted miserably, and stared out of the window to avoid talking.

"How was the film?" Jim asked, trying to get back in her good books. Once Susan was in a strop, it wasn't easy to divert her."

"OK," she said, monosyllabically.

As he turned onto the main road, Susan reached down and picked up a lipstick that had freed itself from beneath her seat.

"Who's is this?" she asked, her reluctance to speak, outweighed by her curiosity.

"Must be your mum's." Jim tried to keep the anxiety from his voice.

"Mum's!" Susan exclaimed with incredulity. She twisted the end to reveal a plum tip. "It's a wet look lipstick in plum, Dad. I hardly think it's Mum's."

"Perhaps the lady I dropped home from the library then?"

"I thought you said she was old."

"An old friend, not 'old' old," Jim explained firmly.

Besides him, Susan twisted the lipstick, pulled down the sunshade to reveal the mirror, and expertly applied it to her lips.

"Susan, I really don't think you should be doing that. It's not yours."

"Finders keepers," she said dramatically, popping it into her pocket and jumping out of the car.

Margaret was waiting at the door when they arrived home.

"I was getting worried about you. Why are you so late?" Margaret asked.

"Ask Dad," Susan sulked.

"And what's that on your lips?"

"I found it in the car. Dad says it belonged to some friend of yours."

Standing in the hall, Jim shifted uncomfortably. Margaret looked straight at him. Her eyes seemed to say 'how could you?'

"I bumped into Betty at the library. It was raining, and I offered her a lift home. I think it must have been a present for her daughter…" Jim's voice trailed to nothing.

"That was kind of you," Margaret replied, and only Jim could hear the steel in her voice.

"Right, Susan, upstairs quickly and get out of those wet clothes. I'll get lunch ready."

As Susan took the stairs two at a time, Jim smiled at Margaret and mouthed, 'Thank you.' The look she gave him as she closed the kitchen door behind her was of sheer disgust.

She made a decision

The drive from London had been a long one. They had taken the A1 and stopped at Cambridge for a cup of tea and a sandwich. Jim insisted on driving the whole way. 'I don't trust female drivers – no coordination,' he'd laughed, as if it were a joke. Christine had been with him long enough to know he meant every word. They had booked a guest house in Kings Lynn, and Jim was keen to get there whilst it was still light. They sat in companionable silence, having exhausted most of their usual subjects of conversation. Christine looked out of the window, seeing the light slowly change. It had been a lovely day, and the fire red of the sky tinged the top of the trees. They were well into the Fens now, and, for as far as she could see, the road was long and straight and flat.

She was looking forward to the holiday. A whole five days when she had Jim all to herself. They had been seeing each other for nearly two years, but it felt far less. Most weeks, they would meet up one night and the occasional Saturday. He always blamed work or babysitters, but Christine worried that the lack of permanence suited him more than it should. More perplexing was his reluctance to introduce her to his children. It was almost as if he were embarrassed by her. The ladies from the Writers Circle were their only mutual friends, and when she suggested going out with her work colleagues, he was equally reluctant. When she asked him directly he would reassure her, promising he loved her and only wanted to be with her. They'd even spoken about getting married, but no ring had been forthcoming. A recent conversation about spending more time together had led to this mini-break. She planned to use the time wisely and show him how good married life could be if only he would give it a chance. He spoke about his wife rarely, and she didn't want to bring back sad memories, but he'd been a widower for nearly eight years now and surely he deserved some happiness of his own?

"Almost there," Jim put his hand on her knee. "Time for a walk before dinner if we hurry." The guest house served a three-course meal at 7 pm on the dot, and it was already nearly 6 pm.

Jim had booked them in as Mr and Mrs Willis – it seemed more plausible than Mr and Mrs Smith. They had chosen the name in tribute to the Leyton Orient goalkeeper, and Christine had borrowed her mother's wedding ring to keep up the pretence. She'd told her mum that Jim wanted to check the size before buying her an engagement ring. Her mother had been delighted. Christine slipped it on her finger. It was slightly large on her, but she had practised trapping it with her middle finger. She wiggled it from below, and it glinted as the gold caught the beam of the street light.

"Perhaps one day I'll have my own," she said quietly, but Jim was already out of the car and didn't hear.

In bed that night they laughed as the bed springs creaked. Jim had placed the bath towels between the bedstead and the walls, but the sound was only softened slightly. Sex had always been the easiest part of their relationship and, for Christine, the time when she felt most connected with Jim. In bed, he was hers alone. There were no distractions. No work problems to respond to. No children to be collected or babysitters to be home for.

She had recently gone on the pill – a friend at school had given her the idea. It hadn't been easy to persuade the doctor, but a combination of a fake wedding ring and a sob story worked their magic. She worried that the lie would jinx her chances of ever having a baby of her own. When she mentioned this to Jim, he'd laughed and said, 'I would have thought your age might have put a spanner in the works already.' He had kissed her and managed an 'only joking!' but his words stung. In her more insecure moments, Christine wondered if Jim had pursued her precisely because of her age. He probably thought she was past wanting a child, whereas the longer she spent with Jim, the more she dared to dream. She'd always been cautious before. Her mother's poor choices sounded the warning klaxon for previous boyfriends. But there was something different about Jim, so she gradually let down her defences and started to believe again.

Time was not on her side. She had turned thirty-seven this year, and her chances of falling pregnant were already declining. The doctor who had prescribed the pill warned about the dangers of a geriatric pregnancy. Christine had decided it was now or never. She was determined to use this holiday to give Jim an ultimatum: only a promise of marriage and a commitment to try for a baby would do. Otherwise, she would end things between them. She didn't know whether she could go through with it. She just knew she had to try.

Breakfast the next day was served in a small room just off the hall. There were four tables, and one was already occupied by a suited gentleman who looked every inch the travelling salesman. The other tables had names propped up against the toast rack. Jim scanned the room and was about to tell the landlady that she'd forgotten to set a table for them when Christine pointed out the one for Mr and Mrs Willis.

"I wonder when they'll arrive?" Jim laughed, taking his seat.

"How about us getting married? We wouldn't have to remember who we are all the time." Christine tried to keep her voice steady.

"Is that a proposal?" Jim countered. He was in a lighthearted mood this morning.

"Maybe?" said Christine.

"Perhaps, one day," said Jim, his words resonating with uncertainty.

That morning, they went on a boat trip to see the seals at Blakeney Point. The sun had yet to warm the September chill out of the day, so they huddled together under the blankets supplied by the skipper and tried to ignore the pervading smell of fish.

"This is nice," Jim said, holding his nose.

"It is nice," Christine insisted, laughing and pulling his hands away from his face. She kissed him and pointed out the seals camouflaged by the shingle.

"Look at those pups – they are so sweet."

"If you say so!"

"I do say so. How could anyone resist?"

"Are you getting broody?" he asked playfully, burying his hands in the pockets of her jacket, and tapping her stomach.

"I am actually." Christine turned back from looking at the seals and looked straight at Jim. He held her gaze for a second, before dropping his eyes and removing his hands from her jacket. Christine felt all the closeness of the morning dissipate. She realised she was holding her breath. She knew she had a choice to make. She could tell him how she longed for a child to satisfy her maternal longing and cement her relationship with him. Or she could laugh it off, grab his hands, and say she was only being silly. Blame it on her age or her hormones.

She did neither. She was too cowardly. Too worried that he would leave her to confront him, and too emotional to disguise it as a joke. Instead, she turned and stared at the island, her eyes stinging in the sea breeze, and, as the captain opened up the engine and started towards the shore, she saw the seals and their pups gradually disappear from view until you would hardly have known they were there at all. The weight of the unspoken truth hung between them as they had lunch at the pub on the harbour. They chatted amiably enough, joked with the waitress about the weather, shared a treacle pudding, and sat afterwards reading the papers. Without acknowledging it, they both knew that they had glimpsed the end – a portent for the road ahead. The ghost of Christmas yet to come. Christine shuddered.

"Are you cold? Shall we walk back?" Jim asked, looking up from the paper and smiling at her.

She loved the crease by his eyes, the slight dimple in his cheek. She loved this man, but she knew it would never be enough. In her mind's eye, she could see what would follow. The inevitable uncoupling. The sex would stop being as satisfying. The jokes no longer so funny. She might even start to dislike the creases and the dimples. The pace at which this happened was entirely in her hands. She'd known enough men like Jim to realise that he would happily continue in an arrangement that suited him, regardless of the emotional dishonesty. He would believe her happy. If he remembered the hurt today, he would think he had misread the moment. Men found it easy to fool themselves. So the timetable at least was in her hands.

"Yes, let's walk back," she said, standing up and pulling her coat from the back of the chair. She placed her arm through his, enjoying the familiarity. She would have to work hard to keep her resolve. Who knew if she'd manage it?

Christine woke early on Friday. They'd left King's Lynn on Thursday and driven down to a village near Norwich to see her evacuee 'parents' Twiggy and Jack. Christine had been keen to introduce them to Jim and for him to meet the couple who had done so much for her as a youngster. They'd arrived later than expected, and after supper, they were shown to the room that had been hers during the war. At some point in the last twenty years, the single bed had been replaced with bunks, and Jim had gallantly agreed to take the top one. She'd slept badly. The warmth of the room had woken her, and a combination of

Jim's snoring and her own thoughts prevented her from dropping off again. She got out of bed quietly and took her clothes to the bathroom across the hall to avoid disturbing Jim. It was still early, and Twiggy and Jack's bedroom door was shut, so she padded downstairs, grabbed her coat, and shut the front door behind her.

Things looked very different from the day she had arrived in 1939. She had never seen the countryside before. The sounds and smells were so different from the greyness and grime of London. She remembered that when Twiggy had taken her by the hand at the village hall, she hadn't understood a word she'd said – the thick Norfolk accent so different from the cockney she had heard all her life. She soon learned though, and even now she found herself reaching for phrases she'd heard back then. She turned right out of the village and headed towards the old farm.

Today was the last day of the holiday, and in some ways, Christine was relieved. The longer she spent with Jim, the more she felt her resolve slipping. Could she really give him up? And for what? The chance she might meet someone else who she could have children with? In the cold light of a beautiful day, it felt like a remote possibility. Perhaps she'd be better convincing Jim to give her a baby? He was ten years older than her and probably thought his parenting days were behind him. But, if he loved her enough, wouldn't he want her to be happy?

She rounded the corner and came across the gate that she'd passed every day on her way to school. Most mornings she had taken an apple in her pocket and held it out to the Shire horse that was always in the field. She loved the warmth of the horse's breath as it gratefully snuffled the apple from her hand, its soft mouth gentle against her fingers, the large teeth receding from the gums to create an equine smile. No horses today, but she still stood at the gate and rested her weight against it, half expecting to see one appearing from the top of the field.

At the end of the lane, she passed the orchard where, as a teenager, she had helped the farmer gather pears and apples into bushel baskets and take them to market in Norwich. How much younger she had seemed than the teenagers of today with their miniskirts and dark eye shadow. Some weekends she and Jack would go into Norwich, and they'd visit the cathedral, or, in the winter months, they'd stand at the River End at Carrow Road and cheer on The Canaries.

They had felt gloriously safe from the war. Their bravado was shattered in 1942 when bombing raids destroyed many buildings around the city, including, to Christine's horror, the local chocolate factory. After the bombings, many of the other evacuees from her school had been called back to London by mothers worried for their safety and missing their company. Her mother seemed to have forgotten she had a daughter, and when Christine had written to ask if she could stay, she never received a reply.

The road curved, and Christine crossed to walk back along the river. In the distance, she could see a small figure determinedly striding towards her. As they got closer, Christine could see that it was Twiggy, and she waved to acknowledge her.

"You were up before I could make you breakfast," Twiggy said, greeting her with a hug.

“I didn’t wake you, did I?” Christine asked, putting her arm through hers.

“Of course not. Nothing wakes me these days. So what’s with the early start? You’re meant to be on holiday!”

“Oh, I don’t know. Probably Jim’s snoring,” Christine laughed unconvincingly.

“You can’t fool me, Chrissie. You were never good at lying.” Twiggy squeezed her hand. “Is there something wrong?”

“No. Not really. I just had high hopes for the holiday. I thought maybe …” Her words drifted off on the dew.

“You love him then?”

“I do. But I don’t think it’s enough. Jim doesn’t want any more children. I didn’t think I’d mind. But now I find I do.”

“Men. They have no idea, do they.”

They walked in silence for a bit.

“What do you think of him, Twiggy? Is he what you expected?”

Christine had told Twiggy more about Jim than she’d told anyone else. She’d explained about his wife dying and how protective he was of his girls. The fact that she had yet to meet either of them.

“He’s very charming,” Twiggy seemed a little guarded.

“Is there a ‘but’?” Christine prompted.

“Not a ‘but’, more of an observation. He seems to like the sound of his own voice too much for my liking.”

“I think he’s just a bit nervous, hoping to impress. He knows how important you both are to me.”

“Maybe. And you say you’ve never been to his house?”

"No, never. He's very protective of his youngest daughter. Perhaps when she's started at the next school?"

"It must have been hard, losing her mother so young. But wouldn't that be the perfect reason to bring someone else into her life? You'd be so good with her, Chrissie. I know you would."

"Everything I ever learned about bringing up girls, I learned from you," Christine said, smiling.

"You were easy to love and quick to learn. Our lives would have been so different without you. We cried and cried when you got on that train back to London."

They walked the remaining way in silence. As they reached the end of the road, Twiggy placed an arm on her sleeve.

"Do be careful, love. Me and Jack would hate to see you hurt."

"Oh, Jim would never hurt me. He's so thoughtful, honestly – when it's just the two of us we're like an old married couple."

"Except you're not," said Twiggy, "and from everything you've said I can't think of one good reason why you're not. Unless, of course, he's already got a wife."

Jim came out of the door smiling.

"I wondered where you'd got to. I see the search party found you."

"She did indeed," smiled Christine. "I just wanted to see how much the village had changed. It's a beautiful morning for a walk."

"Gave me a chance to catch up with Jack. I hear you almost became a Norwich City supporter."

"Hardly, but Jack did introduce me to the beautiful game."

"Or 'bootiful' game, as we say around these parts," laughed Jack, putting on his thickest Norfolk accent.

As they drove home that evening, Christine couldn't help feeling as if time were running out to say all she wanted to say. She felt sure that the moment he dropped her at her flat and kissed her goodnight, she would have lost her chance. Like a latter-day Cinders, all her dreams would become rags. The silence between them no longer felt amiable but like a deep, dark reservoir hiding a secret in its depths. She tried the words on for size in her head and rehearsed different places to start that would not scare him off. Anything to delay the inevitable return to everyday life, to one night in the week and every other Saturday.

She must have dropped off. The rhythm of the windscreen wipers and the warmth of the blow heater proved strangely soporific. She'd woken with a jolt – her head nodding viciously, jarring her neck. For a moment, she had forgotten where she was and who she was with. She'd been in the middle of a strange dream. Her mother had been there, but they were in Norfolk. There had been horses and bombs. She'd been standing with Twiggy and Jack in a field, and she was wearing her school uniform. Across the field, she could see Jim, but he was too far away to see her. He was with a woman and a child, and as she watched, he picked the child up and put her on his shoulders. He turned slowly and looked straight at Christine, and then very slowly, he drew the woman to him and kissed her.

“Christine, are you awake?” Jim’s voice exploded into the fragments of her dream. “I think you must have nodded off. That will teach you to wake up so early.”

“Yes, I’m awake,” Christine managed. Jumping out of the dream had confused her, and for a moment she didn’t know what was real.

Jim went to kiss her, and she pulled away.

“Are you OK?” he asked, looking confused.

“Sorry. Yes, I’m fine. I was just fast asleep and dreaming.”

“Of me, I hope?” he said, the familiar sparkle reflected in his eyes.

“Of you,” she managed, attempting a smile.

He took her chin in his hands and planted a kiss on her lips. “That’s good. See you next week,” he said.

Inside the cocoon of her flat, she sat and closed her eyes, hoping to shift the memory of the dream, but however hard she tried, the after-image stayed strong.

He said "I love her"

"Please get a move on, I promised Gwen I'd be there mid-morning."

Jim was already feeling grumpy before he popped into Christine's, and now she was making him late for a day with Gwen that he was already dreading.

Over Christmas lunch, full of good cheer and a few too many whiskies, he offered to help Gwen move out of the halls of nursing into a rented flat in Acton. Now, on a sleety morning in April, he was thoroughly regretting his offer. Margaret insisted that he go, and reluctantly he loaded the car with boxes of things she thought Gwen might need in her new home.

"Just give me 5 minutes," Christine shouted from the bathroom.

"What are you doing up there?" he shouted back impatiently.

He'd told Christine two weeks ago that he wouldn't make it this Saturday. She'd been disappointed, and they'd had a bit of a row. They had been arguing a lot recently, mainly about the lack of time they spent together. When he'd explained that it was to help Gwen move home, she offered to come with him and help.

“I’d love to meet the real Little Wrinkle, and we could show her some of the books. We might need her onside if we decide to publish them,” she’d argued.

He’d explained why this was not the ideal time and promised to speak to Gwen about finding a date to introduce them. This seemed to placate her. But when he’d seen her on Thursday night, she’d told him she’d arranged to meet a friend in London, and asked if he could drop her in Hammersmith on his way. She hadn’t been feeling too well over the last few weeks, and he couldn’t think of a good reason to refuse, so here he was. If he’d known it would make him late, he would have said no. It was already taking him out of his way.

On the drive to Hammersmith, Christine was uncharacteristically quiet. Having been cross with her for making him late, Jim tried to make up for his snappiness.

“Who is it you’re seeing today?” he asked.

“A friend,” Christine answered.

“I didn’t know you still had any London friends.”

“You don’t know everything about me.”

“I only asked. You didn’t need to bite my head off.” Jim kept his words light. He didn’t want to start a row when he was about to drop her off.

Christine sighed. “I’m sorry. I don’t know why I’m being so miserable all the time. I just don’t feel that great.”

“Perhaps you shouldn’t have come today. Stayed in bed and got over it properly.”

"Maybe. I just thought some fresh air might help, and I usually feel better once I'm up and about and have had something to eat."

"If I finish early with Gwen, I could come over this evening and look after you properly." Jim squeezed her knee suggestively.

"That would be nice." Christine smiled, but Jim wasn't sure she meant it. She'd gone off that too, it seemed. Ever since their trip to Norfolk, she had been a bit distant with him. Christmas, as usual, had been the source of much argument. They'd exchanged presents on Christmas Eve, but for the rest of the holiday, he had been at home with the family. She had bought him a gold-plated lighter and had it inscribed 'with love, Christine'. His first thought was that he would have to be careful to change lighters whenever he was at home. Yet another thing to remember about this complicated private life.

He had bought her a ruby necklace. The man at the jewellers had told him that rubies signified love and undying devotion. He hoped this would show Christine just how much he loved her. She looked excited when he produced the box wrapped in twinkly paper, but she seemed disappointed when she opened it. She'd put it aside and said, "It's lovely, thank you," but her eyes had said differently. There was no pleasing some women.

They came off the A4 and turned into the labyrinth of roads that bordered Hammersmith Hospital. He had visited Gwen a few times whilst she was in the nurse's accommodation, and it was always a pain to park.

"Shall I pop out here?" Christine asked. There was a car behind him flashing his lights, so he turned round at the end and found a place to park on the road, down a little from the flats.

Gwen rolled over to see the alarm clock. It was nearly 10.30 am, and her tummy was starting to rumble. She'd have to eat something before her dad arrived, or she'd be starving at lunch. It had been kind of him to offer to help her pack up and move, and she wanted to be on her best behaviour today. Her relationship with her dad was still a little fragile. When she'd first found out about his affairs, she'd been disgusted with him. They'd had some monumental rows, and in some way, it had been the reason she'd decided to take up nursing so that she could leave home as soon as possible. She still didn't approve of what he'd done, but part of her felt that her mother was partly to blame. Why hadn't she just left him when she found out? That's what Gwen would have done; woe betide any man cheating on her.

In Gwen's opinion, the women's magazines that her mother read were full of bad advice on this sort of thing.

Dear Agony Aunt
My husband doesn't seem to find me attractive anymore, and I think he might be seeing somebody else. What should I do?

Dear Unattractive Wife
Why don't you cook him something special and make extra effort with your appearance – I'm sure you'll win him back.

Anyway, whatever the reason, her mother had forgiven her father, and if she could, Gwen would have to find a way as well. It just wasn't worth the effort required to stay angry at everyone, and she couldn't risk losing touch with her sister Susan, who hadn't been old enough to understand the tension and had been devastated when Gwen left home.

The milk in her fridge had seen better days. Sniffing it made her gag, and when she poured it down the sink, it came out in big lumps. Gwen wasn't the most domesticated of people, and there were times when she missed being at home with dinner ready on the table and her clothes washed and ironed. Perhaps, if things went well today, she could go home for a long weekend and be looked after before she started her new job. Christmas had been OK, and her dad had seemed on good form, so perhaps he'd learnt his lesson and wasn't up to his old tricks anymore. He'd promised to be early, but her dad wasn't known for his timekeeping, so she reckoned she would have time to go to the corner shop for milk. She pulled on her clothes and ran down the four flights of stairs. The corner shop was a godsend for busy nurses who were always running out of everything. She grabbed some milk and then took the fast way home, past the car park. In the far corner under the tree, she could see the distinctive blue of her dad's Cortina. He must have just arrived.

As she grew closer, she saw her dad getting out of the driver's seat. She wasn't sure why, but something made her hesitate from running over to him. The next minute, she saw a woman on the passenger side. Gwen moved behind a tree to get a better look. She was getting that sick feeling in her stomach again. Her dad went to the back of the car, embraced the woman, and kissed her. Not a friendly peck, but a long, lingering kiss. Gwen couldn't see the woman properly, but she looked petite, certainly shorter than Gwen, and slim. She wore a black mini skirt, blue polo neck jumper, and knee-high boots. It was hard to judge her age, but she seemed considerably younger than her dad. Maybe in her mid-30s? She felt like a detective, remembering all the information in forensic detail. In other circumstances, it might have been something to talk to the other nurses about on one of their breaks, but this was her father, and this woman was what? His girlfriend? His mistress? She imagined walking up to them and introducing herself. 'Hello, Dad – this must be your fancy woman. I'm Gwen, his daughter. Where's Mum?' Did this woman even know Mum existed? She wouldn't put it past her father to lie about that. Within seconds, the woman had taken her handbag from the car and was walking towards the main road. Her dad continued to unpack the car. If she was quick, she could go the other way and make it up to her flat before her father pressed the buzzer downstairs. Without further thought, she flew round the corner and knocked right into the woman from the car. The milk bottle went flying.

"I'm so sorry, I wasn't looking where I was going," the woman said.

On closer inspection, Gwen judged her to be in her late-30s. She had a scarf in her hair that made her look bohemian. She wasn't exactly pretty, but there was something about the way she held herself that was warm and natural. It took all of Gwen's self-control to regain her composure.

"No use crying over spilt milk. I shouldn't have been walking so fast," Gwen managed.

"I know how it is to be desperate for a cup of coffee," the woman countered, smiling broadly.

Despite herself, Gwen smiled. What was she doing making small talk with her father's fancy woman?

"Listen, let me buy you another bottle of milk. It was my fault. I was miles away. My boyfriend just dropped me off, and I don't know where the tube is."

"Don't worry about the milk," Gwen replied. She was starting to worry her dad might walk around the corner any minute. It might be amusing to witness the sheer panic on his face, but she needed time to think before that encounter.

"The closest tube station is probably White City. It's about a 15-minute walk, though."

"Oh, thank you. Are you 100% sure about the milk?" the woman asked.

"Yes, I'm sure," Gwen replied, but the woman was already walking away.

When she got back to the flat, her father was sitting outside with three boxes next to him.

"Hello, darling. I was starting to think you'd forgotten," he said teasingly.

"No, I hadn't forgotten. I just popped out for some milk." Gwen's voice was flat.

"Where is it then? I'm parched."

Gwen opened the door, and her dad followed her in.

“Not got a hug for me then?” he demanded.

“I’d have thought you’d had enough hugs for one day,” Gwen replied cuttingly.

Her dad stood in the middle of her flat, looking confused. Gwen was suddenly overwhelmed with tiredness. She sat down on the sofa and put her head in her hands.

“Whatever’s wrong? I thought you’d be pleased to see me. Were you out last night – a bit hungover maybe?”

“If I was, I'd have sobered up pretty quickly,” Gwen replied. “I’ve just run into your girlfriend.”

Jim stood there open-mouthed. Gwen could almost see his mind working. What did she know? What could he say? Would a lie work?

“Don’t even think of lying to me. I saw you getting out of the car. And don’t tell me she's a work colleague, because people don’t put their tongues down their work colleagues’ throats. You disgust me. You promised you wouldn’t do this to Mum again. How could you?”

Gwen’s words trailed off and were replaced by angry sobs. She wished she could shut herself in her bedroom, but there was nowhere to hide in this small flat, so she just stood there with the tears running down her face. After a few moments, there was a tap on the door, and her friend Deidre asked if she was OK. The walls were paper-thin, and you couldn’t keep anything private around here.

“Yes, I’m fine,” Gwen lied, choking back her tears. “Dad’s here, and he was just telling me that my cat had died.”

"Oh, that's so sad. Are you sure you're OK?" Deidre asked. Gwen felt sure that Deidre didn't believe her about the cat. She didn't even have a cat.

"Yes, it's fine. Sorry if I woke you up. I'll see you later."

Her dad had put the box down and was now looking out of the window. He hated any form of confrontation.

"Don't you have anything to say for yourself?" Gwen demanded, but the anger had gone out of her voice.

"You promised Mum after the last time. What's wrong with you, Dad? Surely you can't be so desperate that you're prepared to hurt Mum and Susan … and me."

Her dad turned round, and she could glimpse the hurt and fear in his eyes.

"It's not what you think, Gwen. It's not some tawdry affair. I really love Christine."

"Of course you do. She's ten years younger than you and looks great in a mini-skirt. She's not had two of your children and devoted herself to you for the last twenty years. What's not to love?" Gwen responded bitingly.

"It's not like that, and however much you think you understand everything about your mum and me, you really don't," her dad replied.

"Tell me then, Dad, because I'm finding it hard to understand."

"If you promise to let me talk without judging me, then I'll try and explain. It's not easy. Some of this is deeply personal."

Gwen didn't want to let him off the hook that easily, but she was intrigued.

“I’ll try to keep quiet, but don’t spin me some pack of lies, or I promise I’ll never speak to you again.”

“It all goes back to when your Mum and I met in the war. Things were really different back then. A boy like me would never have met a woman like your mother if it hadn’t been for the war. I know your generation has very modern ideas about all this, but I was a working-class boy from the East End of London and your mum was from a well-to-do family with money. They even had servants.”

“Hardly servants, Dad!” Gwen couldn’t help but interrupt. "Granny and Grandpa might be prim and proper, but they weren’t royalty."

“You know what I mean. Your mum was well out of my league, and her parents did nothing to make me feel differently. They didn’t even come to the wedding.”

Gwen knew this was true. Her parents had married in haste, and Granny and Grandpa hadn’t been able to change their plans. It had been very spontaneous and romantic.

“The difference in our backgrounds shouldn’t have mattered, and, at first, it didn’t seem to. It probably wasn’t helped by conceiving you so early, but after you were born, we just stopped being intimate.”

Gwen felt her face going red. Was her father really going to talk about their sex life with her?

“Your mum still wanted to, but I just found I couldn’t.” Her father was looking at the floor. “I wasn’t experienced before we married, and I just felt your mother was too good for me. With a young baby around, it was easy to blame the tiredness, but day by day and month by month, we just stopped trying.”

"I sincerely hope you're not blaming me for your infidelity."

"No, of course not, Gwen. It was all me. It was me that couldn't give your mum what she wanted. It was me that couldn't be a proper husband."

Her father's voice was subdued. He sounded like he might cry. Gwen had never seen him like this before, and she was uncomfortable with this version of her dad.

"So you couldn't do it with Mum, so you decided to do it with the secretaries at work instead?" Gwen interrupted coarsely. She wanted to shock him into some response.

"I know that wasn't the right thing to do, but I felt it might cure me, in some strange way. That if I could have sex with someone that didn't matter to me, then I could finally be a proper husband to your mother."

"And did it work?" Gwen asked, already knowing the answer.

"No. It just hurt your mum and made me feel more guilty. So, I stopped seeing them. I promised your mum."

"And what about the woman in the car? Or was she a figment of my imagination?" Gwen could feel herself getting angry again.

"That's Christine, and with Christine, it's been different. Your mum and I were getting on well. You know we were. She means the world to me, and despite what you think, we still love each other. But we're just like best friends, living in the same house. We rub along well enough, but it's not a proper marriage."

He paused to gather his emotions and get his stammer in check.

“And then, a couple of years ago, I met Christine. I saw a creative writing course advertised at the local library and decided to join. Christine and I started on the same day. We just hit it off. I’ll spare you the details, but one thing led to another…”

His voice trailed off and Gwen jumped in.

“I suppose you had to ask her for a full rundown on her background to establish whether you’d be able to get it up with her?” Gwen didn’t know where all this anger was coming from. She really wanted to hurt him.

“Don’t be like that, Gwen. I’m not proud of myself, but I couldn’t help but fall in love with her.”

“And does Mum know?”

“No, she doesn’t know, but I think she suspects. Promise me you won’t tell her. I couldn’t bear it”.

For the first time, her father’s words were tinged with something more than regret. There was fear there.

“And what about Christine? Does she know about Mum? About us?”

“Yes, of course, she knows about you and Susan. She’s desperate to meet you both.”

“But she doesn’t know about Mum?” she shook her head, “It doesn’t make any sense.”

Gwen needed some time to think. She left the flat and walked back to the corner shop on autopilot. She picked up a bottle of milk and went to the counter.

“You drink a lot of tea!” The shopkeeper laughed, but she was already out the door. When she walked back into the flat, her dad was sitting on her bed, his head in his hands.

“Gwen, I’m so …”

"Don't. Don't say you're sorry. Don't say anything, because I don't believe you. Just listen to me. I won't tell Mum, but you have to promise me that you'll give Christine up. It can't go on. It's not fair to either of them. If you love Mum like you say you do, then you owe it to her to stop seeing Christine."

"I'm not sure I can do that." Her dad's voice broke with emotion. "I love her too."

"Well then, you'll have to choose," Gwen snapped bitterly, "I'm not going to let Susan grow up thinking you're her hero, like I did, only to find that you're a weak little man who so desperately wants to be liked that he's prepared to hurt everyone else. Now I think you better leave."

"But I was going to help you move. We were going to have lunch."

"I think I've lost my appetite," Gwen replied. "Go and sort yourself out, Dad, before I do something you are going to regret."

Jim went back to his car and wondered what to do. He thought about following Christine into town and turning up unannounced at the restaurant she'd arranged to meet her friend. But in the end, he drove to Kew Gardens and found himself somewhere to sit and think.

He usually hated thinking, preferring instead to act on his instincts. Whenever his actions got him into trouble, as they often did, he was ready with an excuse or a clever way of deflecting the truth. For over forty years, this strategy had worked well for him. He'd been able to have his cake and eat it. And no one had ever got hurt, not really. In the early days, he knew that some of the affairs had upset Margaret, but then they had reached an understanding. As long as it was just a bit of fun and as long as none of their friends or family found out, she would turn a blind eye. All of that had been before Christine. He hadn't been looking for love when he walked into that library. Quite the opposite. He needed a distraction, a way to keep busy and away from temptation. But he couldn't help himself. And the lie he'd told the first night at the pub had escalated, week by week, until he'd written a completely different life story, one in which he was free to fall in love.

From the start, he'd carefully kept his two lives separate. The lie he had told about his sister-in-law and neighbours helping with the children meant that Christine never phoned the house. As their relationship intensified, the fact that Susan was at home meant they always met at Christine's. There had been a couple of close shaves. Once, he and Christine had been in a bookshop in Eastcote, and he'd seen Margaret walking past with Susan. He'd ducked down behind the travel section, bought a book about the great train journeys of Europe, and suggested that they go home immediately and read it in bed. Another time he had pulled into the car park of a local pub, only to see Gwen sitting in the beer garden with some friends. He'd immediately suggested they go somewhere else, conjuring out of thin air a bad lunch he'd had at the same pub only a few weeks previously.

Today's experience had to qualify as the worst possible luck. If they had been five minutes earlier. If Gwen hadn't run out of milk. If Christine hadn't decided to meet her friend for lunch. But in other ways, it was inevitable that his two worlds would collide eventually. He needed to find a solution quickly, or many people would get hurt. The person he was most worried about was Gwen, not Margaret. He'd never felt anything but a proper father to her, and she'd been devoted to him throughout her childhood. She used to come and watch him playing cricket, sitting patiently behind the boundary until tea and then rushing on, her little arms outstretched, begging him to pick her up and swing her around.

"Higher, Daddy, faster, Daddy," she screamed, giggling.

Whenever she got into trouble or had a fight with her mother, she always turned to Jim. He just had a way with her. When he'd first started to write *Little Wrinkle*, she'd been about ten. She was a great reader, but she loved it when he sat on the bed and read her the stories. 'That's me,' she'd say and wrinkle her nose at him to prove it. She hadn't wrinkled her nose today, she'd just looked at him with absolute disgust. Despite all his complicated feelings for Christine and his worries about Margaret finding out, it was the disappointment on Gwen's face that had hurt him. Perhaps this time he wouldn't be able to talk himself out of it. But it was worth one last try.

Back at the flat, Gwen paced up and down like an expectant father, trying to think what to do for the best. Despite the shock of seeing her father kissing another woman, she supposed deep down she wasn't that surprised. 'Once a cheat, always a cheat,' one of her friends had pronounced when she saw her boyfriend eyeing up another girl at a party.

She'd promised not to tell Mum, and to give her dad a chance to decide. But what if he chose this Christine? What would that do to Mum? Or to Susan? No, she couldn't let him do that. And then it came to her. She'd find a way to tell Christine. From what her dad said, Christine didn't suspect he was married. She must be more of a fool than she looked. Or perhaps it suited her as well? Maybe she was playing her dad along and had another man on the go herself? She thought about the women from this morning. She'd seemed nice, ordinary even. Maybe she was just so in love with her dad that she allowed herself to be duped by him. It wasn't fair to her either way.

Gwen knew what she had to do. She picked up the Yellow Pages and searched for Adult Evening Classes in Eastcote. Within a few moments, she had a phone number. Ten minutes later, she has an address for the lady who taught the Writers Circle. She picked up a pen and started to write.

She said "You did me a favour"

It was one of those late April days when whatever you wore would be wrong. Christine had dressed carefully this morning, ridiculously nervous about the impression she would give. As she got older, she worried far less about her appearance. She saw this as a matter of self-confidence, but it could equally be a sign that she had let herself go.

Christine always wanted to make a good impression on people. Even on her trips to the grocers, she went out of her way to be cheerful and friendly to the shop assistants. It wasn't so much that she was desperate to be liked, more that she wanted them to think well of her, to say 'well, wasn't she a lovely lady?' when she walked out of the shop. As if they would! They were probably too busy or bored to care one way or the other. But it mattered to Christine. She put it down to being evacuated as a child. She could still vividly remember waiting in the church hall for a family to 'choose' her. One by one, friends from school were selected. She desperately tried to look like the kind, helpful girl she knew she was, but the more that were chosen, the harder it was to remain positive. It made her feel as if something was wrong with her, that she wasn't pretty enough, or didn't look right.

Being taken in by Twiggy and Jack had been the best thing that had ever happened to her. Where would she be now without them? They had been a tower of strength in the five years since she moved to East Anglia. In the early days, she had lived with them, sleeping in a single bed in the room they still referred to as hers. Twiggy had been so good with her. Giving her space and letting her cry when she wanted to, but always there with advice and a motherly hug. She'd been such a fool. When Kate from the Writers Circle had passed her a letter as she was leaving one night, she'd thought maybe it was some interest from a publisher. She'd popped it in her bag and excitedly opened it as soon as she got home. She had re-read it again last night in bed.

Dear Christine

You don't know me, although we have met once before. I don't know if you remember, but we bumped into each other in Hammersmith, and I dropped a pint of milk. I don't think you knew who I was at the time, but I am Jim's daughter Gwen, and I had just seen him kissing you. I was in a bit of a state because as far as I knew, he was happily married to my mum at the time.

Dad promised me that he would stop seeing you, but he's made promises before that he hasn't kept, and I wouldn't put it past him to find a way out of it. Whatever he has told you, he and my mother are still very much a married couple who share a home, a bed and two daughters. I'm sure you are not intentionally a home wrecker, but I am asking you, with all my heart, to give him up, as he is obviously unable or unwilling to let you go. I also need to tell you that you are not the first affair that he has had, and I think you are unlikely to be the last. I am sorry that I had to be the one to tell you, but I'm sure you can understand why I couldn't let the situation continue – for your or my own mother's sake.

Sorry to be the bearer of such uncomfortable news.

Gwen

The shock at the time had been absolute. The words had stung. The hurt and bitterness had shone through. But nothing had compared to the feelings of guilt and shame that Christine had felt. It had taken her five long years to forgive herself. Twiggy and Jack had helped her see that her only fault was to believe what Jim had told her. For the last few years, she had lost her confidence. She didn't trust herself and she found it hard to trust others. She needed to move on, and meeting up with Gwen today was an important part of that. She grabbed her bag and her coat and set off for London.

Gwen started to pack the baby changing bag as methodically as she could. Until a couple of weeks ago, she had used a list to ensure she hadn't forgotten anything. But even the list miscalculated the multiple changes of clothing required and the ridiculous numbers of spare nappies. Only the other day, David managed a pooh so explosive that it had leaked out of his nappy and covered the whole of his pram. She was still finding smears of mustard yellow weeks later.

There was a misconception amongst Gwen's friends that, as a nurse, she would find looking after a baby the easiest and most natural thing in the world. 'You've looked after a whole ward, Gwen, one baby will be a doddle.' It had surprised Gwen how hard she found it, but her patients were in their beds, not feeling terribly well, and mainly did what they were told. David, on the other hand, hardly slept, had the escapology skills of Harry Houdini, and believed it was his role in life to tell his parents what to do. 'I want a cuddle, I want a feed, I want you to change my nappy.' At least she was starting to understand the different cries and what each meant. Stephen, on the other hand, regularly got them muddled up, and sometimes she was sure he deliberately did this to avoid changing a nappy by insisting it was a 'hungry' cry.

Despite this, she knew she was lucky to have him. He was so good with David and with her. The other mums she met at the clinic didn't seem to have any support from their husbands, and most of them had moved their own mothers in for at least the first three months. As much as she loved her mother, the one week she stayed with them was about as much as either she or Stephen could handle. It appeared that the fundamentals of how to care for your baby changed with each generation. If one generation was meant to breastfeed, swaddle the baby and let it cry, the next was instructed to bottle feed, unwrap, and pick it up the minute it murmured. This seemed to Gwen to inevitably set up conflict between new mums and their mothers just when they most needed support.

David was fast asleep as Gwen washed, dressed and packed the bag. He usually went back to sleep after his 6.30 am feed, and occasionally Gwen joined him. Most of the time, she used the first two hours of the morning as precious time to get things done. If you'd told her a year ago that she would happily be washing before sunrise, she'd have said you were mad. But there was something satisfying about getting all the household chores done before breakfast, and it meant she could enjoy time with her son when he woke up. Doing the washing with the ridiculously convoluted twin tub was a never-ending task with the number of nappies David got through each day. Her mother constantly reminded her how lucky she was to have all the 'mod cons', but Gwen had gone to Radio Rentals on Saturday and ordered herself an automatic machine. She was ridiculously excited about it being delivered next week. She never really understood why people, her mother included, pined for the good old days. Why would you choose to spend your days putting clothes through a mangle? Surely, anything that made repetitive jobs easier was a good thing.

"You're such a women's libber," her mother exclaimed when she caught her reading *Superwoman* the other day.

"Hardly, Mum, although I agree that life's too short to stuff a mushroom," she replied.

"Well, they won't stuff themselves," her mum concluded as if she had won the argument.

Perhaps, Gwen thought unkindly, if her mother had insisted on more help around the house from her dad, he might have had less time for his infidelities. All these men going off to work and leaving their wives at home to deal with the children as if it were the easier option. It made Gwen's blood boil. She heard David cry and checked the kitchen clock. She had an hour before she needed to leave, enough time to get him up and dressed and for them both to have some breakfast.

She was so nervous about today that she'd hardly slept last night. She'd tossed and turned so much that Stephen had got up and said, "I'll go," mistaking her restlessness for David waking. He'd kissed her before he went to work this morning and gave her arm a reassuring squeeze. "It'll be fine," he promised. "And if it's not, just leave and come home".

The phone call had come nearly a fortnight ago now. David was in the pram in the garden, and she was taking 5 minutes to have a cup of tea and read a magazine.

"Hello, is that Gwen?"

There was a slight hesitation that made Gwen suspect the caller was apprehensive.

"Yes, speaking. Who is this?"

"Hello Gwen, this is Christine. You sent me a letter a few years ago. I was a friend of your father's."

Gwen sat down on the chair next to the phone.

"I'm sorry to ring you out of the blue like this, but I want to talk to you about something. I was hoping we could meet," Christine continued.

Gwen wished she had a cigarette. She'd given up smoking when she found herself pregnant with David, but there was nothing she wanted more right now. She quickly gathered her thoughts.

"Is it something we could talk about on the phone? I've got a young baby, and it's not easy to find a good time to meet." Gwen was rambling. Was Christine suggesting she would come to Gwen's house? She didn't want that to happen. It would feel like she was betraying her mum.

Even speaking to her on the phone made her feel deeply uncomfortable.

"I think it would be best to discuss this face to face," Christine sounded insistent, "Perhaps you could ask a friend to have the baby for an hour one day."

It sounded as if Christine had thought about this in advance. She certainly didn't seem surprised that Gwen had a baby. Had her dad told her? Was he still seeing her? The call had come out of the blue, putting Gwen on the back foot. She was irritated that Christine had suggested leaving David with someone, but despite herself, Gwen was curious to know why, after all these years, her father's ex-girlfriend wanted to meet. And what it was she wanted to discuss.

"I suppose if we met at a park, I could bring David with me," Gwen conceded.

They agreed to meet at a local park which had a café. It was neutral territory and walkable from her house, so if things got tricky, Gwen could make her excuses and leave. In the two weeks since the phone call, Gwen had tried her hardest to think what it might be about. Christine had mentioned her letter, and Gwen had been convinced that she and her father were no longer together. Things seemed to have improved between her parents, but she'd been so tied up with the wedding and married life that she'd not paid much attention to her parents. Susan, who might have noticed any increased tension between them, was now away at university. Her short rebellious phase was replaced by a longer 'academic' phase that saw her land a place at Sussex to read English. So perhaps her dad was still up to his old ways, and her mother had simply accepted it? Or maybe the letter had instigated a breakup, and now Christine wanted to restart their relationship. Every idea that Gwen came up with seemed more and more unlikely.

Despite dreading the meeting, it was the not knowing that was really getting to Gwen and she now just wanted to get it over and done with. At 11.25 am she popped David into his pram, shut the door behind her, and started the 10-minute walk to the park.

Despite the length of the journey from Norfolk, Christine had made good time and arrived at the park early. She positioned herself close to the café and was waiting by a small bench that gave her a clear view of both the entrances Gwen might use.

She had only seen a few photographs of Gwen before and couldn't remember exactly what she looked like. She checked her watch. If Gwen was anything like her father she might have ages to wait. He wasn't known for his punctuality. Or perhaps the baby had needed changing before she set off. Babies could be unpredictable like that. Christine was pleased that she had arrived early. It gave her time to run through what she wanted to say. None of it was easy, and Christine found that at moments of stress, she tended to ramble on about irrelevancies or go blank and forget everything she wanted to say. Neither would be ideal today.

"Hello, it's Christine, isn't it?" Despite her clever positioning, the voice came from behind her.

"Yes. Hello, Gwen," Christine stuttered. "Sorry, I was expecting you to come from a different direction!"

Standing before Christine was a woman with dark blonde hair caught back in a loose ponytail. She wore blue slacks and a camel trench coat and was pushing a pram with a changing bag in the wire basket beneath.

"Shall we walk and talk, or would you rather get a cup of tea in the café?" Gwen asked.

"A walk would be good," acknowledged Christine. "Perhaps we could have tea later if you have time."

"Let's see how David does," Gwen said, peering into the pram where the baby was fast asleep. They started walking around the lake in silence, with neither of them quite knowing the correct etiquette to start the conversation. In the end, Christine broke the silence.

"I'm sure my phone call came as a shock, and I feel I owe you an explanation," she began, holding up her hand to stop Gwen from responding. "Please don't say anything or I'll lose my thread, and I want to tell you everything from the start. Is that OK?"

Gwen nodded but said nothing. Christine took a deep breath.

"I know you know that your father and I were seeing each other for several years. I won't give you all the backstory unless you want to hear it, but I want you to know I had no idea he was married."

She paused and glanced at Gwen. She wanted to make sure she was believed.

"He had told me he had two daughters, but until you wrote to me, I was under the impression that your mother had died and that her sister, your aunt, was helping him out and often stayed at yours. It was why I wasn't able to contact him at home."

Christine paused for a moment. Retelling her story was hard, and even as she spoke the words, she realised how stupid she had been to believe the story Jim had told her.

"When I received your letter eight years ago, I was devastated to hear that Jim was married. I hated to think that you thought I was a home wrecker."

"But you still decided to stay with my dad?" Gwen asked caustically.

"The thing was…" Christine began. he took a breath "The thing was that when I received your letter, I was pregnant."

Gwen found that she had stopped walking. She wasn't even sure that her legs worked anymore. She stood rocking the pram, unable to form any reply.

"I know this is a terrible shock for you," Christine started, "At first, I thought that your father would tell you about Paul, but I realise now that I can't trust a word he says."

Gwen was starting to recover her senses. It dawned on her that she had an eight-year-old half-brother whom her father hadn't bothered to tell her about.

"So why are you telling me now?" Gwen managed.

"I need your forgiveness, or at least your understanding. In the early days after Jim and I met, we talked about getting married and starting a family. I can see now that I spoke more about it than your father. But he never said no. He just said 'maybe' or 'later' or 'when Susan is older'. I think I started to realise that unless I gave him an ultimatum, I would never get what I wanted."

"And did you?" Gwen prompted.

"I tried to. We went to Norfolk for a few days. I told him I wanted a family and I wanted to get married. But, as always, he made up an excuse for why it wasn't the right time. That Christmas, he gave me a small box wrapped in glittery paper. I was sure that he was going to ask me to marry him. But instead, it was a ruby pendant. I couldn't hide my disappointment.

He spent Christmas with you, as always, and I had the most miserable time. I caught a stomach bug and was sick for three whole days. He came to my house on New Year's Eve. We were meant to be going to some friends, but I wasn't feeling up to it. So he made me dinner, and we watched a film together, and afterwards we went to bed. He said we should see New Year's in with a bang. The whole time I was ill, I kept thinking that I had to end things with him. But as soon as I saw him, I clung to the hope that maybe this would be the time, this would be the year. So we limped on through January and February. Valentine's Day came and went, and still no ring appeared. I wasn't feeling very well and certainly not up to a confrontation with the man I loved. It was in March that I realised I'd missed my period. The day you saw me, the day with the milk, I was on the way to see my mum, to tell her that I was pregnant and to ask her what I should do."

Christine hadn't intended to tell Gwen the whole story, but once she started, she couldn't stop.

"What did your mum suggest?" Gwen asked.

"We had an almighty row. She called me stupid for getting myself pregnant. Reminded me how having me had ruined her life. Her advice was to get rid of it."

Gwen felt her eyes prick with tears. How alone Christine must have felt.

"And how did my dad react when you told him?" Gwen managed, but she feared the worst.

"He wasn't happy. Suggested that I had tricked him into having a baby. That I had come off the pill deliberately. It was terrible. And then I got your letter."

Gwen felt terrible. She had felt so good sending that letter, being the one to burst her father's bubble, to finally set the record straight. But she hadn't considered Christine's feelings, not really. Now, hearing her side of the story made Gwen realise how little she understood the situation.

"That must have been hard for you," Gwen began. "If I'd known, I wouldn't have been so cruel. I suppose I just wanted it to stop, and it was obvious that Dad wasn't going to end it."

"To be honest, you did me a favour." Christine swallowed hard and continued, "I'd been fooling myself about him all those years, believing he was free to marry me. He was very convincing. I thought he loved me."

"If it's any consolation, I think he did love you. He's just a weak and selfish man who thinks he can talk himself out of anything. Did you confront him with the letter?"

"I did. I was four months pregnant by then, and the reality of having an illegitimate baby was starting to hit home. I knew I couldn't give it up for adoption, so I gave your father an ultimatum. Either he divorced your mother and married me, or we were over. I still thought he would choose me, but he didn't. He kept saying that we could carry on as if we were husband and wife and that no one would know otherwise."

"So what did you do?"

"I ended it with him. I couldn't bear for Paul to grow up thinking that his father didn't love him enough to choose us. I've told everyone that my husband died in a car accident. It's what I'll tell Paul as soon as he's old enough to fully understand. Better a dead father than a fake one."

"And has Dad even met Paul?"

"Yes, but just the once – I thought I owed him that, and I suppose part of me thought that when he saw him, he might reconsider his decision.

"And did he?" Gwen interrupted.

"No, nothing changed. He still wanted us to carry on as before. He said he missed me, that he still loved me, but that he couldn't give up your mum."

"And what about Paul? Didn't he feel any responsibility for him?" Gwen could feel her blood boiling.

"I didn't really want anything from him other than marriage. If he wasn't prepared to give me that, I didn't want him in Paul's life, complicating things for us both. I didn't even put him on the birth certificate. Your dad tried to keep in touch with cards and presents on his birthday and at Christmas, but in the end, I told him to stop and that I'd throw away anything he sent."

They had finished a full lap of the park and were back at the café. Gwen touched Christine's hand gently.

"I think we should have that cup of tea now."

Gwen left Christine with the pram and was touched to see her gently stroking David's face on her return.

“He’s such a bonny baby,” Christine said, “you must love him so much.”

“Well, most of the time I do,” Gwen joked, glad to have a way to lighten the conversation, “Not sure about the middle of the night when he decides it’s time to play!”

“And how’s your dad with him?” Christine asked.

“I wouldn’t say dad particularly likes babies,” Gwen reflected. “He wasn’t at all hands-on with my sister Susan. I was ten, and Mum was glad to have me around to help. He’s fine with David, but we don’t see much of him. My husband, on the other hand, is brilliant.”

After the adrenaline rush of all the revelations, Gwen was feeling a bit flat. She was also wondering what exactly Christine wanted from her. David was stirring, so she picked him up and sat him on her knee.

“I hope you don’t mind me asking,” Gwen began, “but how are you managing? For money, I mean. If nothing else, Dad should be helping you out with that.”

“That was one of the reasons I wanted to talk to you today.” Christine looked awkward as if what she was asking was difficult for her. “I really don’t want anything to do with your dad. The main reason I wanted to see you was to apologise for all the hurt my relationship must have caused you and to promise that if I had known, I would never have continued with it, but …”

Christine hesitated, and Gwen encouraged her to continue.

“When your dad and I were together, I started doing illustrations for the *Little Wrinkle* books he had written. I’ve always done drawings, and the first time your dad read the stories to me, I had a clear picture of the little girl."

"That little girl was me," Gwen said quietly.

"I know. He never lied about that. He clearly adored you," Christine said reassuringly. "To cut a long story short, after your dad made it clear that he wouldn't marry me, I went to live with the couple who had looked after me when I was evacuated. My mother and I had always had a difficult relationship, and I couldn't forgive her for what she had said. They were kind and supportive and helped me get back on my feet. It was why I decided to move to East Anglia, to be nearer to them, and to give Paul more of a family. I'm always popping over for coffee, and they love to see Paul.

"Anyway, I left some of the *Little Wrinkle* books over at their house. They like to read them to Paul when they babysit. The daughter of one of their friends was visiting, and it turns out that she works for a children's publishing company. She saw the stories and loved them, and now the company she works for has asked if they can publish them."

"That's amazing!" Gwen was genuinely excited. She had always loved those stories. "Do you need to get Dad's permission?"

"Yes, and yours. After all, they are based on you! I have no idea how well they will do, but I thought I could put away any money they make for Paul when he's older."

"I think that's a lovely idea." Gwen was glad she could do something to help, given the hurt her actions had caused. "Leave Dad to me. I'm sure he will agree."

“Thank you so much, Gwen. It means a lot to me, and if things go well, it could lead to other opportunities.” Christine’s face was more animated than it had been since they first met. “It feels like a fresh start.”

They’d finished their tea, and David was starting to make it known it was time for his lunch. Gwen got her things together.

“Christine, I hope you don’t mind me asking, but do you think we might try and stay in touch? It’s strange to think I have a half-brother I never knew about.”

“I know, it’s so odd,” said Christine, “and I’d love to stay in touch. I didn’t want Paul to be some dirty secret no one ever mentioned. I was with your father for three years, and Paul is the one good thing that’s come out of it all.”

On the drive home, Christine felt a lightness she hadn’t felt in ages. She hadn’t blamed Gwen for sending the letter, and understood the desire to protect her parents’ relationship, however flawed it was, and however hurt she’d been by Gwen’s father. It was hard when parents didn’t live up to your expectations. She felt differently now she was a mother herself, and she knew she’d do anything to support and protect her son. Paul might not know his father, but he knew he was loved. It had been the right thing to do to come today, and she could finally look forward to the future.

And the consequence was

Margaret

Margaret was sitting on the bed in Gwen's old room, thinking about Jim. It had been two weeks since he'd died, and she had been so busy with all of the arrangements for the funeral that she'd hardly had time to reflect. It helped not to have to think. She'd had enough time to do that when Jim was in the nursing home. It had been hard for her to move him there. In the months after his diagnosis, when he still seemed like the old Jim, he'd made her promise that she wouldn't. He was terrified of being looked after by other people. He just wanted to stay at home with her. In the end, it had been Gwen and Susan who had persuaded her. For two years she had visited him every day, helping to wash and feed him, putting her own life on hold as his slowly ebbed away. She saw it as her penance, but no one else understood. Gwen and Susan would talk about her in quiet whispers. They couldn't understand why she remained so loyal after all he had done. But, of course, they didn't know the whole truth.

When Gwen first found out about Jim's affairs, she went from doting on him to never wanting to be in the same room. And she had done all she could to protect Susan from the truth, in the way that some children keep the secret of Father Christmas alive for their younger siblings. When things had been at their worst between Gwen and Jim, Margaret had considered telling her about Ken. Not to give her a new, improved father to replace the damaged old dad she had lost all respect for, but to explain why she couldn't leave him. In some ways, Gwen's disapproval hurt more than Jim's infidelity.

The first that Margaret had known about Christine was when it ended. She'd had her suspicions, but Jim was careful to be discreet. Then, one week, he just stopped going out. Susan was thrilled to have him around more, but Margaret could tell that something was wrong, and she worried that not talking about it might destroy him. So bit by bit, she gave him permission to tell her everything, and she promised him that whatever he told her, however bad it got, she wasn't going to leave him. They'd come through too much to end things now. As he told her about the lies he'd told, the promises he'd made, the harm he'd done, Margaret could see the relief flood out of him. By the end, she felt she'd almost got her Jim back. Almost.

Over the next twenty years, they built something new together. He changed jobs and they took more holidays. They saw Susan through university and were proud parents when Gwen got married. Jim joined a local cricket team, and Margaret watched him play most weeks. They made new friends. They took up golf. They became grandparents and regular babysitters. Margaret was by Jim's side when his parents died, and he was always there for her when life got hard. They found a way to get over the past and live in the present. And just as Margaret was hoping they would have many more years together, he started to forget things. His stammer returned. His driving deteriorated. He grasped for words and couldn't catch them. She had found his wallet in the fridge. His library books sat unread. She found him crying for no reason. He called her Christine.

She was dreading tomorrow. She'd already said her goodbyes. She rose from the bed, smoothed the sheets, and plumped the pillows. Gwen and Susan were both coming to stay tonight. It would help to have them with her. She shut Gwen's door and went downstairs.

Gwen

Gwen was lying on the childhood bed that had been her sanctuary through her teenage years. Mum and Dad had moved into the 3-bedroom semi-detached a year after Susan was born. She'd been twelve and could still remember the excitement of seeing the house for the first time, picking her room, and being able to choose new wallpaper. She had felt so grown up. She'd opted for a mauve, blue, and green floral pattern, and she remembered her dad trying to hang it, fighting with the long strips of gluey paper, cursing when he cut a piece too short. When she'd gone to bed that night, there had been giant paste bubbles on the paper that he promised would dry out overnight. They never completely disappeared. Over the years, the paper had been covered with posters torn from *Mirabelle* and *Boyfriend*. Adam Faith next to Ricky Valance, and Elvis Presley alongside Cliff Richard. She smiled, remembering how terrible her dad had been at DIY. It was probably why, in the 40 years since, her room had never had a makeover. She wondered what the new owners would make of it. Her mum had put the house on the market a few months ago when it was clear that her dad was never coming home. It was snapped up almost immediately.

She was using the DIY story as part of the eulogy tomorrow. She and Susan had compiled a shortlist of acceptable memories. Overheard phone calls and missing sports days hadn't made it, Father Christmas letters and grandfather duties had. It was weird thinking about what to say about her dad. She'd had such a complicated relationship with him. The early days when she'd idolised him. The teenage years when she saw him in his true colours. That awful day in Hammersmith when she caught him kissing Christine. How conflicted she felt that he'd rejected Christine and Paul for Mum, Susan, and her. And then the years since. The years when he and Mum found their rhythm. The evenings when he willingly babysat her kids. She saw him again through their eyes. The fun he was. The way he chased them around the house and tickled them until they couldn't breathe. It wasn't easy to sum all that up in a few words. Let alone to read it out without breaking down.

The last few times she had visited her dad at the nursing home, he hadn't been awake at all. She'd wanted to sit with him quietly and hold his hand. Instead, the nurse had wanted to get everything in order. Was there a Do Not Resuscitate in place? Who were the Funeral Directors? Who would be responsible for clearing his room? It felt heartless, as if her father was already gone, which, in a way, he was. Her mother dealt with it all with her usual practicality. She was good like that. On their last visit, her mum had asked her if she'd forgiven him. And she realised that she'd forgiven him a long time ago.

Christine and Paul were both coming tomorrow. It seemed ages ago that she had broken the news to Mum about Paul. Despite everything, her dad had never told her. She'd taken it remarkably well and asked Gwen questions about him. She'd given her blessing to Paul visiting Jim in the nursing home. And she hadn't hesitated to invite them to the funeral.

"Are you sure it won't be awkward for you?" Gwen had asked. "After all, not everyone knows about Dad's extramarital activities." Gwen had squeezed her mother's hand.

"Well, maybe it's about time they did," Margaret had replied. "I'm getting too old for secrets."

Christine

Christine found it hard to decide between the red jacket and the blue suit. She hated the modern fashion of wearing colourful clothes to funerals. It was so much easier to wear black. It reminded her of those awful non-uniform days they used to have at Paul's school. Just an excuse to show off your latest trainers or hoodie.

How many of the older generation even had colourful clothes? She had found a red jacket at a charity shop – it was a good make, and a bargain too, but she didn't feel comfortable in it. When Gwen had phoned to tell her that Jim had died, she'd felt strangely numb. Over the years, she'd almost managed to forget the hurt he had caused, and that he had caused the family. Paul was a walking reminder. As he'd grown up, he'd become more like Jim. The same smile and the same eyes. Where would she have been without Paul? Sometimes, it felt as if wishing she and Jim had never been was like wishing away her own son. Instead, she pushed Jim to the back of her mind.

Being happily married to Andrew had helped. It had been Andrew who had convinced her to tell Paul about his father. By then, he was old enough to understand some of what had gone on, and Andrew felt it was important not to hide the truth from him. When Paul was growing up, he had shown little interest in meeting his father. She had heard him asking Gwen questions about him on their occasional meetups. She knew he had some photos of Jim that Gwen had given him, but she hadn't thought much more about it. The first realisation that she may have got it horribly wrong was when Gwen phoned to tell her about Jim's dementia and asked if she wanted to see him. She got off the phone to find Paul sitting at the kitchen table.

"I think you might have asked me for my opinion," he'd started. "Or perhaps you weren't even going to tell me he was ill."

Christine had been taken aback by the emotion in his voice.

"You've never given me any reason to think you wanted to see him," Christine replied.

"Well, perhaps that's because you've made it clear to me from the start that wanting to see him would be a massive betrayal of you and Dad."

"That's not fair," Christine countered. "If you'd shown any interest we would have talked it through with you – you know we would."

"You'd have convinced me it was in no one's best interest, you mean. Reminded me how much it would hurt Aunty Gwen and her family," Paul railed.

Christine could hear the anger and hurt in Paul's voice. How could she have got it so wrong? Had he been sitting on all this resentment for years without her knowing? When he calmed down, she suggested he meet up with Gwen. If he still felt that he wanted to meet Jim, she wouldn't stand in his way.

"Well, that's good of you, Mum, allowing me to meet my own father!" he'd exploded.

She really didn't know what had happened to him. He was a grown-up man with a flat and a good job, and yet he was behaving like a teenager. Christine had spoken to a friend who was a psychologist, and she had suggested family counselling. It hadn't been easy to open up some of the doors that Christine had firmly closed when she'd left Jim. It was hard as well to let Paul see her vulnerabilities. Through the counselling, she realised how much she'd hidden away, thinking it would protect him when, of course, it had had the opposite effect

And she learned so much about Paul. He had heard so many bad things about his father that he believed he had inherited all his bad traits. He was wary about forming any relationships with girls because he thought he might be hard-wired to cheat on them. Rather than ask questions about his dad, he'd kept all his concerns and worries to himself. Part of the homework that the counsellor gave them was for Paul to find out more about the good side of Jim. For Christine, this had involved letting herself remember why she had fallen in love with him in the first place. It had been hard. She still felt guilty about the hurt she had caused, mortified that she had not realised he was married. But once she put that behind her, the memories and feelings flooded back. The way he was the life and soul of any party, lighting up the room with his stories and jokes. The evenings they sat comfortably next to each other, reading. Paul had sat there, listening. Occasionally he asked a question or commented on a detail. And as the memories tumbled out of her, Paul soaked them up. The counsellor felt that to help him process everything, Paul needed the chance to meet Jim. Christine felt her heart sink at the suggestion, but, deep down, she knew the counsellor was right.

Christine was roused from her thoughts by Paul shouting up the stairs. She had decided on the blue suit with a red scarf, and glancing at herself in the mirror, she felt she had made the right choice. If Jim had been alive, she thought he would still have recognised the 35-year-old he'd fallen in love with, albeit she had put on a few pounds and her hair had greyed. The time with the counsellor had helped her as well as Paul. She no longer felt the enormous sense of guilt that she had carried with her for too many years. She had been naïve certainly, but she'd been a victim too. And, despite everything, she'd found a way to forgive Jim. If counselling had taught her anything, it was that no one is perfect, she thought, as she picked up her bag and went to join Paul in the car.

Paul

Paul was at the wheel today. He was glad he was driving. Mum wasn't a good driver on the best of days, and today wasn't one of those. He could tell she was nervous about how the day would turn out, and she was now sitting quietly in the passenger seat with her eyes closed, though he doubted she was asleep. They had Radio 2 on, not his choice, but he let it play in the background. He felt strangely emotional. Jim had never been a father to him, but there was something about the finality of it all. By the time he had met him, Jim was just a shell of his former self, physically and mentally. The Jim his mother had described must still have been somewhere within that shell, but there was no way of reaching him.

He had visited Jim in the nursing home with his half-sisters, Gwen and Susan. It was just after Jim had moved there, and he was warned that Jim would probably have no memory of him.

"This is just so depressing," Susan had observed as they'd walked up the corridors filled with bland paintings of flowers, a heady mix of cabbage and disinfectant lingering in the air.

"Please put a pillow over my face, if I ever get to this point," she'd continued, with the confidence of youth and good health on her side.

"Shhh," Gwen had interrupted. "Just be grateful that there are people who care enough to look after Dad. Otherwise, it would be you and me that would be wiping his bottom."

Paul enjoyed the relationship between Gwen and Susan. It was something he had missed out on. He hoped in time that he'd be able to join in the banter, but perhaps that was wishful thinking as they had forty years of shared experience to relax into. The most he could hope for would be to become friends. At least they had welcomed him, if not with open arms, then at least with warmth and acceptance.

They'd entered the too-hot room, filled with memorabilia designed to trick the residents into thinking they were still at home. Paul didn't know what he expected, but he was shocked to see Jim propped up in the bed, his cheeks hollow, his eyes sad.

"Hello, Dad. It's Gwen and Susan," Gwen had begun, giving him names and a relationship to grasp in the shifting sands of his memory.

"And we've brought someone to meet you," Susan piped up.

Jim turned his head in the direction of Paul.

"Who's this then, one of your boyfriends? Is he going to ask for your hand in marriage?" Jim had spoken slowly as if remembering the right words was an effort.

"No Dad, this is Paul. Christine's Paul. Do you remember Christine? She was your good friend for many years," Gwen intervened.

"Christine, of course, I remember Christine. We used to go to the youth club together. She was a fine-looking girl. I wonder what's happened to her?"

"Well, Paul is her son," Gwen explained, "And he very much wanted to come and visit you."

"Hello Jim," Paul had started, a lump forming in his throat. "It's lovely to meet you. Mum has told me so much about you."

"Has she?" Jim had rallied. "I'm sorry, but I can't remember anything about her. My bloody brain, it just doesn't work anymore." His eyes had filled with tears.

Gwen rubbed his hand to calm him down, and they had sat amiably enough for another half an hour chatting about nothing in particular. When it was time to leave Gwen and Susan kissed Jim goodbye, and Paul had gone to shake his hand. As the girls left, Jim had gripped his hand tightly and pulled Paul towards him. Then Paul had felt his father's dry lips press gently against his cheek.

"I wasn't a good man to your mother," Jim had confessed. "But I loved her with all my heart. Tell her this, won't you, son."

Paul would never know whether this was just a turn of phrase, or if somewhere deep within that small kernel that was still Jim, he had made the connections. It had been a fleeting moment, and there would be no way to know one way or the other, but for Paul, who had come with no expectations, it was enough.

"I think we might have just missed the exit."

Paul was torn away from his memories by his mother's voice breaking through the soporific tones of Radio 2.

"I don't know how you know that, as you've been asleep for the last hour, but we're fine. We'll be there in 5 minutes," Paul reassured her.

Woken from a light sleep, Christine was suddenly surrounded by once-familiar street names and landmarks. The park where she'd met Gwen that day, the library where she'd met Jim. It was a shock to her system, and the closer they got to the crematorium, the sicker she felt. As they turned in, she took a deep breath and let it out slowly to try and calm the mounting sense of panic she was feeling.

"Paul, I really don't think I can do this," she whispered.

"Of course you can, Mum, and you'll have me by your side the whole time."

The meeting with Jim had helped Paul, and Christine was the first to admit she'd been wrong. But despite Gwen trying to convince her otherwise, Christine and Margaret had never met. Christine could see Margaret standing in a group with her family. It felt to Christine like some awful soap opera scene with the mistress and the wife meeting over the coffin. The family grieving, and everyone turning to stare at the scarlet woman. She suddenly realised that this whole thing was a mistake. Why had she let Paul convince her to come? What possible good would it do? She felt her mouth go dry and her chest tighten. She wasn't sure that her legs would even work, and she was grateful for Paul's arm as they walked from the car to the chapel of rest.

The funeral

Gwen spotted them first and strode over with a warm smile. She embraced Paul and wrapped Christine's arm under hers. It was a kind gesture, and Christine felt her eyes prick with tears.

“We’re all so glad you came. And we've already decided that you’re going to sit with us at the front,” Gwen whispered as they walked to meet the rest of the family.

“I can't do that. What would people say?” Christine managed.

“If I’ve learnt anything over the years, it’s not to worry about what people say. It wasn’t your fault you fell in love with Dad. It wasn’t your fault he pulled the wool over your eyes for all those years,” Gwen answered.

“But it was my fault that I kept Paul from knowing him, from having any sort of relationship with him until it was too late.”

“You did that out of love. Love for Paul. Love for Andrew. It's natural to protect the people we love. We can never change the past, only learn from it. Now, hold your head up high and walk with me into the chapel.”

Susan walked in first, with Margaret next to her, followed by Gwen and Christine, and finally Paul. They walked up the aisle, past the pews where friends and family were sitting. If people were staring, Christine didn't notice as her eyes were firmly fixed on the back of Margaret’s head. They had briefly acknowledged each other outside, and Margaret had squeezed her hand reassuringly. There would be time to talk afterwards. For now, they were focused on getting through the next hour.

When it was time for the eulogy, Gwen and Susan rose to their feet. They were a good double act, Christine thought to herself. Gwen had always been the mature one as if the weight of Jim’s infidelities had made her old before her time. Susan, by comparison, was a much lighter character, always ready with a funny remark to lighten the atmosphere. She reminded Christine more of Jim. His ability to put people at ease. His charm. Susan did most of the eulogy, striking the right balance between remembrance and celebration. She told stories about Jim and reflected on his zest for life. And she spoke movingly about his dementia. She then passed over to Gwen.

"Thank you, Susan," Gwen began.

Christine could hear the nervousness in her voice.

"I hope that most of you will recognise Dad from Susan's words, and it's lovely to remember the good days before he became ill.

" She paused and took a few seconds to compose herself.

"I want to talk about a different side of Dad, a side that few of you will have known. He was a complicated man, and he wasn't always the best husband to Mum."

A shocked hush went round the already silent room.

"A few years ago, he met and fell in love with another woman. Her name was Christine. For most couples, this infidelity might have meant the end of their marriage, but Dad was still in love with Mum, and so he kept it from her. He also failed to tell Christine that he was married."

Christine could feel herself getting hot. She was grateful for the scarf hiding her reddening neck. She felt Paul reach for her hand.

"When Christine found out Dad was already married, she left him. She moved on with her life and found happiness. But Christine and Dad also had a child together. And for many years this was a secret. But secrets cause all sorts of hurt and pain, and we don't want that for

our family. I don't think Dad would have wanted it either. Paul, would you join us to say a few words?"

Christine hadn't noticed that Paul had taken his hand away from hers and was already rising from his seat. His shoes squeaked on the wooden floor as he walked the few steps to stand beside Susan and Gwen. They both embraced him.

"Thank you, Susan, Gwen and Margaret, for welcoming me into your family." Paul's voice rang out into the emptiness. *"I don't think I'll ever forget how it felt to be accepted by you. And to have a second family to call my own – I've always wanted two big sisters to look up to!"*

A sense of collective relief spread amongst the mourners, as if they had all been holding their breath and could finally relax.

"I'm sad that I never had a relationship with my dad until it was too late. I know my mum feels terrible that she unknowingly caused so much hurt to Margaret, but I'm sure our dad wasn't the first person to fall in love with two people. And he won't be the last."

The three siblings hugged each other and returned to their seats whilst the vicar invited everyone to stand and sing a hymn. As they stood up, Margaret turned round and smiled at Christine. She mouthed, 'OK?' and Christine nodded in reply.

At the wake afterwards, everyone went out of their way to welcome Christine. Gwen had booked a room at a pub, and there was a good spread of sandwiches and cakes that most were tucking into. Christine knew she needed something to eat to soak up the two glasses of wine she'd already finished. But her appetite had deserted her.

"Fancy some fresh air?" Margaret asked, spotting Christine playing with a smoked salmon sandwich. They walked around the pretty pub garden in quiet companionship.

"Do you miss him?" Christine asked.

"I do," Margaret said, her eyes fixed on some faraway point. "I'd always known he wasn't perfect, but it's hard to love perfect. I think we just understood each other. And that's what I miss. Although the dementia robbed me of that. Now, I just feel relieved that he's not trapped inside that hopeless brain anymore. I feel I lost my Jim quite some years ago."

She tucked Christine's arm under hers.

"And what about you, Christine? Do you miss him?"

"I'm not sure. I spent so long hating him, that it was hard to remember that I'd loved him once. Paul and I had counselling. I don't know if Gwen said?"

She looked at Margaret, who nodded kindly.

"It reminded me that I had loved him. It brought back the good memories. It helped Paul. It helped me. I just wish it hadn't hurt you so much."

"I'm a tough old bird. You don't have to worry about me." Margaret laughed. They finished the circuit of the pub and walked back into the conservatory. Margaret picked up a glass of wine and handed it to Christine.

"To Jim," said Margaret, bumping her glass against Christine's, "and to all his mistakes."

"To us," said Christine, "and putting them right."

Part Three: 2004 - 2023

David
And Erin
Met online
She found a letter
He told his mum
She said "I'm sorry"
He said "And now we're here"
And the consequence was …

David

David was busy mowing the lawn for Grandma Margaret. She had moved to the one-bedroom bungalow soon after his grandpa had died, telling everyone that she didn't need a big house at her stage of life. David suspected she'd found the memories hard to live with. He had been a baby when his mum found out about Paul, and at university when she'd finally told Grandma. She'd taken the news of an additional stepson remarkably well. After Jim had died, she'd welcomed Christine and Paul into the family with open arms. David didn't think he would have been as forgiving; he'd left his latest boyfriend as soon as he caught him eyeing up someone else.

David and his grandma had always been close. His mum worked shifts at the hospital; his dad kept unpredictable hours in London, so she was regularly asked to look after him. He loved going to her house with its large garden and the flower patch he was allowed to tend all by himself. He looked forward to the sunflowers growing taller every year. He used them as a horticultural measuring stick, judging their success by how much they'd outgrown him. When he wasn't in the garden he'd be baking biscuits and cakes with his grandma and throwing a tea party for his parents when they came to collect him. When he'd started school, she would be waiting at the school gates to collect him. As he sat at the kitchen table frustrated with his homework, she'd patiently help him through it. When she noticed he was struggling with his reading, she'd demanded a meeting with the headmistress and proceeded to fight David's corner. Years later, when he told this story as part of his interview for Oxford, he was sure that it had impressed them into offering him the place. As if his grandma's spirit and determination must be part of his DNA.

Yesterday, he'd taken his grandma over to his parents to celebrate Mum's birthday, and he'd offered to stay over on the sofa-bed in the lounge and help in the garden today. Since his grandpa had died, David made sure he popped over regularly to do any odd jobs around the house. At first, it had been decorating, but now it was mainly gardening. Most days, David worked and Margaret chatted, but today she had left him alone.

She was a remarkable woman. At eighty-two, she still drove herself to the shops and the library. Some months ago, David had noticed a scratch on the bumper and suggested it might be time to stop. 'Surely that's what bumpers are for,' she'd retorted, before letting him know, in no uncertain terms, that older drivers were statistically the safest. She always had an answer for everything. It was what made her so easy to confide in.

Even before David had come out to his parents, he'd discussed it with her. He could still remember the conversation during the summer holidays of his third year at Oxford. David had started university unsure of his sexuality. After a 6th Form party, a close girlfriend had taken him to one side and asked if he thought he might be gay. It had surprised David because he'd never been very interested in either sex. But she was right. His social life had improved at university, and things became clearer. It started with a few drunken snogs during fresher's week. After years of worrying about what was wrong with him, he'd found it liberating to be surrounded by people who didn't care whether he was gay or straight. They just liked him for who he was. He found it hard to keep up the constant partying and merry-go-round of partners, so he was pleased when he and a guy from his course started dating. As they approached Christmas, his boyfriend had suggested they get together during the festive break. This put David in such a tailspin of anxiety that he'd ended up finishing their relationship just so that he didn't have to tell his parents that he was bringing a guy home.

He was grumpy and argumentative all that Christmas. He'd even had a row with his mum, which was unheard of. After Christmas, he had gone to see his grandma. She immediately knew something was wrong and refused to believe it was exam stress.

"Whatever's wrong? You aren't yourself at all. You know you can tell me anything. Remember I'm unshockable." She'd opened her arms and gave him a hug.

And he had told her everything. It had poured out of him. How angry he was with himself for being a coward. The fear that his parents would be disappointed in him. His grandma had listened carefully before giving her famous words of wisdom.

"Your parents love you. And they are not going to care one jot whether you are straight or gay or any other LGBT letter."

David had smiled. He hadn't realised how well-versed she was in the correct terminology.

"What they care about, is you being happy, and you won't be until you tell them. You can't go through the rest of your life finishing with boyfriends just because they want to meet your parents! It will tear you up inside. You know how hard you find it to keep secrets."

David had done what she'd advised. He'd gone home, sat his parents down, and told them. It had all been a bit of an anticlimax. His mum said they had known for ages. And when he seemed surprised, his sister had said, 'Duh, no straight guys like Kylie Minogue.' So his gran had been right, as always. Since finishing university, he'd found it hard to find anyone he wanted to bring home to Mum and Dad. Most nights, he was more likely to be at home watching television than out at a club. At the weekend, he visited his grandma. David recognised that this might not make him the most exciting of catches.

He stopped the mower and inspected the alternating lines of dark and light green. His grandma would be impressed. He wandered into the kitchen to find her.

Margaret was in her bedroom, sitting at the desk she positioned in front of the bay window. The last owners used this room as their lounge, but Margaret liked the light flooding into her bedroom in the morning. With the lawn mower running outside, she went into her bedroom for a lie-down. She hadn't wanted David to see her slowing down. The family were so used to telling everyone how remarkable she was for her age that she felt a responsibility to live up to their aspirations, however tired she felt. The last few months had been difficult. She probably should have gone to the doctors a year ago when she first felt the lump, but she told herself it was nothing, a gland perhaps. She'd finally made an appointment in April. The doctors were so busy, and she hated to waste their time. She didn't want to make a fuss. Tests followed, and now a prognosis. She hadn't told the family yet. Cynthia was coming over soon, and she wanted to tell her first. For now, it was her secret to guard.

She took the card out from the top drawer of the desk. Every year, she chose a different picture. Usually, they were arty, sometimes with flowers or a countryside view. No words inside – they were for her to add. She had written fifty-eight of these already, this was the fifty-ninth. She'd never posted any of them. All the others were in the bottom drawer of her desk in a large buff envelope. Some years ago, she'd had to buy a bigger envelope to fit them all in.

She'd started this year's card yesterday. A birthday card, not to Gwen, but to Gwen's father. The words were Margaret's, but the subject was Gwen. A round robin for her not-so-little girl. The highs and the lows, but mostly the highs. In the early days, it had been easy. First smile. First words. First steps. She shared her school reports, the English prize she'd won and her 11+ results. The teenage years were more testing. There was always something to say, but never enough words to fill the gap that grew wider and longer and deeper over the years. In the early days, Margaret had imagined giving these to Gwen when she told her about Ken. And then, when she knew she never would, they became something else entirely. A diary of her guilt. A monument to her shame.

It had been the cards that she thought of when the doctor had sat her down and explained what she'd already guessed. She couldn't keep them. She couldn't let Gwen find them when clearing out the bungalow after she'd gone. Only a monster would do that. So what to do? Should she shred them with her bank statements? Or burn them on a bonfire? She knew she wouldn't be able to do either. They had taken on too much significance. Her annual purging to an unknowing pen pal. Last week, she'd woken from an afternoon nap with absolute clarity. She would choose palliative treatments over rounds of chemotherapy. And this year she would send the cards to Ken. Give him his daughter as a manuscript. Let him decide whether to read the book.

The doorbell rang, and David got up from his seat in the kitchen to answer it. He'd called for his grandma a while ago but assumed she was having a doze when she didn't reply. He noticed she was getting more tired recently. He expected to find one of the neighbours at the door. They were so good around here, always checking up on each other. It was a surprise to see Cynthia.

"Hello, David," Cynthia seemed surprised to see him. "I didn't know you were going to be here."

"I stayed last night. It was Mum's birthday. Gran hadn't told me you were coming either! What's the occasion?"

"You'll have to ask Margaret that," Cynthia replied. "She rang and asked me to pop over for a chat. So here I am."

"Ask me what?" Margaret came out of the bedroom and hugged her friend.

"I just wondered why Cynthia was here. She says you asked her to come over."

"Does there have to be a reason to see my best and oldest friend?" Margaret asked, raising her eyebrow teasingly.

"No, of course not." David wondered if he'd said the wrong thing.

"Don't be silly," Margaret continued. "There was a reason, and I'm glad you're here too, David. But first, let's put the kettle on. I could do with a cup of tea."

David took it as his cue to go to the kitchen. He made a pot of proper tea and found some posh chocolate biscuits.

"So what's it all about?" David asked, trying to make his voice sound nonchalant.

"The fact is…" started Margaret. "The fact is that I've gone and got bloody cancer. After all these years of being hale and hearty and thinking I'd avoided it, it's snuck up on me without me knowing."

David, who was kneeling on the floor pouring the tea, stopped and sat back on his heels, his face ashen.

"Oh, Margaret, I'm so sorry," Cynthia said, shocked by the news and the matter-of-fact way Margaret had delivered it.

"I know. I know. It's rotten bad luck. But at our age, we know something is going to finish us off. Rather this than Alzheimer's."

"What has the doctor said?" David asked, desperately trying to feel more in control of the situation.

"Well, apparently, it has spread, but it's not the most aggressive form of cancer, and at my age, it could take months or years to finish me off."

"Don't talk like that. I'm not ready to lose you yet," David replied. A lump was forming in his throat, and he thought he might burst into tears. Losing Grandpa Jim was one thing, but in the end, it had been a relief more than a sadness when he'd died. Seeing his beloved grandma sitting in front of him talking so openly about no longer being here was too much for him to bear.

"So, what are you planning on doing?" Cynthia asked, her own eyes welling up with tears.

"I've decided that I don't want all the malarky with chemotherapy. I plan to put my affairs in order, and then I plan to live a little. I've already written a bucket list of all the things I want to do before I can't do them anymore. And, David, you'll be pleased to know you feature in many of them."

Despite his sadness, David was intrigued.

"Go on then, what's on the list?"

"I'd toyed with the idea of going to Canada. I've always wanted to go, but it's never been quite the right time."

David thought he saw something flash between her and Cynthia, but it was over in a second.

"Unfortunately, it seems my insurance won't cover me flying, so I think I'll have to put that one on ice. Perhaps a weekend in Cornwall instead."

"And anything else?" David prompted.

"I want to be in the audience for an episode of 'Mastermind'. Better still if I could meet John Humphrys. I like him."

"I'll see what I can do." David hoped he could pull some strings with the production company.

"And I'd like to go to a gay club and see a drag act."

David spluttered his tea out of his nose.

"I knew you'd like that one," Margaret laughed. "You gays don't get to have all the fun."

They talked for another half an hour, and then Margaret asked David if he'd mind leaving her and Cynthia alone for a while.

David returned to the garden and started trimming the hedges, his mind all over the place. It was all so strange. An hour ago, he hadn't known any of what his gran was going through. He strongly suspected that if he hadn't been at hers today, he wouldn't have known for months. And yet now that he knew, he couldn't unknow it. And, as his grandma had once said, he was terrible at keeping secrets. When his sister had told him she was having her ears pierced, he'd blurted it out at the earliest opportunity. His mother had stopped her having them pierced, and she hadn't spoken to him for three months. He hoped his grandmother wouldn't do that. She had been adamant that she didn't want Gwen to know. However difficult, he would have to respect her wishes and keep this all to himself.

Margaret and Cynthia walked into the bedroom and sat down on the bed.

"We've come a long way from South Kensington," Margaret said. She grasped Cynthia's hand. Cynthia put her arms around her. It felt like only moments ago that they had shared digs and dreams. Cynthia was the only person who knew everything about Margaret, and it felt fitting that she was the first to know about the cancer.

"What will I do without you?" Cynthia asked, her eyes damp with tears.

"Don't write me off quite yet. I've got a few good months left, and I need a friend to help me through the bucket list."

"You know I'd do anything for you," Cynthia replied, the sadness welling up in her voice.

"There is one thing." Margaret hesitated momentarily. You're not going to like it, but you're the only person I can ask. The only one I trust." Margaret picked the card up from the desk. She handed it to Cynthia.

"What's this?"

"Just read it, dear," Margaret added softly.

Cynthia read the whole card and then replaced it in the envelope.

"Does this mean …?" she started.

"I don't know. I think so. I don't know what to do for the best." Margaret paused and sighed. "What would you do, Cyn? What's the right thing to do?"

"I don't think there is a right and wrong thing to do. Does Ken have a right to know? Maybe. Would it break his heart? Probably. And what about Gwen? She might hate you for keeping this from her."

"I know. I know." Margaret felt the weariness of carrying a secret for so many years. She couldn't cope with spending her last months without the love of her girls. That would be too much to bear.

She stood up and retrieved the buff envelope from the bottom of the desk. She placed the final card inside, licked the strip with her rough tongue and then planted a soft kiss across the seal. The envelope already had Ken's address on the front. It hadn't been hard to track down. Everything was easy with the internet.

She handed the envelope to Cynthia.

"After I'm gone," she said. "After I'm gone."

The heat had gone out of the day, and David felt overwhelmed by the news his grandma had shared. He went into the house and saw the bedroom door ajar. Heard the quiet conversation of friends. He picked up his keys and left. He'd ring Gran later, once he'd had time to think.

The drive home on a Sunday was easy, and he allowed his mind to drift. Now he was alone, there were so many questions he'd wished he'd asked. There would be time for those. But not that much time. When you are approaching the end, even a long life is short. Gran had done so much with hers, but what had he done with his? Since university, he'd let his social life drift. He would never end up with someone special unless he did something about it. He needed to find someone he could make plans with and trust not to disappear in the morning with a brief kiss on the cheek and a 'see-ya later'. Someone he could share bad news with, who would hug him and tell him everything would be OK. Someone who would love him unreservedly, and maybe, in the future, someone he could have a child with.

When he arrived home, the space he usually parked in was already taken by a small removal van. Angrily, he drove around the block before finding a space two streets away. Distracted by looking for his house keys, he nearly bumped into two girls carrying a sofa into the first-floor flat next door to his.

"Oi, watch where you're going with that," he said, irritated that they hadn't seemed to notice the near collision.

"I'm so sorry," said the blonde-haired girl with jeans and converses, looking mortified. "Tilly, we almost knocked this guy out."

They put the sofa down, clearly struggling with the weight of it and exhausted by the prospect of carrying it up the steps.

"Do you need some help with that?" David asked. Despite his simmering irritation, he didn't want to get off on the wrong foot with his new neighbours.

"That would be amazing!" the girl he gathered was called Tilly replied. She was an attractive girl with a cut-glass public-school accent. He'd met a whole world of those at Oxford.

"We're moving in, you probably guessed," she laughed, "and I had no idea how heavy sofas would be?" David took one end, and they took the other.

"Is it just the two of you?" David asked.

"Just the two of us moving in, but my brother Toby is helping with the removal. I'm not sure where he disappeared to. He's probably sitting down watching TV while we're doing all the heavy work," Tilly laughed.

The three of them managed to get the sofa into the front room, and David was just about to leave when they were startled by a shout of help from one of the bedrooms. They hurried down the corridor and were met by the sight of a young man half hanging out the window.

"What on earth are you doing, Toby? Tilly asked

"I was trying to reach the aerial, but now I've got my hand on it, I can't pull myself back in. Stop asking stupid questions and give me a hand."

The girls were laughing so hard, it was David who grabbed the back of his jeans and dragged him back into the room. When he turned around David could see he was gorgeous.

"My saviour," Toby said dramatically, collapsing onto the bed. "And who are you?" he asked flirtatiously.

"This is David. We found him on the street, and he's our new next-door neighbour," Tilly responded.

"Well, I think David deserves a proper thank you for helping with the sofa, and for saving my life," Toby continued.

"Oh yes, absolutely he does," said Tilly. "How about joining us later for pizza and fizz?"

David didn't hesitate.

"I'd like that a lot," he said, thinking how easy it would be to say no after the day he'd just had. It had taken Margaret's bucket list to make him realise that life was too short not to grab your happiness when you could. And there was something about the twinkle in Toby's eye that made him think, just maybe, he would be worth grabbing.

And Erin

Erin sat in the waiting room of Primavera Fertility, flicking through the pages of magazines that had been selected for their ability to be as inoffensive as possible. She imagined the receptionist removing anything that might be triggering; no *Mother and Baby* or *First Time Parenting*, even though that was what everyone in the clinic was there for, one way or the other. All that remained was an endless selection of celebrity gossip magazines alongside *Canadian Gardening* and *House and Home*. She looked around the waiting room to see who was reading what. Most of the single women were scrolling through their phones, whilst the two couples ignored the magazines and whispered to each other as if they were in a library or a church.

A smiling nurse in a neat white uniform pushed open a side door, and a sudden burst of laughter from the nurses beyond broke the vacuum of expectation in the waiting room. The nurse glanced at the name on the top of the buff-coloured folder, and everyone looked up. Two women sitting anxiously in the corner holding hands stood up and followed behind her. The others exchanged friendly half-smiles and then returned to their scrolling. Erin had been waiting for nearly half an hour and had resorted to wondering who on earth came up with the names of these clinics. All so light and feminine and hopeful, when in fact, the whole process of IVF was horrible and dehumanising.

Not that she was there for IVF. No, at 35, and having been unable to find anyone that she wanted to have children with, she'd reluctantly decided to harvest and freeze her eggs. For the previous week, she'd been injecting herself every day with hormones, and today she had to go into the clinic at 7 am for a checkup. Usually, she was good at early starts, but getting up at 6 am with only a 'full bladder' ultrasound to look forward to was a different prospect altogether. She had decided to freeze her eggs now, not only because they were starting to get to their 'use by' date, but because the tech company she worked for was offering to pay for it. This could either be seen as a genuinely helpful perk for 30-somethings who didn't want to have children yet, or some Orwellian nightmare where companies track your fertility, know exactly when your period is, and control your whole reproductive life.

Today, she felt like a particularly angry koi carp, lopsidedly walking around with what she imagined were thousands of eggs weighing her down and bursting for the loo. The worst thing about the whole process was that any exercise beyond a gentle walk was banned. This, together with the mood swings caused by an excess of hormones, had turned Erin into an irritable mess. The only consolation was that the end was in sight, and sometime next week, she would come back for egg retrieval, and finally get her life back. At least until she felt ready to have a baby. If she ever did.

Sitting on the designer couches in the carefully curated waiting room, she wondered what Grandma Laurie would have made of it all. She had been a Farm Cadet during the war and had waited four long years for her sweetheart Ken to return from England. Erin imagined their meeting again after the war as a hugely romantic episode, where Laurie had flung herself into his arms and begged him never to leave her again. But Gramps said it hadn't been like that at all, more a growing realisation that they both wanted the same things from life: home, children, and a quiet life on the farm. They'd had children almost immediately, no uncertainty for them. No waiting for the right time in their career. And, with little in the way of birth control other than abstinence, no way to enjoy some time as a couple before falling into motherhood. They married in 1949, and Erin's father was born soon afterwards, conceived on a trip to England where her grandpa had taken Laurie on honeymoon. He had wanted to show her where he had been stationed during the war. Laurie had died over ten years ago now, and she knew her grandpa still missed her.

That was the sort of love Erin wanted to find with someone. But it wasn't easy in the age of Tinder. People made decisions in a fraction of a second – too small, too tall, too geeky. Too much hair. Not enough hair. And even when you matched, there was all the game playing that followed. Being too keen or not keen enough. How soon do you sleep with them? Whether you were exclusive? Erin felt as if she had been born in the wrong era. Too late for the comfortable relationships of her parents and grandparents, and too early to feel at ease with the new dating rules. Just like her eggs would be, she was frozen in limbo, waiting for something or someone that would get her life started. In the meantime, she went through the motions. She'd always struggled to stick with boyfriends. After a few months, she got bored with them, usually because they wanted her to do 'their thing' at weekends, when all she wanted was to go out for a run or a cycle. And when she'd dated other triathletes, that hadn't worked either. She knew her family was keen for her to settle down, but she'd seen enough friends end up in disastrous relationships. She'd rather be on her own and happy than have to compromise her lifestyle for some insecure idiot with a huge ego. As if sensing her innermost thoughts, her phone vibrated angrily.

How much longer are you going to be? x

The passive-aggressive tone and the meaningless kiss at the end, made her clench her jaw. She took a deep breath before replying.

Not long now, I hope. My bladder is about to explode, and they won't want to clear up the mess

She resisted adding a kiss and added a laughing emoji instead. It was wrong to describe her latest boyfriend as an insecure idiot with a huge ego. It had been kind of him to offer to drive her this morning, but now she wished he hadn't. They'd met at work, and after one drunken Christmas party, they'd moved from being acquaintances who smiled at each other during the weekly Town Halls, to colleagues with benefits. At the start, the sex had been worth the workplace gossip, but even before the enforced

Fertility Clinic no sex ban, she found herself going off him. She hoped it was the hormones that were giving her the ick but suspected it was a symptom of something more terminal in their relationship. Unfortunately, abstinence had made his heart grow fonder. As she'd become rattier and taken to her least flattering PJs at 8 pm each night, he'd become more rampant. She regretted showing him the pamphlet that suggested other ways they could be intimate during this time. Last night she'd got tetchy when she'd woken up in the night and found his hands massaging her enlarged boobs and his 'fondness' stabbing her in the back. She'd gone for a pee and then slept the remaining hour on the sofa. The car drive to the clinic had been a little frosty. Her phone buzzed again.

I'm going to have to head to work. Will you be OK to get a cab after?

No kiss this time, and to be honest, it was a relief to make her way into work afterwards. She wouldn't have to address last night's activity or lack of it. And hopefully by Friday, they'd have both forgotten about it. They tended to spend most weekends together, although between her training and his lacrosse, this usually meant getting a take-out and watching Netflix, like an old married couple. It suited Erin that they both had their own lives, and it was a relief to be off Tinder, but deep down, she knew it shouldn't feel this convenient this early in a relationship. And if she'd thought he might be the one, surely she would have delayed the whole egg-freezing thing? She quickly pinged him a reply:

Fine with me. Sorry, it's all taken so long. Coffee later?

She hesitated before finally adding a kiss. The door opened again, and a different nurse stood there, notes in hand.

"Ms Jackson." The nurse emphasised the 'Mzz' in a way that made Erin self-conscious. Her neck felt warm, and she instantly felt hirritated – a word her boyfriend had made up for her hormonal mood swings. 'It's like being hangry – hormonal and irritated – hirritated,' he'd explained unnecessarily. One more notch on the bedpost of ick. Despite her irritation at being singled out as a desperate singleton, Erin found herself defending herself to the nurse as they walked along the lavender-blue corridors of the clinic.

"I'm having my eggs frozen …. No one on the scene at the moment … Company perk … Hard to find the one these days …"

She knew she was rabbiting. Why did she always feel the need to fill a silence gap? If she'd been braver, she'd have suggested that the nurse use first names rather than Mrs or Ms and told her how it made her feel. Instead, she had used the time to apologise for being an unmarried woman in a fertility clinic to a nurse who was half her age and looked like she was already having Botox.

30 minutes later, she was on the bus heading through Stanley Park. The doctor had assured her that her eggs were doing nicely. She resisted the urge to flap her elbows and say, 'cluck cluck'. Instead, after the scan, she wiped the sticky goo from her stomach with a wad of blue paper

towels and checked she had the details for next week. It was weird how transactional it felt. They expected her to make life-changing decisions about how many eggs to keep and how long to freeze them for. They asked her what to do with them if she died. They made her eggs sound like products, not potential people. Not the building blocks of life.

Erin imagined the fertility storage facility as a cross between IKEA and an ice rink. She had once been stuck in IKEA for over an hour when she'd foolishly tried to bypass the kitchen displays and go directly to the marketplace. Hopefully, when the time came, her eggs would be easier to find. She checked the messages on her phone. One asked if she'd join a few friends for drinks tonight. Another, whether she would lead a club ride at the weekend. The last one was from her dad, reminding her she was dog sitting for them while they went to the theatre.

She moved on to her email and found the usual mix of admin and spam. It was amazing how quickly late-night scrolling for birthday presents led the algorithms to assume she was now a gin aficionado or a keen gardener. It was lucky she'd resisted the urge to buy her best friend a vibrator, or who knew what her Instagram would have made of that. Nestling amongst the clickbait was an email from 23+Me that piqued her interest. A few years ago, in an attempt to understand more about her health and wellness profile, she'd taken a DNA test. Her best friend was told her genetic muscle composition was that of an elite athlete, and Erin wanted to know if hers was as well. Her results had shown a propensity to lactose intolerance and normal muscle composition. It had all been a little disappointing. She'd ticked the ancestry box, which revealed a handful of distant relatives dotted around North America and Scotland. In the intervening years, she'd received the occasional alert when another distant relative had signed up. She hoped she might be connected to a minor royal or a celebrity, but nothing interesting thus far.

She opened the email. The introductory text explained that a close match with her had recently been tested on 23+Me. She skimmed over a long explanation about how close relations were predicted. Towards the end, there was a second link to identify the close relation. She clicked.

Close Relation Match: David Armitage
Living in: London, England
Your Predicted Relationship: Cousin
Shared DNA: 12.5%

Erin stared at the page. She struggled to understand what it meant. She had cousins, but none were in England, and she'd never come across this name before. It must be some sort of mistake.

The bus stopped at Coal Harbour. She jumped off and started her walk along the sea wall. There was a chill in the air, and the skyscrapers were casting long shadows across the wide walkway. She briefly turned her head to see a seaplane lift into the air and turn steeply towards Vancouver Island. Lost in thought, she was brought back to earth by the sound of a tinny bell and realised she'd strayed into the cycle lane. She raised her hand in apology, embarrassed by her faux pas. They'd think she was a tourist, not a keen cyclist who knew these lanes better than most. She bought a flat white and sat down on one of the benches splattered with seagull droppings. The email had rattled her. She scanned it for any suggestion it might be a scam. It was odd timing, arriving as it had whilst she was in the middle of egg retrieval. Maybe it had been generated by an algorithm – no need to freeze your eggs, you have a whole new family waiting to meet you across the pond. The email seemed genuine enough, but how could she have cousins in England? Apart from her great-grandfather coming to Canada from Scotland, she didn't believe any of her grandparents had links with England. Her phone pinged again.

Everything OK? Still on for lunch? xx

The kisses had returned. He'd obviously forgiven her for last night. He might give her the ick sometimes, but he wasn't one to hold grudges, and he was usually fun to be around.

Yep, all good. Just on my way in now xx

Resisting the urge to reply to the email straight away, she finished her coffee and popped her phone back into her bag. It was probably a scam anyway.

Met online

"Remind me why it's my job to decorate the nursery?" David shouted down the stairs to Toby in the kitchen.

"Sorry, can't hear you," Toby replied, instantly turning the volume up on the football.

David had expected painting and decorating to be a shared chore in a same-sex relationship. But, according to Toby, anything remotely creative was David's domain. Since they married, Toby had divided all chores into creative or practical, based entirely on the fact that David had a History of Arts degree, and Toby had graduated in Maths. David could understand that cooking was creative, but surely decorating was practical.

"It's got the word painting in it," Toby had joked. "That's got to be creative."

Ultimately, it wasn't worth arguing about, and with his audiobook playing and the rest of the afternoon free, there were worse things he could be doing. He and Toby had chosen the colour scheme together – a subtle green on the wood panelling and a sweet wallpaper with monkey illustrations on the walls. Painting had been easy, but, as a wallpapering newbie, David found it all a bit stressful. He'd borrowed the pasting table from his parents. Despite their offers of help, David decided that this was a parental rite of passage and was determined to decorate the baby's room by himself. He'd given himself a couple of weeks to get it done, but, as usual, he'd procrastinated, and he was worried it wouldn't be finished when the cot arrived later.

He imagined that if a pregnant partner were wandering around the house, it would be a constant reminder of the urgent need to complete the task. But they only saw Tara in person at scans or consultant appointments, so the imminent arrival of their son felt a little less pressing. Perhaps someone would invent a tracker for surrogate babies, so you'd get a text every morning saying things like 'we received your order and will let you know when the heads engaged' or 'your order is sitting in our depot and could be delayed by three weeks', before the final 'your order has shipped and will be delivered within a two-hour window.'

The surrogacy process had been a rollercoaster. It had taken years for David to even admit he wanted to be a dad. It wasn't exactly a chat-up line, and since he'd come out at university, David had encountered a fair few partners who would run a mile at any commitment, let alone a lifelong one! When he met Toby, he knew he was the one. He was such a positive person – charming, high energy, an extrovert to David's introvert. David couldn't believe that someone like Toby would ever fall in love with someone as cautious and anxious as he. But love him, he did. So the last thing he'd wanted to do was scare Toby off with baby talk.

Toby came from a large, bohemian family. His parents had both had high-power city jobs and owned a large house in Surrey. He had three older sisters who doted on him. It was at one of the regular family get-togethers that the subject of children was first mentioned. David had been playing badminton with Olivia, Toby's middle sister. He was showing her four-year-old how to hold the racket and connect with the shuttlecock, a frustrating experience for all involved. After ten minutes, the children got bored and ran off to find their cousins, and he and Olivia continued to play.

"You are so patient with the children, David. You're a natural. I'd have just told them they were useless and sent them off to their father," Olivia had started.

"I know that's not true, Liv. You're a great mum," David replied.

"So when are you going to tell Toby?" she continued.

"Tell him what?" David blushed, knowing exactly what she meant.

"Tell him you want children, silly. Although he probably knows already. It's obvious to all of us."

So that night, sharing the small double bed in Toby's childhood room, surrounded by the ephemera of his youth, David plucked up the courage to tell him. And, of course, Toby hadn't been phased at all. He just kissed him on his nose and said yes.

Getting from the idea of wanting children to the reality of having a baby had not been as easy. Initially, they had copious advice from friends and family, some helpful and some not. They looked into adoption but after much deliberation they agreed they wanted a child of their own. David spent his evenings researching different options and trying to decide between agencies. But how do you make a decision like that? Even worse, some of the agencies asked you to scroll through profiles of potential surrogates, swiping left or right like some terrible dating app. Toby had started to write a list of the characteristics he wanted from his egg donor: intelligent, artistic, empathetic, and kind to animals. It was like an interview for Miss World.

"You missed out big boobs, and does a lot of work for charity," David said sarcastically. They were just about to sign up with an agency when a phone call from Olivia changed everything. Since their conversation over badminton the previous summer, she had thought long and hard about how she could help. In the end, she decided to offer them her eggs.

"I've got loads of them left, and they'd just go to waste otherwise," she joked, trying to lighten the weight of the moment.

Olivia had even found them a surrogate. Tara was a dear friend of hers from university who had sailed through two pregnancies of her own. When Olivia talked about donating her eggs, she'd offered to 'babysit the embryo' for them. David burst into tears at the generosity and then felt positively sick that the dreams he had thought so distant, now felt within reach. They agreed to take a month to think things through and discuss any potential ramifications with their families and loved ones. If they still felt the same way, they would take the next step. Using Toby's sister's eggs meant that, with David's sperm, the baby would be genetically related to them both. During the 'cool down' month, David used an online DNA service to check for inherited health conditions. Toby had laughed at him for being a hypochondriac, but with so much at stake, David didn't want to leave anything to chance. The process had been easy, and he was relieved when the results came back clear. A month later, David, Toby, Olivia, and Tara had sat together in the garden of a Richmond pub. One by one, they agreed to go ahead with 'Project Bambino' as Toby named it, and, miraculously, less than a year later, they all sat down together again in the kitchen of Tara's house as the blue line emerged on the pregnancy test.

When they'd spoken on the phone yesterday, David had been ribbed for the slow work on the nursery.

"I've been working on this for 9 months, and you can't even pull your finger out with the decorating," Tara joked. "Well, you better get your pasting table out because I don't think it will be long now."

It seemed unbelievable to David, looking around at the freshly painted skirting boards, the feeding chair, and the new changing table in the corner, that their little boy would soon be here. Before long, he'd sit in the corner of the room in the small hours, giving him a bottle or kissing the downy hair on the back of his head. Toby came bounding into the room.

"Wow! This looks great," he said, putting his arms around David. "You're good at all this DIY, aren't you? I'm impressed."

"Flattery will get you everywhere," David replied. "Although I think we need to get a man in for the rest of the house."

"As long as he's fit and will work with his shirt off," Toby joked

"No time for any of your fantasies once we're parents, Tobes. We'll be too exhausted for any of that," David countered.

"Spoilsport. How about a quickie now before your parents get here?" Toby said, only half joking.

"Get out of here, you've got way too much energy. You could always grab a paintbrush and help out."

"I think that's my phone ringing downstairs," Toby lied as he left David to finish off.

Gwen and Stephen had spent the last two hours in John Lewis, looking at prams and pushchairs until they both lost the will to live.

"We're too old for any of this," Gwen grumbled, as they got in the car and made their way to David and Toby's. "I mean, how many features does a pram need? They're like cars these days. And you need an engineering degree to even operate them."

"At least the cot was easier," Stephen intervened.

"Only because Toby had ordered it, and all we had to do was click and collect," Gwen laughed. "Frankly, I don't understand why they can't have secondhand. It's all we could afford when our two were born."

"It's not quite them though, is it? I can't see Toby pushing anything that wasn't the latest trend," Stephen answered.

Gwen smiled to herself. When David first told them he was marrying Toby, what had surprised them most was that he'd chosen someone quite so polished as his life partner. Toby was many things that David was not – private school not local comprehensive, confident and self-assured rather than shy and self-effacing. Gwen was sure he voted Tory, although they never actually discussed politics. But clearly opposites attracted, because Gwen had to admit she had never seen David so happy. It would be interesting to see how they both took to fatherhood. She imagined David would be the one getting his hands dirty – literally with the nappy changing, and metaphorically taking the lion's share of the baby work. He was taking the paternity leave anyway, which meant she would have a lot of time to get to know the new baby.

She wondered what her mum would have thought about two men having a baby together. It would have been unthinkable in her youth. But her mother had constantly surprised Gwen with her liberal views. She and David had been very close, and it had hit him hard when she'd been diagnosed with cancer. Her mother had drawn up a bucket list of things she wanted to do whilst she still could, and David had helped her through it, making memories along the way. Shortly after her diagnosis, David had started a serious relationship with Toby, the first boyfriend he had ever brought home. Perhaps his grandmother's diagnosis had been a reminder of his own mortality, and the fact that you only get one shot at happiness.

Just before she'd died, Margaret had revealed the final item on her bucket list – to find David a husband. It had been early days in his and Toby's relationship, but, with a confidence he rarely displayed, David had held his grandmother's hand and said, 'I think you can cross that one off the list.' No matter how surprised they had initially been by the charming Toby, Gwen and Stephen were now fully on board and excited about being grandparents again.

Stephen dropped Gwen off and went to park the car around the corner, murmuring 'bloody residents permits' as he did. Ringing the bell on the Edwardian semi in St Margaret's, Gwen remembered the weeks before David had been born. She'd been scared to leave the house, worried that her waters might break in Sainsbury's, or a sudden contraction might cause a car accident. Having your baby delivered by a surrogate sounded like a much better idea; but what if the worst happened and Tara couldn't bear to give up the baby?

Gwen didn't think she'd have it in her to pass a little bundle over, even if it had nothing to do with her genetically. There was something about carrying a baby for nine months that made you feel pretty attached to it. Gwen felt tears well up in her eyes. She didn't know what was wrong with her lately. The slightest thing set her off, and she was often struck by negative thoughts as if something awful was about to happen. She couldn't even put it down to the menopause, as she was well over that. Maybe it was just old age doing it to her, but she couldn't shake the feeling that something was missing in her life. Perhaps a new grandchild would be just the thing.

David could hear his mum and dad downstairs, showing Toby how the new pram worked. That would keep them busy whilst he changed into something more fitting than his decorating clothes. He'd managed to grab a shower before they arrived and washed off the wallpaper paste that seemed to have found its way into all his crevices. He sat on the bed and grabbed his iPad to check for any updates from Tara. Toby had made him promise not to keep messaging her, but Tara usually sent a short update through in the afternoon. It was reassuring to hear from her, and it meant they could have a beer without worrying they might need to dash to the hospital.

The text from Tara was positive on the beer front, with no twinges, or Braxton Hicks to report. He was just about to close his laptop when a new email message popped up from 23+ Me, the company he'd used for his DNA health checks. The original report hadn't shown any inherited conditions, so why were they sending him messages now? In a blind panic, he clicked through to the secure part of the website and saw that he had a new message. When he had sent his sample off for analysis, he'd opted into the ancestry part, interested to see if he could unearth any long-lost family. It all proved slightly disappointing. A couple of his dad's cousins were on there, but since then, he'd completely forgotten about it. But now, out of the blue, there was a message from Erin Jackson. And she lived in Canada. He clicked to read the message.

Hi David
I recently received an alert from 23 + Me that suggested we might be cousins. I've done some online research, and apparently, we share a grandparent. This seems unlikely because I grew up living next door to my grandparents, and I'm in Canada. I can only assume this is some sort of mistake. Before I do my usual and put my foot in it by asking my granddad if he's got something to tell me, I wanted to see what you thought? As far as I know, the only time either of my grandparents were in England was when my grandfather, Ken Jackson, was there during WW2, as a radar operator. Do either of your grandparents have any

connections to Canada? If you can shed any light on this, I'd be really grateful to hear from you, as this is a real mystery. Thanks in advance.
Erin

David's immediate thought was it was a scam. He'd seen something similar where a long-lost relative had pleaded for money for a lifesaving operation. Perhaps that was how these things started – a friendly email and, before you knew it, you'd been conned into giving away all your money or donating a kidney. Despite his suspicions, he was curious. This Erin didn't sound like a scammer, and it was interesting that her grandfather was a radar operator. He'd have to check with his mum, but he thought Grandma Margaret was in the RAF, too. It was still a puzzle – for him and Erin to be related, it would mean Grandpa Jim wasn't Mum's father. Perhaps he needed to be careful before blurting it out to his mum. As he contemplated what to do, a WhatsApp message pinged through.

Hope you've finished the nursery. My waters just broke!

The email would have to wait. He was about to become a dad.

She found a letter

Erin couldn't remember the last time she had such a good night's sleep or a day when she'd still been in bed at 9.30 am. Her flat wasn't conducive to lie-ins. It was either boiling hot in the summer or freezing cold in the winter, and she usually set her alarm for early morning training at the weekend. Her friends thought she was completely mad to forego nights out, lie-ins and a social life for swimming, running and cycling, but she couldn't help it; she was completely addicted.

Jumping out of bed, she was immediately pounced upon by Maple, her mum and dad's new puppy. After running the farm all their adult lives, her mum and dad had sold the farm last year and moved into a new build by the river. It was quite a change, and her mum thought a puppy would be a good distraction and give them a reason to go on long walks together. Maple was the reason for Erin's sleepover last night. Her parents had miscalculated how much of a tie a new puppy would be, and Erin had been called upon to puppy-sit so they could go on a theatre trip they'd booked long before Maple was a consideration. The good thing about not having a social life was that Erin had most of her Friday nights free, and it was a treat to have a whole house to herself for once. After a busy week at work, nothing compared to being able to lie on the sofa with no one else to steal the remote. She hadn't reckoned how much of a handful Maple would be. But after several games of tug and a couple of 'accidents' on the kitchen floor, they had both zonked out.

The puppy-sitting request had come at just the right time, as Erin had something important she wanted to discuss with her mum and dad. There was no noise from her parent's room, so she made three cups of coffee and some sourdough toast and went upstairs.

"You don't have to knock," her mum called. "Your dad and I are much too old for any of those shenanigans."

"For goodness sake, Mum!" Erin replied. "I just thought Dad might be naked."

"And what would be wrong with that? We always used to walk around naked when you were a child," her dad reminded her.

"I know, but I'm 35 now, and it traumatized the postman," Erin laughed.

"This is nice," her mum started. "I wasn't expecting breakfast in bed! What's the occasion?"

"No occasion. I just wanted to talk to you about something."

"Pregnant, Gay or Moving Abroad?" her dad joked.

"Surprisingly, none of those, but thanks for speculating. No, the thing I want to talk to you about is all a bit odd. You know I did one of those DNA tests a couple of years ago?" Erin continued.

"Oh my God" her mum interrupted. "Don't tell me there's something wrong with you?"

"No, nothing like that. The health checks were all fine. It's just that occasionally I get an alert when someone matches my DNA. Last week, I got an alert about a guy in England who it says might be a cousin."

"A cousin? That can't be right. You don't have any cousins in England," her mum interrupted.

"I know. That's what I thought," said Erin.

Her dad was busy googling relationships.

"A cousin would mean Erin shares a grandparent with this guy."

"That can't be right," her mother interrupted. "Surely we would know if our parents had a child we didn't know about?"

"Exactly. We lived next door to my parents for 30 years. I think we'd have known if that were the case," her dad concluded.

"I know, I thought the same," Erin agreed, "but these tests don't often get it wrong. I've been reading up on it."

"So what are you saying?"

"I don't know. I agree it seems unlikely, but then I remembered something. Do you remember when I helped Gramps move after Grandma Laurie died?"

"Yes, of course. It was when we were away."

"Yes, exactly. A few days after Gramps moved out of the barn, I got a phone call from the new owners. They had some mail for him, and I went and collected it. I'm sure I mentioned it. Anyway, it was a large buff envelope."

"That's odd. What did you do?" her dad prompted.

"I thought about opening it, but I was in a rush, so I just popped it in my bag. When I got to Grampa's, the flat was so full of packing boxes that I popped it at the back of his desk for safety."

"Did you tell Gramps about it?" her mum asked.

“That’s the thing. There was so much going on, people popping in. I think it slipped my mind.”

“Why do you think it has anything to do with this potential cousin in England?” her dad asked.

“I’m not sure, but I think the return address was in England. Did Gramps ever mention anyone during the war?”

“I don’t think so. I never heard of anyone special. He hardly spoke about his time over there. I know he took Mum to England for their honeymoon. Would he have done that if he’d left someone special behind?" her dad asked.

“I suppose not. It’s just a bit strange. Maybe I’m making too much of it.”

“Let’s assume that there was a special someone.” Erin’s dad wasn’t prepared to let it rest, quite yet. “We know he got posted to France a few months after he'd been in Cornwall."

"And?" Erin and her mother said together.

"What if this girl was pregnant with Dad’s baby?”

“Ken wouldn't abandon her if he’d known she was having a baby. That’s not like your dad at all,” Erin’s mum intervened.

“I agree, but what if this girl didn’t tell him she was pregnant?” he continued.

“That would be a terrible thing to do. What sort of person does that?” Erin asked.

“You’ve got to remember they were very different times,” Erin’s mum began. “Having a baby and not being married was shameful in those days. Her parents might have disowned her. She was young, she probably had no idea what to do. They didn't have morning-after pills or abortions then, at least no legal ones." Her mum paused. "And what if she had told him? What would he have done? Stayed in England and left his parents to work the farm on their own, or dragged her over to Canada away from her family? There were no happy endings with that one."

"Let's not get ahead of ourselves," Erin's dad implored. "We need clear heads to work out what to do – if we do anything, that is. I mean, Dad's ninety-four. What possible good will it do to bring it up now? Surely it's better to forget all about it."

"But if it is true, Michael, you have a half-sister you've never met and cousins and nephews. Wouldn't you want to know more?" Erin's mum asked.

"I don't know. Maybe. I just have no idea how we raise this with Dad. What do you think, Erin? Shouldn't we try and get more clarity first? I can't imagine how I would feel at his age. Pleased to know that I can still do something about it, or regretful of all the lost years. It might break his heart."

"We do need to be careful," Erin agreed, "Perhaps we should try and find out more from Gramps. See if he ever opened those cards? And I can ask this guy in England if he knows anything more."

"Let's talk to Dad next week and see if he'll open up any more about his time in England. It might help us decide what to do."

Ken was having a lovely dream when Alexa rudely interrupted him.

This is your reminder. Erin. This is your reminder. Erin.

"Alexa, stop," barked Ken, not for the first time wondering whether the benefits of technology really outweighed the irritation of being bossed around by an inanimate object. Yes, he had asked Alexa to wake him up in time for Michael and Erin's visit, but he'd have preferred a soft shake of the shoulder, or a kiss on the cheek, over the strident tones of Miss Bossy Boots.

Quite a few of the residents were being cared for by Alexa, reminding them to take their medication or to switch the cooker off. He supposed they were the lucky ones. At least they were able to live independently. Quite a few of his friends at Longlake had moved into the care home that shared the grounds with the retirement village. There was a certain amount of black humour amongst the residents about the inevitability of moving from apartment to care home and then finally to the place upstairs. The older he became, the less amusing he found it.

When he moved in, he'd been one of the younger residents, but now, at 94, he was the second oldest. The new residents were a lot younger. Women in their seventies who were able to take advantage of the activities and the wellness centre that had been built a couple of years ago. Erin had said that some of them were probably looking for a husband. She said he'd be a great catch. As if! Maybe a few years ago he would have enjoyed the companionship, but now he'd take his chances with Alexa. At least she didn't talk through the hockey or expect him to compliment her on her dress.

Laurie had spoilt him for any other woman. She had been so easy to live with, so dependable and kind. Since she died, he had missed that closeness, the familiarity that came with living with someone for so many years. He had only had two loves in his life, something the youngsters of today would find hard to believe. Perhaps monogamy was in his DNA. It might explain why Erin had yet to find 'the one'. He wondered if it would have been the same if he had married Peggy. He could still remember the way she had fitted into his arms. His inexperience hadn't mattered. He didn't know why he was thinking about Peggy again after all these years. Initially, he'd hoped they might keep in touch, but he'd heard nothing from her in years. He still had the love letters she wrote him during the war, he'd never been able to throw them away. Since Michael phoned last week, he'd been thinking a lot about the past. Michael had said he wanted to know more about his time during the war as part of research for their family tree. He hoped he wouldn't disappoint him. His memory wasn't that great anymore, and it was all such a long time ago. Ken saw the car pull up, and Michael and Erin got out.

"Hello, Dad," Michael hugged him warmly, "How are you feeling today? How's the knee?"

"Mustn't grumble," joked Erin, impersonating Ken and leaning in with a kiss.

"You're lucky I don't grumble, Missy," Ken responded, "You should hear most of my neighbours around here."

"Are you up for a walk, Dad?" Michael asked. "I thought you and I could go for a stroll around the lake, and Erin can make us some lunch."

"I've brought some salmon, your favourite," Erin laughed, "and some ice cream for pudding."

"That sounds lovely. I think I can manage once around the lake," Ken replied. "Perhaps we could stop for a beer at the café on the way back."

"Take all the time you want," Erin insisted, "But give me a ring when you're nearly back, and I'll get lunch on the table."

Ken got his stick from the hallway, and Michael opened the patio doors that took them into the grounds. It was a beautiful day, unexpectedly hot for April. Michael waited until they got to the path around the lake before gently asking his dad about his time during the war.

"Why the interest suddenly?" Ken asked, "Is it because you think I'm on the way out?"

"Don't be silly, Dad. I've just been thinking about our family history and getting it written down for future generations. I realised I know nothing about your time in the war."

"I'm not altogether sure I can remember it now."

"Just your memories, Dad. How you felt about it all. Were you homesick? Were you frightened? It's hard for us to imagine what it must have been like to leave your home, travel nearly 5,000 miles and fight in a war that must have felt like somebody else's."

"I did feel like that when I was doing my training in Canada. It all felt so far away. And I was horribly sick on the boat over, most of us were. But as soon as I got there, sitting in a room with all the others, operating the radar systems, then it became my war too."

"Why do you think that was, Dad?" Michael prompted.

"You were part of it. At the base where I was stationed, you could see the brave pilots and crew getting into their

Spitfires and Hurricanes each day, and you knew that many of them wouldn’t come back. They weren’t the anonymous numbers of the newspaper reports. These were your friends, your colleagues. So you wanted to do everything you could to protect them, to give them the best possible chance.”

“Did you mainly stick with the other Canadians when you were off duty?” Michael asked.

“Not really. It wasn't like that. We were all together – the British, the Americans and us. It just depended on where you were stationed. My first proper posting was with two guys I’d sailed over with, and we used to go to dances together. It gave us someone to stand at the bar with. Not so different from young men these days!”

“You had time to go to dances and socialise then?”

“Oh yes, we had a great deal of fun. When you never know what’s around the corner, you tend to live life to the full. For a country boy like me, it was a real eye-opener. The dancing. The drinking. The girls!”

“Wow, Dad, I had no idea! Did you end up making good friends then? People you’ve kept in touch with?”

They had come to the top of the lake where a wooden bench faced the water. Ken hesitated and leant on his stick, catching his breath.

“Are you OK?” Michael worried that they were walking too fast, but when he looked at Ken he saw a wistful look on his face. “Let’s sit for a moment.”

“I’m sorry, son,” Ken began, “It’s a long time since I thought about any of this.” He paused and wiped his brow with a handkerchief. “I did make one special friend, my first love, I suppose you’d call her. We met at a dance.

You could say we bumped into one another! She was so beautiful, like no one I'd ever met before. She had such a twinkle in her eye. And she drank beer – none of the Canadians could get over the fact the English girls liked beer!

"The girls I'd known before the war were just girls, but Peggy, she was a real woman. You have to understand that it was all new to us. These women were working alongside us, so the relationships we had with them started out as friendships. Then, if there was an attraction, things usually progressed pretty quickly. It was thrilling."

"I take it there was an attraction with this Peggy?" Michael hardly needed to ask.

"Oh, there was, Michael. And it was mutual. But it was a brief fling because, within a few months, I'd been selected for special duties. And it wasn't as if you could say no."

"Was that the last time you ever heard from her?"

"We kept writing to each other whilst I was in France, but eventually she called it off. I was heartbroken, of course, but I suppose it was a bit like a holiday romance. Who's to say if it would have survived the reality of Canadian winters or a lifetime of warm beer!"

As Michael helped his dad up off the bench, he gave him a long embrace and was surprised at how frail he felt in his arms. He gently took his arm.

"Come on, Dad, let's get you home for lunch. You can tell me about the D-Day landings on the walk back."

Erin waited until they had been gone for a good ten minutes before she made her way over to the desk in the corner of the lounge. She felt like a petty thief, worried that her victim would return to pick up his keys and catch her in the act. The desk had been Ken’s mother’s writing desk. It was pretty impractical in this day and age, but it had the benefit of three deep drawers. She knelt down, opened the bottom drawer and slipped her hand to the back. Sure enough, beneath other folders and files, she felt the shape of a thick envelope. Her heart was pounding as she pulled it out. As far as she could see, it hadn't been ever been opened. She examined the back of the envelope and saw that the return address was to Cynthia Clarke in Windsor.

She promised her dad that she would look through the cards, but now it felt wrong. Whatever lay within, these were private intimacies meant for him, not her. She took out her phone and took a quick photo of the address on the back. That would be enough, wouldn’t it? If it turned out Cynthia was the London guy’s mother, then she would have proved a connection.

She returned them to the bottom drawer and noticed a small tin box close to the front. At least this was something her grandfather knew about and had chosen to keep. She opened it. There were souvenirs from the war. His Canadian Air Force medal, a small diary, and a prayer book. Folded at the bottom was a letter. She sat back on her knees and read the neat blue handwriting. It seemed to be a reply to a proposal, presumably from her grandfather, to come to Canada and make her life there. The words in the reply were kind, the emotion palpable, but ultimately, she said no. And there, so easy to overlook, in blue ink made lighter by the tears that her grandfather had shed, were some final words.

'I will always love you, Ken, and some part of you will always be with me. Yours forever. Peggy xxx'

Erin's eyes filled with tears. She felt a part of her reach back through time to this other woman. Did the words mean what Erin thought they might or was it just a turn of phrase to reassure her sweetheart that she would never forget him. Erin quietly replaced the letter and closed the drawer. Her phone pinged with a text from her dad.

We're on the way back. Lots to tell

She walked into the small kitchen, put the salmon in the oven, and prepared a salad. When she got home, she would email the guy in England and explain about the package from Cynthia and the letter from Peggy. She wondered if the two were connected and if one of them was his mother. Twenty minutes later, she saw her dad walking across the lawn. Her gramps was holding his arm. He suddenly looked frail and vulnerable, a trick of the light perhaps. To see him now, it was impossible to imagine him living any other life than the one she knew. But if Peggy had accepted his proposal and followed him to Canada, there would be no Laurie, no Michael, no Erin. One decision, one yes rather than no, and an entire family tree would be uprooted. Erin caught her father's eye over her grampa's head. He nodded, imperceptibly. It seemed that they had a choice to make. Who knew what the repercussions might be.

He told his mum

David was bathing baby Seb when his phone rang insistently in his pocket. It told you everything that his ringtone was the theme tune to Peppa Pig. It was meant ironically, but Seb laughed every time it rang, so he'd decided to stick with it. When Seb first came home from the hospital, David thought he'd never get used to holding such a small person, let alone bathing him. But a few months in he was getting more and more assured. Not quite confident enough though to answer the phone and bathe him with one hand, so he let it ring through and saw that whoever had phoned had left a voicemail.

Things were finally settling back into a routine after the whirlwind that had been the first few months. When the call came that Tara was in labour, he and Toby had raced to the hospital and spent all night camped out on chairs in the maternity unit waiting room. Baby Seb had been born the following morning. From that moment on they'd hardly had time to breathe. At first, everyone had rallied around, and the house had been full of family, giving advice and cuddles in equal measure. His mum had stayed with them for a week, but it got to the point where they wanted the house to themselves.

At the start, he and Toby were nervous about everything, and they were lucky to have their sisters on speed dial for emergencies. Tara had been brilliant throughout, and for the first few weeks, she'd popped around regularly and expressed her breast milk, giving Seb the best possible start in life. At four months old, Seb was starting to grow into his skin. He'd lost the grumpy old man look and had learnt how to smile broadly at anyone who paid him the slightest bit of notice, charming everyone from shop assistants to Deliveroo drivers, of which there were many. Toby did most of the buggy walks to the local park, grabbing the attention of the yummy mummies of West London. 'It's a good thing I'm gay,' he'd say, 'because a straight single man with a baby would be eaten alive by that lot in Bushy Park.

They had agreed early on that David would take a year's parental leave. It was an easy decision – the BBC had policies for adoptive parents, and Toby earned considerably more than him. Toby took two weeks off from his job as a fund manager when Seb was first born but was happy to go back to work for a rest! Despite their best attempts to share the workload, David ended up doing most of the day shift and all of the night feeds.

"If I went to sleep on the job, peoples' pension pots would crash and burn, and you wouldn't want that on your conscience," Toby had said as he reached for the earplugs and turned off the bedside light.

Four months on, David was just about getting used to the sleep deprivation and lack of social life. It was one of the drawbacks of being a male mum. Despite going to all the baby classes, he just hadn't made the friendships other mums had. They weren't unwelcoming, he just wasn't part of their gang. He was starting to miss work, where all the relationships were already in place and where drinks at the pub made it easy to form friendships. When he had mentioned this to Toby, he'd been pretty dismissive.

"It was you who wanted a baby in the first place," he'd said unhelpfully, or "Just invite them all to the pub after Baby Yoga, I'm sure they'd love it."

"I've had a baby, not a personality transplant," David had replied to this suggestion. Toby had roared with laughter and then gone back to reading the paper.

Once he'd finished bathing Seb, he popped him down for a sleep and played his voicemail. It was from Cynthia. A few weeks ago, he had received another email from Erin, the girl in Canada who claimed to be a cousin. She had explained that as she'd heard nothing back from him, she'd done more investigating. She had spoken to her father, and they had spoken to her grandfather about his time during the war. Erin had also found two things in her grandfather's desk – a large package containing cards with a return address in England, and a love letter from a girl called Peggy. Erin had sent him a photo of the return address on the package. It was Cynthia's address. He phoned her immediately.

Cynthia had just got back from her afternoon walk when David phoned her. She was a firm believer in using it or losing it, when it came to mobility. Whatever the weather and however tired she felt, she always managed at least one walk a day. In her seventies and eighties, she had been proud of her good health. She saw it as a testament to a life lived with few vices. In fact, like most people, she had smoked like a chimney and drunk like a fish during the war. As a driver in the ATS, it was almost part of the uniform and suited girls like Cynthia, who were tomboys at heart. Now that she was in her nineties, the 'good health' label was hanging around her neck like an albatross. One by one, her friends were succumbing to some illness or another. The lucky ones dropped down dead on the golf course. A good death, not the slow decline of dementia or the invasiveness of cancer. Living independently in her own flat, Cynthia knew she was one of the lucky ones. However, she wondered what the point of good health was if you had no friends and family left to enjoy it with.

She went to the cabinet in the corner where she kept her drinks, found a large bottle of Remy Martin at the back and poured herself a glass. She wasn't usually a mid-day drinker, leaving her daily gin and tonic until she heard the theme tune for Eggheads. The call from David had shaken her, and she would need some Dutch courage for when he and Gwen came round later. She hadn't seen either of them since Margaret's funeral. They always invited her along to family celebrations, but Cynthia felt such a fake. She wasn't a real aunty, and although they always seemed pleased to see her, she had so little in common with the younger generations. The latest invitation had been to David's son's naming ceremony. She had a soft spot for David. She'd always known he was gay, of course. Such a sensitive child with very high emotional intelligence. She'd heard a programme about it on Radio 4. But she also felt a touch of resentment. Why was it OK for two men to live together today? They were able to marry, even to have a child, when so many of her generation were forced to hide how they felt.

How differently her life might have panned out if living with a woman had been acceptable back in the day. A few of her lovers had ended up married to men, so they could have the children they so yearned for. But not Cynthia. She hadn't been terribly interested in sex and certainly didn't have any desire for children. It would have been nice to have a life companion. Someone to cuddle up with by the fire, to share the ups and downs of the day, to watch Eggheads with.

Margaret had been her first love. She remembered the day she'd turned up at her digs in South Kensington, looking glamourous with her hair freshly waved and a new dress she'd bought to impress the landlady. When she left, Cynthia begged Mrs. Pearce to choose her. She had interviewed four girls that day, but there was something about Margaret. Cynthia knew that they would hit it off and become best friends. 'Well, I liked her too,' Mrs Pearce had said. So it was agreed, and Margaret moved in that Monday. There had never been anything romantic between them, and if anyone had told Margaret that Cynthia had a crush on her, she'd have laughed loudly, thrown her arms around Cynthia and said, 'I don't think so, she knows all my disgusting habits.' But the truth was that Cynthia had found everything about her intoxicating.

When they first signed up, Cynthia hoped they might be posted somewhere together. But Margaret had made it into the WAAF, and Cynthia had joined the WTS and travelled the world. They'd kept in touch throughout the war. Margaret's letters were full of fun and gossip, Cynthia's more serious, and self-censored so as not to give anything away should they fall into enemy hands. She had always been good at keeping secrets.

She had kept Margaret's secret for over seventy years. Now, it seemed that modern science had, in a lickety spit, uncovered the carefully covered tracks that had kept this secret safe for over seven decades. When Margaret was dying, Cynthia had begged her to tell Ken and Gwen the truth. In the end, Margaret made Cynthia promise to send the letters. They were written for Ken, but truthfully they were love letters to Gwen. Cynthia read them all after Margaret died. She hadn't known what to do for the best, but she'd kept her promise and sent them off. She'd included her address on the back, and for months, she expected him to call. But he never did.

Cynthia had found Margaret's funeral hard. Not just because she had lost her oldest and best friend but because that secret weighed heavily on her conscience. She was ashamed of her part in keeping this from Gwen, but still strangely reluctant to break the confidence, even with Margaret and Jim both dead. When David rang, it had been partly relief that she had felt. She'd kept the secret, but the truth had come out anyway. She had answered his questions the best she could. Even knowing it to be true, David had found it hard to believe. In the end, they agreed to talk to Gwen together.

David rang as he and Gwen were leaving Harrow. He was going to tell his mum the basics on the drive over. Cynthia would be able to answer questions when they got to hers. They were at the door within minutes of Cynthia putting the brandy away. One look at Gwen, and she got it out again.

“I just can’t take it in,” Gwen admitted. “Is it true Cynthia? Did you know all along?”

“I did.” Cynthia had decided to answer honestly, without embellishment.

“And you never thought to tell me? Not when I opened up to you about how I felt about Dad? I mean Jim. I don’t even know what to call him anymore.” Gwen broke down, sobbing into her hands.

Cynthia got a tissue, and David gently stroked his mum’s arm, letting her cry. As she composed herself, David gently repeated some of the information that Cynthia had told him. The affair itself. The impossibility of being an unmarried mother. The kindness of Jim’s proposal. The promise she had made to him. The white lies they had told about the baby being premature. The deep love she’d felt for Gwen. The sorrow she’d felt when the marriage didn’t work out. At points Gwen asked questions, but mainly she sat and listened as if the story was about a stranger. Which, in many ways, it was.

David hadn’t known what to expect from his mother. She wasn’t very demonstrative, and usually kept her feelings to herself, so the tears had been a surprise. It was the shock, he supposed. Eventually, Cynthia put the kettle on to give them time to talk.

“How are you feeling, Mum?”

“I don’t know how to feel. I’m numb. It feels like there’s been an unexpected death in the family. I have so many questions, yet the only people who can answer them are dead. Why couldn’t she have told me? How could she have kept this from me? I blamed Dad for everything, and yet Mum lied to me my entire life. I can't get my head around any of it," Gwen cried.

"I suppose she wanted to keep her promise to Grandpa. He might have been a bad husband, but he always loved you as if you were his own," said David.

"I know, but in later years, after we found out about Paul… or after Jim died… she could have told me then."

They sat in silence while Gwen slowly processed everything. When Cynthia came in with the tea, David handed her the messages he'd received from Erin.

"I know it's a lot to take in, Mum, but I've been talking to Erin in Vancouver. Her father, Michael, is your half-brother, and her grandfather Ken, is your father. They haven't told him about you yet. They wanted to know how you felt first. She's sent me photos of some of the letters your mum wrote, and a few photos of Ken. Do you want to see them?"

"You mean my dad is still alive?" Gwen took another sip of the brandy that Cynthia had topped up.

"He is. He's ninety-four, and still pretty independent from the sounds of things. Here, look at the photos. I think it will help."

When David finally got home, Toby and Seb were fast asleep on the sofa with an abandoned pizza box on the table and one of Seb's bottles next to Toby's craft beer. He opened the door quietly so as not to disturb them and stood in the doorway, his heart bursting with love. Toby wasn't Seb's real father either, but he loved him just as much as if he were.

And Jim had loved Gwen, even though she'd hated him for most of her twenties. David had thought the problems between them might have made things easier, but his mum said it made them worse. If she had known the whole story, she might have been able to forgive him. In the end, David concluded, you need to tell people the truth and let them decide how they feel about it. They'd certainly do that with Seb. But in Margaret's situation, would he have felt the same?

Before he'd left Cynthia's, he'd asked his mum if she'd decided if she wanted to meet her dad. Her answer had surprised him. It was time he took his head out of the sand and replied to Erin. Leaving Toby and Seb sleeping, he went upstairs to his PC and started to type.

After David left, Gwen phoned her husband and asked if he would pick her up later from Cynthia's. She needed time to process everything she had just heard before she answered his questions. He would want to know how she felt, and she had no idea. She went to sit in the lounge, and Cynthia brought her a large glass of red wine.

"I'm hoping this might help," she said, handing Gwen an envelope.

"Not more revelations," Gwen managed, putting the glass down tiredly. "You're not going to tell me that you're my mother, are you?" She laughed unconvincingly.

"Just read it, dear," Cynthia said kindly. "Your mother asked me to give this to you if you ever found out about Ken. It might answer some of your questions."

Gwen opened the envelope with trepidation and read.

My darling girl,

I have started this letter many times and never had the strength to finish it. I fear if I don't find the words now I never will. I'll start with the simple truth.

In 1944, I fell in love with the most wonderful man, a Canadian called Ken Jackson. After less than six months together, he was posted to France. After he left, I found out I was pregnant. I didn't know what to do for the best. My parents would have disowned me, and with no prospect of Ken returning before you were born, I decided to accept a proposal of marriage from an old boyfriend. That boyfriend was your dad, Jim.

Other than Jim, only Cynthia knew that you weren't his child, and we all promised to take the secret to our graves. The rest, you know. Jim loved you as if you were his own. And whilst he might have been unfaithful to me, he loved **us** *more than anything. He gave up his chance of happiness with Christine for a life with you, me and Susan. And for that, I will always be grateful.*

What can I tell you about Ken? I knew him for such a short time, and yet I know I would have been happy to spend a lifetime with him. You remind me so much of him. So strong, and kind and loyal. He loved the outdoors – we spent our days walking on the moors and our evenings drinking beer in the pub. You were conceived just before he was posted to the South of France, and I named you Gwen, after Merlin's wife as a reminder of our first magical weekend together in Tintagel.

He would have been a wonderful father to you, Gwen, but it would have torn him apart to decide between us and his family in Canada. His letters from France showed me how much he missed them and how much they relied on his return. So, I made the decision not to tell him of my pregnancy. It wasn't an easy decision, and there wasn't a day when I wondered whether I made the right choice. There were many times I considered telling you about Ken, but how could those six months compare to the fifty years of Jim being your father. When he proposed, he wasn't just asking me to marry him, he was asking you to be his daughter. However, conflicted I felt at times, I couldn't take that from him. Perhaps after Jim had died, I should have told you about Ken, but it was so long ago. I had no idea whether Ken was still alive, and the last thing I wanted to do was for you to get hurt. So, I kept my secret.

For many years, Cynthia has tried to persuade me to tell you the truth, so please don't blame her for keeping silent. All the blame is on my shoulders. In the end, we all have to stand by our decisions and accept the consequences. But know that everything I have done, every decision I have made, has been out of love for you. You have been the best thing that has ever happened to me, and I will love you for eternity.

Mum x

Gwen put the letter down and wiped her eyes with her handkerchief.

"Did it help?" Cynthia asked.

"A little," Gwen replied.

She could hear her mother's voice in every word. When David had told her the news today, she had thought her mother selfish – too wrapped up in her own life to care about what Gwen wanted. This letter told a different story.

The secrecy wasn't an act of selfishness but of sacrifice. She had sacrificed her own happiness for a life of stability for Gwen. She had spared Ken the enormity of choosing between her and his family. And, even though he never truly deserved her loyalty, she had kept her promise to Jim. It couldn't replace the emptiness she was feeling, but perhaps with time, it would help her to forgive.

Erin had taken a couple of days off work. After the hormonal rollercoaster of egg retrieval, she had planned a mini-break with her boyfriend to thank him for his support and make amends for her snappiness. Unfortunately, they hadn't got that far. They'd had a monumental row over something trivial, and he had messaged her saying it wasn't worth the drama. Erin did her best Bridget Jones impression – sitting in her pyjamas, drinking wine and eating chocolate. She hated that she was in her mid-30s and still single, and she missed having a significant other to do things with at the weekend. But she couldn't really say she missed *him*. The situation with David and the DNA test had unsettled her more than she realised. It felt like the sand was shifting under her feet, and the world wasn't as predictable as she always believed. She loved her gramps with all her heart, but keeping such seismic news from him made her reticent about visiting.

She had heard from David last week. He'd apologised for the time he had taken to reply, but his email contained the answers she and her dad had both needed and feared. The Peggy from the letter was the WAAF that her grampa had spoken of as his first sweetheart. She had been posted to Devon at the same time as Ken and had a child eight months after he left for France. Peggy had married an old boyfriend soon after Ken left, and the baby, named Gwen, had always believed that he was her father. The name on the return address on the package was Peggy's best friend, Cynthia. She had been the only other person to know the truth, and Peggy, or Margaret as she was known to her family, had asked her to post the package after she died.

Erin phoned her dad as soon as she heard. It had taken a while to process the news that he had a half-sister on the other side of the world. Erin wondered whether she had done the right thing getting in touch with David. When she initially found out about a possible family in England, it felt like something you might see in a film. She imagined her relatives living in large stately homes and welcoming her into their lives, in a mix of Pride and Prejudice and Notting Hill, whereas these revelations had the potential to ruin people's lives and change their relationships forever. How would she feel to discover Michael wasn't her father, and that her mother had kept it from her for her entire life? It was unthinkable. And, just like Gwen, she would want to meet her father.

Now that it was becoming real, she worried about the impact it might have on her grandfather. Even before she found out about the DNA match, he seemed frailer. His mind was sharp, but his body was diminishing. More and more he was happy to stay in the apartment rather than joining the others for social activities that, only a few months ago, he'd have looked forward to. It was as if he was preparing himself for the end, slowly discarding the ephemera of the day-to-day and focusing instead on only the essentials of life. He loved it when she and Michael visited but he no longer wanted to tell them about the funny thing that had happened last week, instead drinking in their experiences and taking pleasure from that.

How, given this, could they possibly introduce the enormity of a daughter that he had never known? Maybe a year ago, this would have felt like the right thing to do, but now they worried that it would do more harm than good. Ken might be Gwen's biological father, but what did that mean in this day and age? She and her dad needed some time to think. It would be hard for David and Gwen to wait, but this was one decision they weren't going to rush.

She said "I'm sorry"

There was nothing quite as terrible as machine coffee Erin decided, getting two cups from the vending machine in the corner of the closed cafeteria. In two hours, the café would be open, serving a bewildering range of coffees from flat whites to pumpkin spiced lattes to thankful nurses finishing their shifts and outpatients waiting for routine blood tests. But here, in the small hours of the morning, this tepid watery-brown liquid was the only drink available to the next of kin, rudely awakened by the unnaturalness of a 3am phone call.

Erin had been at training last night, a swim and a hard track session, followed by a trip to a bar for a quick beer with the others. Even when work was busy, she tried to make time for training. It made her feel good and helped her sleep better. The conversation last night had been about which triathlons they were doing and what times they were aiming for, followed by gossip about who was sleeping with whom. Erin had a core group of friends who had joined the club straight out of college. As the years passed, more of her girlfriends took a year off to have children. The gossip was now centred on the new crowd of twenty-somethings who were the only ones with the energy to do triathlons and still have sex on a school night. Erin had announced the end of her latest relationship, and these youngsters had tried to get her to sign up for the latest dating app to find a quick rebound hook-up. It wasn't for her.

She was in bed by 11pm. Erin always slept with her phone next to her bed, and it was 50/50 whether she remembered to turn it to silent. Last night, thankfully, she had forgotten. The ringtone had ripped her straight from her dreams, and she was still half asleep when she heard the voice on the other end of the phone tell her that her grandfather was in hospital. Erin turned on the bedside light, suddenly wide awake. She urgently searched for a pen to write down the hospital address. In the confusion, she forgot to ask any important questions. Was he conscious? Would he be OK? Had they phoned her dad? But by the time her brain had caught up with her body, the nurse had hung up, leaving Erin struggling to think what to do.

In the end, she phoned her parent's landline and waited for nearly 30 rings before her dad picked up.

"Hello. Who is this? Do you know what time it is?"

Erin could hear the mix of anger and fear in her dad's voice.

"Dad, it's me," Erin said gently, "It's Gramps."

She pulled on tracksuit bottoms and a jumper and drove to her parent's house, where her dad was waiting in the hallway, anxiously looking through the glass panels for the car headlights. By 4.30 am, they were in the ITU, sitting next to Ken's bed. Heavily sedated and hooked up to tubes and monitors, he looked so much smaller than he was. Without his false teeth, his face looked hollow. Erin had never seen a dead body, but she imagined it wasn't much different from this. It was only the slight movement in his chest and the numbers on the monitors that told her that he had survived the heart attack.

Throughout the journey, she had said silent prayers to a God she didn't believe in. 'Just let him live. Just let him live.' But now, sitting amongst the beeps and the bleeps, she wondered if she had done the wrong thing. After all, what would life be like for him now? The prayers had been selfish, born out of her need to see him again, to be able to speak to him, to kiss him one more time. She hadn't thought about his wishes, his desire to live independently and his fear of moving into the care home. 'Three steps to heaven' he'd called it – retirement village, care home, upstairs. When he finally woke up, she knew she'd see that realisation dawn on him, and it was this that finally brought tears to her eyes.

An hour later, the doctor came and spoke to them. Ken had been lucky, he said and pulled the alarm chord by the toilet when he'd woken in the night. The onsite medical team and the defibrillator that the Friends of the Care Home fundraised for last year had saved his life. By the time the paramedics arrived, he was conscious, and they were able to transfer him to the hospital.

"With a cardiac arrest out of hospital, there's only a 10% survival rate, particularly in such an elderly gentleman," the doctor had continued. "He must have a strong survival instinct."

Erin and Michael sat by the bed, watching and waiting. It reminded Michael of the nights when Erin had been poorly at home, where he and Marie had taken turns sleeping on the mattress beside her bed. They'd anxiously watch for any change in her condition, ready to fetch a sick bowl quickly or to administer Abenol if her temperature got too high.

His father had always seemed like a big man to Michael, full of life, and full of fun. Seeing him so diminished and vulnerable, was almost too much to bear.

"I'm going to get some air," he told Erin, squeezing her hand, "and phone Mum to let her know the news."

"OK," Erin replied. "And maybe get us some decent coffee. The café should be open by now."

The nurses had said that even though he wasn't able to respond, her gramps would be comforted by her being there. He might even hear what she said, so Erin held his hand and gently stroked his thumb. She was careful to avoid the tubes stuck haphazardly around his hands, regulating his pain and keeping him in the land of the living. She felt silly holding a one-sided conversation but forced herself to do it anyway. She told her grampa about her run last night. How pleased the coach had been with her. She told him how terrible the coffee was. She told him about the oldest fossils in the world that had just been found in the supracrustal belt in Quebec. She told him what a wonderful grandfather he was and how much she and everybody loved him. And when she'd run out of things to say, she kissed his hand and sat there quietly, the beeps and whirrs of the machinery creating a strange symphony in the background.

It was bizarre how time ticked on relentlessly. It felt like she had been sitting by the bed for minutes, but the buzz of activity outside the unit and the sun creeping through the blinds said otherwise. Her smartwatch told her to 'MOVE

NOW' so she obediently stood up and stretched. When Dad returned, she'd take a walk and phone work to tell them she wouldn't be in today. She felt guilty as if she was taking an undeserved day off. She knew everyone would understand. They knew how close she was to her grampa. But the world moves on, and within days, they'd expect her to be back to her usual self. Compassionate leave was capped at 3 days a year. Not terribly compassionate, thought Erin as she retook her seat and reached for her grandfather's hand.

When he woke in the night, he immediately knew something was wrong. He was sweating heavily and had a terrible sense that something awful was about to happen. By the time he got to the toilet, the pain was intense, and he instinctively pulled the blue chord hanging in the bathroom. He'd mistaken it for the light switch once and been embarrassed at bothering them unnecessarily. Today he was grateful it was there. It was a relief when he heard the front door opening and unfamiliar voices calling his name. He must have passed out because he had no recollection of anything until he woke up, and the paramedics were there. He remembered feeling ashamed that his trousers were around his ankles and the smell of excrement – his own, he realised – was all around him.

He remembered being taken into the ambulance and hooked up to all sorts of drips and devices. He hoped someone would call Michael. They must have sedated him because now he was trapped in some weird dream world. Occasionally he could hear voices around him. At one point, he was sure he heard Erin complaining about the coffee. But try as he might, he couldn't open his eyes.

Something told him this was for his own good, so he stopped fighting and drifted into a world of peculiar dreams where real memories merged with bizarre fantasies. The dreams came from different parts of his life, faces and places flashing into view, some almost within reach.

Playing cards with some of the other residents, but rather than being at the retirement village, they were on the top of a mountain, a precipice on either side.

A walk in the park with Laurie and the dogs with all the trees in bright dayglo colours. Without warning, Laurie disappears. He runs into the forest to find her, but the further he gets, the more lost he feels. He hears a voice saying, 'You're not out of the woods yet,' and when he looks at the trees they start laughing at him.

A day he spent fishing when Michael was eight or nine. Seeing the float bob under the water and striking perfectly. He tries to reel the fish in for what seems like hours and then finds that he is pulling up the bottom of the ocean itself.

Each memory takes him further back in time until he finds himself in England with Peggy. They are at a train station, and he is leaving with thousands of other men in uniform. They are on different sides of the tracks, and Peggy is frantically trying to tell him something. She is shouting as hard as she can, but the words are lost by the whistling of the trains and the noise from the crowd. Suddenly, she throws a bundle across the tracks. He thinks it will drop short of him, but he catches it and looks down to see that it is a baby. Before he can do anything, the baby is snatched from him by a dirty-faced child, like a character in a Dickens' play. The urchin runs off, and when he looks across the platform, Peggy has gone.

Even in his befuddled state, he knows that these memories are important. His body is in limbo, but his brain is trying to tell him things that he has somehow always known. Memories that were hidden so well in the folds of his cerebral cortex that they have been impossible to find. He wants to wake up now before he forgets it all again. He wants to share some of these dreams with his family so they can help him make sense of them. He wants to find a way through this maze of memories to the solid ground of consciousness. If only he could work out how.

Erin and Michael were in the café, eating sandwiches they didn't want and working out what they should do next. They had spent all morning at Ken's bedside, trying to interpret the different beeps and numbers and waiting for any sign that he would come around. 'He's not out of the woods yet' was all the doctors would say. The ITU nurses were monitoring his vital signs – checking the drips and the catheter, writing up their notes and replacing them in the wallet at the end of his bed.

When Erin asked how things were looking, they smiled kindly and told her the doctor would speak to them later. It felt wrong that there was so little going on. She was used to watching TV hospital dramas, where white-coated junior doctors made a diagnosis on the back of the smallest piece of information and consultants performed open heart surgery in the corridor because there was no time to get to the operating theatre. The reality was hour after hour of waiting and feeling helpless. In the end, one of the nurses told Erin and her dad to go and get something to eat, promising she would get them if anything changed.

“Do you think we should tell Gwen and David?” her dad asked, putting down a barely eaten sandwich.

“I don't know," Erin answered honestly.

"We haven't told Grampa about Gwen yet, and the last thing we want is for them to hop on a plane and turn up for a deathbed reconciliation.”

“We don’t know he’s on his deathbed," her father snapped. Erin could see how much he was struggling.

“I’m sorry.” The lack of sleep and too much coffee had made Erin less sensitive than she should be. “I only mean we need to think about whether this is the right thing to do for Grampa.”

Erin had been conflicted since she received David's email. In the last month, Gramps had slowed down considerably. His mind was still sharp but going to the bathroom or taking a short walk left him breathless. He had promised Erin that he would visit the doctor at the retirement village, but she wasn’t convinced he had. Recently he'd fallen and though he explained it away as a momentary loss of concentration, she wondered if there was more to it. She blamed herself for not insisting he saw a doctor.

And it wasn't just the falls. Every time they visited, Grampa wanted to give them things. 'How about these for the charity shop,' he’d say, handing over books and records that had once been his pride and joy, or, 'Do you think Marie would like these figurines?' as he offered them family heirlooms.

"What's this all about, Dad?" Michael had asked, worried his behaviour was out of character.

"You can't take it with you," he'd replied.

Only last week, he'd shown Michael a notebook with ideas for what he wanted played at his funeral.

"I've been to some awful affairs recently, and I just want to make sure everyone enjoys themselves at mine," he managed when Michael told him to stop being so morbid. When Erin told her mum about his behaviour, she said that her mother had been the same in the months before she died. She likened it to the nesting instinct mothers get before childbirth, an innate need to get everything in order, to leave no mess. In hindsight, perhaps there had been signs they should have noticed if they hadn't been so distracted by whether to tell him about Gwen.

They had gone around in circles trying to answer the unknowable question: 'Would he want to know?' The more people they asked, the more confused they became. Those who advised against telling him said, 'What possible good would it do?' while those who advocated for telling him would say, 'He has a right to know.' Some felt it would be cruel not to let his daughter meet him if she wanted to, and a few warned about potential problems with his will.

After listening to all the opinions, Erin and Michael decided it should be his choice. They had been planning to tell him about Gwen at the weekend. When Michael first heard the news, he wondered if they had somehow caused the heart attack, as if their decision had sent shockwaves straight to his arteries.

“The heart attack changes things. He's going to need months of convalescence, and finding out he has a daughter he never knew about will cause so much additional stress. I don't think we should tell him yet.”

Deep down, Erin agreed with her dad, but she dreaded telling David. She knew he'd understand, but she couldn't help feeling guilty. If she hadn’t messaged him in the first place, he’d be none the wiser. She wondered how Gwen would feel, knowing this might be her last chance to see the father she never knew she had. Would she understand and want the best for him? Erin hoped so.

“I’ll call David in the morning and tell him about Gramps. We'll know more by then. I'll explain that we want to wait until Gramps is stronger to tell him about Gwen. I just hope he understands.”

Erin looked at her dad to get his agreement, but he wasn’t looking at her. The ITU nurse had walked into the café and was signalling for them both to come.

The manager at Longlake Retirement Village turned the key in the lock and walked into the hall. The last time she had been here was to respond to a chord call. It was never good news when she was woken in the middle of the night. The paramedics had got here quickly. All she had to do was sit with Ken until they arrived. She tried to make him decent as the older generation feared the loss of dignity more than anything else. He had been their second oldest resident, and she had a soft spot for him, so it hadn’t been a hardship to hold his hand and try and make him feel less afraid.

She was going in to make sure everything was in order. Ken's relatives were coming over later to clear out the flat. It had sold quickly, and the new owner was having it decorated before she moved in. The cleaners had done an excellent job already, so all she needed to do was open the windows to give the place an airing. She went into each room for one last check. It was never easy for the relatives, and she wanted them to feel that things were in order. As she left the bedroom, she glanced back. The bed was made, but she noticed something peeping out from under the valence. She knelt down and pulled out a buff-coloured envelope full of birthday cards. One individual card was on the floor next to it. She wondered what it was doing there. Perhaps Ken had kept birthday cards from over the years. She popped the card back into the envelope and put the whole thing into the desk drawer in the living room. Just one more thing for Ken's son to sort. She walked down the hall saying 'night, night Ken' to herself as she did. She turned off the hall light and locked the door behind her.

He said "And now we're here"

Michael gripped the handrest between the seats and took a deep breath as they hit some turbulence. He had flown all his life, but the older he got, the more nervous he became. He glanced across at Erin, who was fast asleep and snoring lightly. He admired her ability to sleep through anything. Since his father had died, Michael struggled with insomnia. During the day, he found he could distract himself, but as soon as he closed his eyes, his mind went straight to thoughts of his dad. He missed him so much. Everyone said his dad had a good innings and had lived a good life, but none of that stopped the grief. It crept up on him unawares. He'd be taking Maple for a walk and suddenly be overcome with sadness or watch a film his dad had liked and feel tears prick his eyes.

To Michael, it was logical that you would miss someone more the longer they had been in your life. There was more to miss. He still had his dad's voicemails on his phone, and sometimes he went into the garden and played them, just so he could hear his voice again. He was glad that he hadn't come around from the heart attack. The doctors promised he would have felt no pain, just slipped away into whatever came next. His dad would have hated a long convalescence. He was never a man who liked any fuss, and he wouldn't have wanted to give up his daily gin and tonic or move into the dreaded care home. Better the way it happened. They didn't have the chance to say goodbye, but his dad knew they loved him. They told him often enough. And they were never in any doubt about how Ken felt about them. And while Michael felt sad for Gwen, he was glad they had decided not to tell Dad about her. He knew it was selfish, but he'd been his dad for sixty-eight years, and he didn't want to share him at the end. He supposed if he hadn't had the heart attack, they would have felt obliged to tell Ken about his daughter, but this way it was taken out of their hands, and he honestly thought it was for the best.

Despite everything, he was excited to finally meet Gwen in person. When Ken died, Erin phoned David to explain. She told him they never had the chance to tell Ken before he passed away. It was a white lie, given they had procrastinated for at least a month, but it felt right in the circumstances. A few weeks later, David had asked Erin if he and Gwen could have a Skype call with her and her father. They had so many questions they wanted answered, and Gwen was keen to meet her half-brother, however sad the circumstances. Michael was dreading it, but the minute the camera sprang to life, it all felt easy. Having David and Erin there really helped, and not for the first time, Michael marvelled at how easy the younger generation found it to chat with near strangers. He supposed it must be something to do with social media and online dating, both of which he would have been terrible at. David had baby Seb on his lap, and they spent the first ten minutes cooing at him and playing peekaboo to make him laugh. By the end of the first call, they already felt comfortable with each other, so when Gwen asked if she could call Michael again, he didn't hesitate to say yes.

They spoke every week for the next couple of months. Gwen was hungry to discover everything she could about the man she never knew. She revelled in understanding the minutiae of his life – was he a reader (yes); did he go bald (no); what was his favourite food (meatloaf); which sports did he follow (ice hockey and soccer). In return, Michael spoke about Ken in all his ordinary glory; it helped him to process his grief and come to terms with how he was feeling. And it let him remember how much he loved him. Marie called it his weekly therapy session, and he supposed it was.

His friends had been great, but he felt a responsibility to be his old self again as if their sympathy had a time limit attached. Marie had been wonderfully supportive, but after the funeral, even she seemed to think that normal life should resume. The problem for Michael was that since his retirement, normal life had revolved around the twice-weekly visits to his dad. They were woven into his life like coloured threads which, when removed, made the fabric of his everyday life unravel. It wasn't a dramatic unravelling – he wasn't on the verge of a breakdown – he just felt he was missing something, missing someone.

The calls with Gwen helped. As he told his stories, it was as if he breathed life back into his dad and banished the final memories of him looking so diminished, so unlike the father he'd known all his life. In the first few weeks, their calls had been all about Ken, but as they grew more comfortable with each other, the conversation turned to Gwen's mum, Margaret. Gwen had been careful about discussing her at the start out of respect for Michael's grandmother. But Michael found that, just as Gwen had wanted to know more about Ken, so he wanted to know more about Margaret – as if she could unlock even more about his father. It's like discovering a new song from your favourite artist, he'd explained.

Finally, a couple of months ago, Gwen had suggested they meet. He had sent her the cards and letters his father had received from Margaret, and she immediately suggested he should come to the UK and visit some of the places that were mentioned. He discussed it with Erin and Marie, and they decided they would visit during the summer. Marie wanted to stay at home, citing the need to look after Maple, although, in truth, she didn't want to play gooseberry to Michael meeting his sister for the first time.

"As we will start our descent into Heathrow, please ensure your seat backs and tray tables are in an upright position, and your seat belt is securely fastened."

Michael gently prodded Erin's arm to wake her.

"Are we nearly there yet?" Erin asked, like some toddler bored on a long car journey.

"We certainly are," Michael replied, popping his book back into his backpack.

"And are you OK?" Erin asked.

"I will be," Michael replied, holding her hand tightly and closing his eyes for landing.

Gwen was waiting at Terminal 5 arrivals, holding a handmade sign she had created that morning using cardboard and bamboo canes. It read 'Welcome Michael and Erin', and she kept raising it expectantly as the sliding doors opened and a new set of bleary-eyed travellers emerged like a cheap version of Stars in Your Eyes – 'Tonight Matthew, I'm going to be an exhausted Brazilian who hasn't slept a wink'.

She had arrived ridiculously early, tracking the plane as it made its way across the North Atlantic, and leaving home a good hour before it landed, just in case of bad traffic on the M25. In the end, it had only taken her twenty minutes door to door, and there was still no sign of them, even though the plane had landed ages ago. Erin had sent a text saying they were waiting for their bags. Hopefully, they would be through soon, or she'd roll over into the next exorbitantly expensive time zone on the short-term car park. She probably should have suggested they got a taxi.

It was weird to think she was about to meet her brother and niece. Some people corrected her, saying they were her half-brother and half-niece, but she didn't feel that way. She had already missed out on them for most of her life, so she would fully claim them for the time she had left. When she had first found out about Ken, she'd struggled to take it in. She'd been angry – with Cynthia for not telling her, at herself for wasting all those years hating Jim. But mainly at her mother for keeping it from her all her life, and then dying, and taking away any chance for answers, for closure.

She hated that word – closure. So American, such psychobabble, but it fitted how she felt, like a book only half read, abandoned on the bedside table with the spine cracked. The chapters so far lead you in one direction, and then, out of the blue, a new character is introduced, an unexpected turn of events. She had thought that meeting her father might help, and then this was snatched away from her.

In the months since Ken had died, she had gradually come to terms with the situation. In particular, it had made her think about her relationship with Jim. One of the benefits of age is that you realise that very few things are black and white. She'd seen enough friends have affairs, get divorced, and lie to their partners, to know that nothing is cut and dried when it comes to affairs of the heart. She had created a narrative for her mum and dad that painted her father as the criminal and her mother as the victim. Her mother, unfulfilled, at home bringing up two girls with a husband who had countless affairs and then got one of them pregnant. But equally, you could have painted it as her mother tricking a young, single man into a loveless marriage whilst pregnant with another man's child.

The truth was neither of these. Cynthia, who had known them the best, had helped fill in the gaps. Jim, she told Gwen, had been hopelessly in love with Margaret and was heartbroken when he returned from Italy to find her in love with another man. When she admitted her predicament, he'd instantly offered marriage. Like many couples who married during the war, they'd struggled to adapt to civilian life. Margaret, who had enjoyed new freedoms and revelled in her work in the WAAF, was thrown back into the dullness of domestic duties and baby care. Jim, an ordinary man with few qualifications, found it hard to provide for his middle-class wife and new family, with all the expectations that came with it. And in the bedroom, it just didn't work.

In the early days, when Margaret was pregnant and then nursing a baby, their lovemaking was first put on ice and then, to Margaret's distress, abandoned altogether. Jim put Margaret on a pedestal and found it impossible to see her as someone who could fulfil his desires. Finally, after a particularly boozy night at the pub, he went to bed with his secretary, enjoying a physical relationship unburdened by the complexities of his feelings for Margaret.

Today, they would have divorced, but things were different then, and they still loved each other, just more as friends with a shared past, than as husband and wife. Gwen had witnessed the affection between them. She knew they loved each other, but she could never forgive her father for his infidelities. If she had known then what she knew now, would it have helped? Or would she have hated them both? Hindsight is a wonderful thing, Gwen thought as her phone vibrated, announcing a new text.

We are through and waiting by M&S

After all that bother with the sign, she had missed them anyway. She strode towards the shop. Within a few seconds, she could see them. The faces so familiar from Skype calls were now transformed into real people, her flesh and blood. Not half-anything, but her whole family and it felt good.

It had started with an off-the-cuff comment on one of their regular Skype calls. Gwen had said how sad she was that she couldn't attend Ken's funeral. Michael had sent her the eulogy to read, and she had been touched that mention was made of his time in England during the war and a special friendship he had made with a beautiful WAAF called Peggy. They had agreed not to mention that he had a daughter with her, not wanting to start rumours amongst the tight-knit Vancouver community.

“We know the truth,” Michael had said, “and that’s all that matters.”

Even so, Michael admitted to Erin that he felt sorry that Gwen had nothing to remember her father by. When they were clearing out Ken's flat, they put aside all the old photographs. Later, Erin created an album for Gwen that showed Ken from a cheeky young boy sitting on the back of the tractor to one a few years ago, when he caught the baseball as it flew into the crowd at the Nat Bailey stadium. You could see how surprised he was that he could still react so quickly. It was whilst she was creating the album that Erin had another idea.

“What if we take some of Grampa’s ashes to England with us?” she suggested to her dad. “That way we can scatter them in his and Margaret’s memory.”

“I think that’s a lovely idea,” said Michael. It had always struck him how strange it was to keep a person's ashes – putting them on the fireplace like a trophy, or worse still, in the attic. Moving from idea to reality had proved more difficult than Erin had expected, and anyone reading her Google history might have wondered what she was planning.

How many ashes does an average body create?
3-4kg for a man – surprisingly heavy!

Can you take cremated ashes on a plane?
Yes – but you need all sorts of paperwork!

Are you allowed to sprinkle ashes anywhere?
Yes, in most places, but you sometimes need permission from the landowner.

Erin had bought an eco-urn designed for taking ashes overseas and carried it onto the plane in her hand luggage. She hated to think what the customs guys would say when the ashes went through the X-ray machine. Now, in the bedroom of a Premier Inn just on the outskirts of Bath, Erin was re-packing her suitcase and trying to keep her dirty running kit away from the container with its precious contents. Since they'd arrived a week ago, she'd had very little time to herself. Going out for a run this morning had been a priority. The last week had taken its toll, what with the jet lag and the emotions involved in meeting this new extended family in real life.

They had spent a couple of nights in London with Gwen and her husband. On the second evening, they'd been joined for dinner by David, Toby, and baby Seb, alongside David's sister Helen. On Thursday, she, Michael, Gwen, and David had driven to Bath. Gwen was keen that they saw some of the sights while they were in England, and Bath was a good place to break their journey to Cornwall. When they had mentioned the ashes to Gwen during the Skype call, she'd been so emotional. Erin thought she even saw tears in her eyes, but it was difficult to tell on screen. Armed with the letters, Gwen had created a road trip that took in Hawks Tor and Harrowbeer and ended in Tintagel, where they decided they would scatter Ken's ashes together with Margaret's, which Gwen had never been able to let go.

Erin enjoyed the romance of the gesture, but to her it felt like the closing scene of a film she had watched. The Ken she was scattering wasn't her Gramps, but a character from a different age, a black and white version, not the high-resolution, technicolour man she had loved all her life. She tenderly touched the outside of the urn, then shut her case, and walked down to reception to meet the others.

The drive down from Bath had taken them over four hours, and David was relieved to finally be at Tintagel. His mum had offered to share the driving, but he would rather endure her backseat driving than spend the whole journey worrying every time she pulled out into the fast lane. Or, worse still, driving along in the middle lane as cars overtook her on the inside, oblivious to their flashing lights. They had stopped for lunch at the Exeter services, forgoing lunch at a nice English pub for a tasteless and uninviting meal deal to get to Tintagel before it closed. Now, sitting in the car park waiting for Gwen and Michael to get their walking boots on, he thought about the symbolism of what they were about to do.

Since having his own child, David found himself getting more sentimental. Sometimes, even watching Peppa Pig brought a tear to his eye, and the lyrics of love songs he'd previously regarded as trashy now brought a lump to his throat. He'd always thought it was hormones that made expectant mothers so emotional, but it was clearly something deeper, more profound – an unsettling mix of fear, connection and responsibility that went straight from your heart to your tear ducts, making your shoulders ache on the way.

"Are you sure you're not describing a heart attack?" Toby had commented when David had explained how he felt. Dear old Toby, always making light of everything and grounding him in the day-to-day reality of fatherhood. Even so, David knew how he felt when he looked at Seb asleep in his cot at night, and he couldn't imagine the pain of having a child that he knew nothing about. Wouldn't there be some cosmic tug through the years, across the Atlantic, telling Ken that Gwen existed? They had started their walk from the car park to the castle, Michael and Gwen in front chatting quietly to each other, their backpacks bouncing in unison, the slope of their shoulder and their stride length strangely similar.

"Do you think how you walk is genetic?" he asked Erin.

"I wouldn't think so, surely it depends on your height and weight and stuff," Erin replied. "They do have the same laugh, though. And the way the lines crease around their eyes."

"I think that's just old age," David laughed, although he could see the likeness too.

"It's nice that they've found each other, though. At least something good came from doing those tests!"

"I know! When I first got your message, I thought it was a scam, and then, when I realised the implications, I'd have done anything to turn back the clock."

"And now we're here."

"And now we're here," agreed David, squeezing Erin's hand.

There was a queue waiting to go up the 100 steps to the castle, and while they waited, they read about the new footbridge that would join the two sides of the castle together.

"I'm glad we're experiencing this like Peggy and Ken did," Gwen said.

David noticed that she'd started using the diminutive Peggy rather than Margaret when she talked about her mum to Michael and Erin.

"And look, they are fundraising for the new bridge. For £5 we can sign one of the Cornish slates that's part of the walkway," Erin announced excitedly.

"We should do that," Michael agreed, "and have Ken and Peggy here for posterity."

It took them another half an hour to get to the highest point. Then, slightly out of breath, they found a quiet spot overlooking the Atlantic Ocean.

"When you look at all this beauty, you realise there's not much that separates us," Michael said, breathing in the sea air.

"Apart from the Atlantic and most of Canada," laughed Gwen.

"I know, but it's people that count. The connections between people. The love we have for each other. The shared experiences. That's what really matters."

"And yet that's what often keeps us apart," whispered Gwen.

"Well, now we've found each other–" said David.

"We'll make sure we don't lose each other again," finished Erin.

Gwen took the flask from her backpack, and Erin handed her the urn from hers. Gently she tipped one into the other, joining their DNA together for eternity. With the next gust of wind, she raised the flask and let its contents blow out towards the sea, drifting past Merlin's cave and to the beach beyond.

And the consequence was ...

Erin had never believed in fate. She was far too practical for that. But what else could you call her meeting with Alex? If she hadn't taken the 23+ me test, she would never have known about her family in the UK. If they hadn't decided to scatter Grampa Ken's ashes with Margaret's, she wouldn't have come to England. And if she hadn't added two weeks to her trip to do a triathlon in Weymouth, she might never have met Alex.

After the trip to Tintagel, they had driven back to David and Toby's, and she had stayed a week with them. Her dad had flown home on Tuesday, keen not to leave her mum for any longer than necessary. It had been such an emotional time, but as she and Gwen waved him off from Heathrow, it felt as if they had bonded as a family. It would usually take years to reach this level of connection, but the hours of Skype calls had speeded up the getting-to-know-you phase and cut through any awkwardness they might otherwise feel. And, of course, underneath it all they were related, and the traits that had attracted Ken to Margaret must be somewhere in their own DNA.

She had loved her time with Toby and David. They were easy to get along with and made her feel so welcome. David hadn't been the Hugh Grant figure she originally imagined. And their house in St Margaret's wasn't a stately home, more an Edwardian semi-detached that had been given a contemporary update, all glass skylights and bifold doors. You could tell that David had an eyes for design, as it had all been done so tastefully. The type of house you might see on the pages of some upmarket-style magazine.

And Sebastian was a wonderful baby. At 18 months, he was into everything, navigating his way downstairs like a pro and, happiest of all, sitting in the paddling pool in the garden. Erin hadn't had much experience with babies. None of her friends had made that leap yet, although she didn't imagine it would be long, given that all her single girl friends had now found partners.

At the end of the week, she had hired a car to go down to Weymouth. It had been an impulsive decision to book onto the triathlon, and she was lucky there were spaces available. Rather than taking her bike with her, she'd decided to hire one instead, so having checked into her hotel, she went to the bike shop to pick it up. The triathlon had attracted hundreds to this beautiful seaside town, so she wasn't surprised that some of them had found their way into the bike shop, eying up the latest merchandise. The atmosphere was friendly, with conversations about the likely weather the next day.

"As long as they don't ban wetsuits for the swim, I'll be happy," Erin had joked in response to someone saying that it was going to be windy.

"You don't have to worry about that in England," the guy standing next to her laughed. "You're clearly not from around these parts!"

“How did you guess?”

“Must be that accent of yours. Canadian, I assume – what brings you to sunny Weymouth?”

She was impressed. Most people automatically assumed she was American.

“I was over visiting family and thought I’d tag this one on”. Erin smiled, realising that the family word had felt so natural. “How did you know I was Canadian?”

“My job takes me out there all the time, and I wouldn’t have made it out of meetings alive without being able to tell my Canadian from my American. It’s almost as bad as calling a New Zealander an Australian! It’s Alex, by the way.”

The guy held his hand out to her.

“I’m Erin” she replied.

They had ended up chatting idly for the next fifteen minutes, and when she was about to head off to get her bike, he’d asked her if she wanted to meet up after the race.

“If you’ve got nothing else to do,” he added quickly.

“Apart from a massage and a long hot bath,” she had replied.

In the end, they’d agreed to meet up in the athlete’s village at around six, assuming they both made it around without any incident. The race itself had been tough. They had been treated to rain, wind and finally sun – ‘three seasons in one day’ and Erin had never felt as sick as she had in the rolling waves of the sea swim. She ended up Top 10 in her age group, which she was pleased with given the conditions.

After dropping the bike back to the shop and having a bath at her hotel, she popped on some jeans and a hoodie and made her way to the Athlete's Village. People were still streaming through the finish line, the sound system was pounding out loud tunes, and the announcer was as enthusiastic as when she crossed the finish line several hours earlier. She was worried she wouldn't recognise Alex, they had only spoken for a few minutes, but she spotted him as soon as she walked in. Alex would joke in years to come that their eyes had met over a row of overpriced Ironman merchandise and that it was love at second sight. For Erin, it felt as if the stars had aligned, and Ken and Margaret's love story was unfolding all over again. Knowing how badly that love story had ended, Erin was determined not to repeat the same mistakes.

At the end of the first night, they'd agreed to meet the following day. Alex had taken some holiday and promised to show her around. They drove onto Portland Island. Still aching from the previous day's race, they left the paddle boarding and kayaking for another day and opted to stretch their legs with a long walk on Chesil Beach. In the afternoon, they walked around Portland Castle, and Erin was struck by the crossovers with Ken and Margaret's story – just replace Tintagel with Portland and King Arthur with Henry the Eighth. Finally, they sat and had a beer at the harbour.

"You know this is where they embarked for the D-Day landings," Alex said. "My grandfather left from this very spot."

"So did mine, for Operation Dragoon," Erin replied, and she felt the hairs on her neck bristle.

They'd ended up spending the next three days together. Alex phoned in sick for the final day and drove Erin back to London for her flight the next morning.

On the journey back, they engaged in a speed dating game – eager to get all the important stuff out in the open.

Alex
Age: 38
Occupation: Management Consultant
Siblings: 1 sister; 1 brother
Longest relationship: 3 years
Last relationship ended: 9 months ago
Who ended it: I did
Why: I didn't love her
Best quality: calm and supportive (that's 2!)
Worst quality: untidy
Favourite holiday destination: New Zealand
Do you want children? Yes
When: soon
How many? 4 (you've got to be joking)
Favourite tri discipline: bike
Have you ever been in love? Yes

Erin
Age: 36
Occupation: Information Security Analyst (is that really a thing?)
Siblings: 2 brothers
Longest relationship: 18 months
Last relationship ended? 1 year ago
Who ended it: I did

Why: too many arguments
Best quality: loyal
Worst quality: clumsy
Favourite holiday destination: Canada (Very adventurous)
Do you want children? Yes
When: soon
How many: 2
Favourite tri discipline: run
Have you ever been in love? No (Really?) Yes, really
Do you think you could fall in love with me? Maybe (Really?) Yes, maybe

She'd stayed at his flat in Clapham and had been relieved and disappointed when he took the sofa bed in the lounge. As he hugged her at the airport, it was obvious they both felt the same way. It had all been such a whirlwind, and in normal circumstances, Erin would have written it off as a holiday fling, but she couldn't shake the idea that this was meant to be. By the time Erin landed in Vancouver, she already had a lovely email from him, and within a month he had organised a three-month work secondment at the Vancouver office that got extended to six.

In June 2019, just a month before Alex's secondment was due to finish, Gwen, David, Toby and Sebastian came over for a visit. It was the first time that Toby and David had met Alex in person, but they got on so well that when Erin was busy at work, they hung out together.

'Just making sure that he's good enough for our Erin,' David had said, making Erin unbelievably happy that she had been taken under their wing. She now knew what it felt like to have two gay best friends. In the last few months, she and Alex had talked about what might happen when he returned to London in July. Erin had spoken to her work about doing a spell at their London office and knowing that she had family there had made her feel more comfortable about the whole thing. But it was still a big move with no certainty about how things would ultimately work out with Alex. Not for the first time she thought back to Margaret making her decision. It wasn't easy, even when you really loved someone.

The gang were staying until after the Victoria triathlon on Vancouver Island that Erin and Alex were both competing in. Having a race to focus on had taken their minds off Alex's imminent departure and training for the event had brought them even closer together.

As they lined up in different pens for the swim start, he reached for her hand, mouthed 'see you at the end' and blew her a kiss. When she crossed the line about an hour after him, covered in sweat with ice still in her bra top, she saw him down on one knee. Behind him, Toby and David were holding a banner saying, 'Will you marry me, Erin?' The announcer shouted over the tannoy, 'Well, will you Erin?' It was as much as she could manage to nod her head in agreement before collapsing in a sweaty bundle into his arms. The loudspeakers boomed out *It's a nice day for a white wedding* and all the supporters waiting for their loved ones to finish broke into spontaneous applause.

Although she hadn't realised it, the proposal of marriage helped quell any nerves she was having. It was the commitment she'd been looking for, even though she hadn't realised it. And it meant a lot to her that everyone who met Alex seemed to think they would be perfect together. Even her parents, who were devastated she was moving to England, gave their blessing and promised to visit often.

They ended up getting married in London in December of 2019, and unknown to her friends and family who had lined up to throw confetti outside Chelsea Town Hall, like Margaret she was hiding a secret under her wedding dress. Even with eggs past their 'sell by date' she was already 3 months pregnant. In preparation for the baby, they moved from their flat in London to a three-bedroom house in Cheam. This proved to be the best decision ever when, a month later, the whole world went into lockdown. It wasn't the pregnancy that Erin might have hoped for. Explaining your concerns about your nipples or your perineum to a midwife over Zoom felt way more embarrassing than doing it in a doctor's surgery.

As lockdown took hold, Erin's hopes of making friends by joining antenatal classes and popping along to coffee mornings disappeared in a puff of corona. Her friends tried to give her an online baby shower, but it wasn't quite the same. They were lucky to live so close to Nonsuch Park, and right up to the final weeks, she and Alex managed a morning run together as their legal daily exercise. When Gus arrived in June, it turned their lives upside down, although having Alex on a mix of paternity leave and working from home gave them much more time to bond as a family. Instead of rushing for the early commute they got up together and enjoyed a walk in the park with Gus before Alex went to work in his temporary study in the spare bedroom, and Erin went back to bed.

In one way, it was perfect, but as new parents, they longed to show Gus off to friends and family. Erin's parents missed out the most as their planned visit when Gus was born was replaced with Zoom calls, which, even when the technology worked, could never replace an actual cuddle with your first grandchild. By Christmas, they were well and truly into a routine with Gus, who, against all expectations, had turned into a placid baby. Their social life revolved around weekly Zoom quizzes. These started with Toby, David, Gwen and Stephen, but were expanded to include Christine and Paul; Alex's brother and his wife; Toby's family, and Seb's birth mother.

"If anyone had told me that I would be playing Stop the Bus with the illegitimate son of my wife's cousins' grandfather, I'd have never believed them," Alex liked to joke – every week finding more and more obscure relationships to describe.

"It's a shame we don't have a quiz on naming different family relationships," Erin countered, "We'd absolutely nail it."

"I can't believe Boris has cancelled Christmas this late," Alex moaned, looking up from his iPad. Gus was still asleep next door, and they were enjoying a coffee and a couple of minutes of peace before getting up.

They had been invited to spend Christmas with David at Toby's family in Virginia Water. After all the months of barely seeing anybody, they were ridiculously excited about it. Toby's father loved Christmas and went out of his way with decorations. These included a herd of life-sized wicker reindeer and outside lights which a local electrician wired up every year.

"How the other half live," Alex commented, but secretly they were happy to give Gus the best first Christmas ever.

"We'll have to go to Tesco's and see if there's any turkeys left," Erin grumbled. The idea of cooking her first Christmas dinner and not being waited on hand and foot put her in a sudden grump.

"It'll be fun," Alex countered, trying to snap her out of her mood. "We'll get to see Gus opening his presents without thousands of onlookers."

"You do know that he'll be as interested in the cardboard boxes as any presents?" Erin laughed.

"I know, it's me that's excited about the presents," Alex said, pulling Erin towards him in a big hug and kissing her ears.

"Gus was telling me that there was one thing he wanted for Christmas though," he continued.

"You do know that he isn't actually speaking yet," Erin replied, kissing his nose.

"I know, but I am fluent in baby speak and happen to know that 'goo, goo, goo, ga, ga, ga' means 'could I have a little brother or sister please, Mummy and Daddy'."

They had always talked about having a second baby, but Erin had expected to wait a bit. With another lockdown looming, perhaps it did make sense to get on with it.

"Before I agree to anything, I need a signed contract saying that we are stopping at two," Erin demanded, remembering full well that Alex had always said he wanted four.

"I promise," Alex said, kissing her neck.

"I need it in writing," Erin insisted, but already her resistance was waning.

"Just as soon as I can find a pen," Alex answered, his foot pushing down her pyjama bottoms as his hands explored under her top.

"You'll not find one up there," Erin thought as she sighed deeply and gave in to the moment.

Erin narrowed it down to two dresses. She couldn't decide between the maxi floral green dress or the midi blue dress with the yellow bow pattern. Despite spending the last four years in England, she still didn't understand the dress codes, which seemed to involve some weird algorithm that triangulated occasion, age and class. She had already attended two weddings, one where the bride wore flip flops, and one where the groom had worn a kilt in the wrong tartan, which led to whispers from some in the congregation. It seemed that wearing the wrong clothes was a social faux pas unless you were incredibly wealthy, in which case almost anything went. Her choice today was restricted by the fact that she was still breastfeeding and needed to be able to get her boobs out quickly if she needed to keep Evie quiet during the service. She chose the midi-dress and reflected on how lovely it was to get dressed up for once. She'd spent the whole of lockdown in tracksuit bottoms and a T-shirt (hot weather) or a hoodie (cold weather). Even the race T-shirts she had sworn to only wear at the gym or in bed, were a regular part of her weekly attire.

Alex was downstairs keeping Evie and Gus entertained, which probably meant he had sat them down in front of CBeebies and got himself a beer. One of the downsides of being permanently pregnant for the past few years was that she was always on driving duty. She would remind Alex of this in future years, although he'd probably still find an excuse not to drive. She was so looking forward to today. She had never been a godmother before and was unsure what she would have to say or do during the ceremony.

"You have to renounce the devil and stuff like that," Toby had said in his usual throwaway style.

"And promise you'll love her forever and ever," David had clarified.

Well, that shouldn't be a problem, thought Erin.

She had come up with the idea while pregnant with Evie. About halfway through she had heard from her old employers asking whether she wanted her frozen eggs stored for another five years, or whether they could be donated. She could hardly believe how much her life had changed since she had chosen to have her eggs frozen. If anyone had suggested then that she would be living in London with the love of her life, about to have baby number two, she'd have told them they were mad.

For her, egg freezing had been a safety net she no longer needed. For a couple desperate for their own baby they could be a chance for happiness. Throughout lockdown, she and David had met as often as the rules allowed, pleased to be able to get Seb and Gus together. On one walk, the conversation had turned to babies, and David admitted that he and Toby were desperate to have another. David explained how everything had worked the first time around. Tara, the friend who carried Seb for them, was happy to babysit another, but Olivia was now too old to donate her eggs. Erin hadn't told David about her frozen eggs, she wanted to discuss the idea with Alex first.

"As long as you don't have to have sex with Toby," Alex laughed, kissing her on the cheek.

"Not in any meaningful way," she replied. Not for the first time wondering where she had found a man quite so wonderful as Alex. Offering her eggs to David was like giving somebody the best present ever. The sheer joy on Toby and David's faces confirmed they had made the right decision. When finally, Tara sent them a photo of the pregnancy test, with the caption, 'First time in lockdown I've been pleased of a positive result,' they were overwhelmed with happiness.

Erin had enjoyed her second pregnancy. Having Alex with her at pre-natal appointments and scans made her more relaxed, and once she had the vaccine, even her fears of catching Covid were reduced. It was tough with a toddler, but with Alex working from home, they managed to juggle things between them pretty well. By comparison, the last six months had been an eye-opener. Alex was back in the office a couple of days a week, and Erin had to balance the needs of a hyperactive toddler with getting Evie into a routine. Some nights, when Alex got home, they were all fast asleep in front of CBeebies.

"Perhaps we should have waited until Gus was toilet trained before having Evie," Alex said one day, having changed his gazillionth nappy.

"I'm not sure that was on your mind at the time," Erin reminded him.

She had never received a signed commitment to stop at two, but she felt that the current situation should prove adequate contraception for now. They didn't have enough time to sleep, let alone have sex, and despite Alex occasionally suggesting she could put him on the naughty stair anytime, she suspected that spontaneous sex was out of the question for at least the next fifteen years.

Today was the christening of David and Toby's little girl. Erin was delighted they had a girl, and with only a six-month age difference, she and Evie would be great playmates for each other. It was both weird and not weird that they were related. Erin had felt no maternal tug. Even when she gently kissed her cheek, it felt no different to kissing a friend's baby. It helped that she was born with a shock of dark hair that marked her as Toby's child and that Erin was in a breastfeeding love bubble with Evie.

When they asked her to be a godmother, it had felt natural, as if something otherworldly had intervened to enable this wonderful baby to be born.

"You'll be suggesting she's the daughter of God next!" Toby had laughed.

"Well, it was the immaculate conception," David added.

Erin couldn't shake the feeling that something other than coincidence had brought them together and allowed this miracle to happen.

"Are you nearly ready?" Alex shouted to her, "I'm just going to get the car loaded up."

There was no doubt today would be a logistical challenge. If she managed to get home without getting sick in her hair, she'd count it a major success. She had a nightmare last night that she was at the font, just about to renounce the devil, when her boobs started leaking. Not just a dribble but a huge fountain emerging from her nipples and spraying like a broken nozzle into the holy water and drenching the vicar.

“Just coming,” she shouted down to Alex, hastily stuffing a mega pack of breast pads into the already full changing bag.

The christening was at a church local to Toby’s parents in Virginia Water, with a party afterwards in their garden. On the way there, Erin sat in the back, keeping Gus entertained by calling out the colours of all the cars they were passing. Within the first five minutes, Evie had fallen fast asleep, which was fine for the journey but meant she would be a hot, grizzly mess when they woke her up.

David and Toby were already at the church when they arrived, and Seb ran to meet them as soon as he saw Gus.

“It’s the Godmother,” Toby announced in a mock Italian accent.

“If you say that again, I’m going to punch you,” David threatened.

Erin found somewhere quiet in the church to breastfeed Evie before the ceremony started. They agreed that Alex would take her outside if she cried, and Gus would come to the font so he could see. The service was lovely, and the church was packed with friends and family. Erin felt herself well up during *All Things Bright and Beautiful* but recovered before making her way to the back for the baptism itself. They gathered around while the vicar took the baby from David. He held her in the crook of one arm and cupped the holy water with the other. He gently poured it over the baby's head and started the blessing.

Faith is the gift of God to his people. In baptism, the Lord is adding to our number, those whom he is calling. People of God, will you welcome Maggie Erin and uphold her in their new life in Christ?

When they had told Erin they were naming her after David's grandmother, it brought the story full circle. They felt Margaret was too stern and Peggy too personal, so Maggie it was.

"I think my Great Aunt thinks she's named after Margaret Thatcher," Toby said, "and she's going around telling everyone that she's going to be the next Prime Minister."

"I'm just glad we had a girl. I'm not sure I could have got used to Ken," said David.

It had been David who asked her permission to use Erin as the second name. They had gone for a walk a few months ago.

"I still can't believe we've ended up here," Erin had said, gently touching David's arm.

"To think I thought you were some sort of scammer! 23+me has a lot to answer for. Good and bad," said David.

"Just think what would happen if we hadn't taken those tests. There would be no Evie, no Maggie."

"It must be fate, I suppose."

"Or the opposite of it. If Margaret hadn't kept her baby secret from Ken? If she'd followed him to Canada?"

"Or he'd come to England?"

"Then we would be writing a whole different story. It makes you realise how important the choices we make are. How do we know that donating my eggs to you was the right choice? Maybe in a hundred years, someone will be cursing us for derailing their path, their journey?"

"At the end of the day, we just have to own our choices and deal with the consequences."

"I suppose we do."

After the christening, they went back to Toby's parents' house. It was a perfect English July day. There were jugs of Pimm's, and gin cocktails, croquet on the lawn, and smoked salmon sandwiches in the fridge waiting to be dispatched. Baby Maggie had been put down for a sleep in the coolest room in the house, and after breastfeeding Evie, Erin popped in to check on her.

Next to the cot were some christening presents, including the *Little Wrinkle* book from Great Aunt Christine. At eighty-eight, Christine was the last of that generation to still be with them. Sitting quietly in the room, Erin felt surrounded by the love of those who had gone before. Of Cynthia, whom everyone spoke of so fondly. Of Ken, her wonderful grandfather, who loved her grandmother the way she hoped Alex loved her. And of Margaret, Maggie's namesake, who had made an enormously difficult decision and then made the best of the life that followed.

As she read Christine's inscription aloud to Maggie, she could picture all three sitting in their uniforms, raising a glass and making a toast.

Love who you love,
Live how you live,
Stay close to your family,
And learn to forgive.

Downstairs, listening in at the baby monitor, David raised his glass in a silent toast and wiped away the tears he could already feel gathering.

To play consequences

1. Give each person a sheet of paper, and ask each player to write down a word or phrase to fit a description (e.g. 'a character')
2. Each player folds the paper over to hide the most recent line, and hands it to the next person.
3. The players are then asked to write down a word or phrase to fit a second description (e.g. met 'another character')
4. The game continues in this vein with different prompts for each turn of the paper ('at'; 'he said'; 'she said'; 'he wore'; 'she wore' etc.)
5. On the final turn of the paper, players are asked to add a summary phrase ('the consequence was…')
6. At the end, the stories are read out to much amusement.

About the author

Bridget Roe grew up in the 1960's in the London suburbs. She went to Harrow Weald Grammar, where she met her future husband and developed her love of creative writing. After attending the prestigious Watford Copywriting Course, she moved into branding and communications, where her main claim to fame was naming Wispa for Cadbury's.
In 1978 she found out that her father had a second life that she knew nothing about. Nearly 40 years later, she stopped working for long enough to write about it in her debut novel Consequences. Bridget now lives under one roof in a multigenerational house with her husband, one of her daughters, her son-in-law and their two dogs. When she's not writing, she runs a private hire swimming pool that she hopes might give her enough ammunition for her next book.